AF422077

Trafficking In Murder

A Sydney Riley Provincetown Mystery

Jeannette de Beauvoir

Trafficking In Murder

Copyright © 2026 by Jeannette de Beauvoir
Book Eleven

Published by Beckett Books
PO Box 326
Provincetown, MA 02657

ISBN 979-8-9925942-5-6
eISBN 979-8-9925942-6-3

Cover Design by Miladinka Milic

Other Books
by Jeannette de Beauvoir

Mysteries:
The Abbie Bradford international mystery series:
> *The Everest Enigma*

The Sydney Riley Provincetown mystery series:
> *Death of a Bear*
> *Murder at Fantasia Fair*
> *The Deadliest Blessing*
> *A Killer Carnival*
> *A Fatal Folly*
> *The Matinée Murders*
> *The Lethal Legacy*
> *The Fine Art of Deception*
> *The Honeymoon Homicides*

The Martine LeDuc Montréal mystery series:
> *Deadly Jewels*
> *Asylum*
> *Trapped*

The Trinity Pierce Boston mystery series:
> *Murder Most Academic* (as Alicia Stone)

Assignment: Nepal (co-authored as J.A. Squires)

Historical Fiction:
> *Lethal Alliances*
> *Our Lady of the Dunes*
> *Légende (as Jeannine Allard)*

Chapter One

"Americans," said my goddaughter, licking cheese and tomato sauce off her fingers, "eat twenty-three pounds of pizza every year."

I looked at her suspiciously. There's no doubt in anybody's mind that Lily is precocious for a seven-year-old, but she also sometimes falls prey to what in artificial intelligence is known as hallucinations, and makes things up if she believes they'll create a better story. "I don't eat twenty-three pounds of pizza," I said, even though we were in fact sitting at the Provincetown House of Pizza and contributing to the statistic.

"Not every American," Lily conceded. "It's an average." She brightened. "So that means, some people eat way *more* than that!"

"That's a lot of pizza," I agreed. The truth is, I do regard it as a treat of sorts. I am part-owner of the Race Point Inn in Province-town's East End, and pizza is *never* featured on our Michelin-starred restaurant's menu.

Besides, I like spending time with my goddaughter. When my best friend Mirela brought Lily back from Plovdiv in Bulgaria— where her sister had regarded the baby as an inconvenience and readily signed adoption papers so Mirela could bring Lily to the States—I hadn't been quite as enthused. (To be fair, neither had Mirela: if there were ever someone who manifested zero maternal instincts, it's her. As a mother, she's something of a work in pro-gress. That had not, however, stopped her from once becoming the fiercest mother bear ever out in the dunes when the baby's life was threatened.)

In my defense, there aren't that many non-parents who can truly embrace the demands of a baby, which morphed into the demands of a toddler, which finally metamorphosed into the very smart conversations one could now have with the girl sitting at the table with me.

"Did you know," she said, "that some indigenous people call the earth Turtle Island?"

"I did not," I said. *She knows the word indigenous. Of course she does.* "Are you going to eat that piece?"

She shook her head, intent on her thought. "The way the turtle shell is curved works okay for half the earth," she said. "That makes sense. But what about the bottom half? And where does the turtle sit, or stand, and how come people don't fall off the turtle? And if we're on Turtle Island, why don't we just float away? But if we did, what would we be floating on top of?"

"Good questions," I said. Somewhere in the back of my mind an expression flitted by, *turtles all the way down,* but I couldn't remember who said it or what it meant, and didn't want to further complicate the conversation. I picked up the last slice of pizza and took a bite. "You could look them up and see."

"Aunt Sydney," she said to me with dramatic excessive patience, "I already did. I *know* how to do *research!* But no one knows."

When I was seven, I probably didn't even know the word research. I sighed. Maybe she could make it her dissertation topic. At the rate she was going, that was probably going to happen sometime next year. "It's their story," I said. "Lots of cultures have stories to explain how things work."

"But if everybody's got a different story, how do we know which one is true?"

We'd gone from alimentation to geography to metaphysics in under four minutes, which had to be a record of some kind. I was rescued by the arrival of my husband. "I see you didn't save me any pizza," he said, sitting down at the table and reaching over to tousle Lily's hair.

"Didn't know you were coming," I said.

"Uncle Ali," said Lily, "How do we know whose story is true?"

"Story?" He raised his eyebrows, amused, and gave me a smile, which always—even after twelve years together—takes my breath away. Ali is Lebanese-American, and is the most beautiful man I have ever seen.

"Origin myths," I told him. "Turtle Island."

He said to Lily, "Truth can be different from facts, you know? Different stories are true for different people. In my religion, we don't think the world started with a turtle. We think Allah created it, and did it in seven days." He paused. "Does that sound like a fact to you?"

She shook her head. "My mom can't even do a *painting* in seven days, sometimes," she said.

"So they're not facts, our stories, but even if we know they're not factual, they tell us some truths about who we are," he said.

"What truths does *your* story tell?"

He considered the question. Ali always treats Lily like a miniature adult. It works okay more often than not. "Well, it tells me that Allah is good, because the earth is good. It tells me Allah pays attention. It reminds me that he wants me to live in a way that I pay attention, too. And I think that people who tell the story of Turtle Island must be very close to the earth and nature, and the turtle reminds them of that."

"Okay." She was probably filing it all away to ask Mirela about later. "Are you going to order a pizza?"

Ali smiled. "I think not," he said. "I was just passing and saw your Aunt Sydney's car here so thought I'd stop in to say hello, because I haven't seen you in forever."

"It hasn't been *forever*, Uncle Ali," Lily said seriously. "It was last week."

"Well, it *feels* like forever," he said. "What are you ladies doing after lunch?"

"I don't know about Lily," I said, "but this lady has work to do."

"You have to take me home first," Lily said.

"I know."

"My mom gave me the key," Lily said.

"I know. She told me. And you haven't lost it?"

She made a face. "Of course not, Aunt Sydney. I'm responsible."

"You certainly are," I said, smiling. I stood up and began clearing the table. "Want to help me with this? What time's your mom coming home?"

She finished her soda, sucking noisily on the straw. "When she's done at the gallery."

That could be anytime. Mirela isn't just any artist; even in Provincetown—itself an important art colony, the oldest continuous one in North America—she's one of the town's hottest artists. She came to P'town from Bulgaria one summer to work, back when Bulgarian students came here in droves; they still come, but in somewhat smaller numbers; Provincetown is changing. She spent that first summer waiting tables at Joon Bar and The Mews, driving a pedicab, and painting seascapes, mostly of the harbor. The paintings sold, and she stayed on, eventually becoming a US citizen; but over those years her style changed. Now she creates abstract works that sell for tens and even hundreds of thousands of dollars. She's also marginally psychic, and some of her paintings carry eerie messages that scare the hell out of me.

Lily is, of course, her loudest critic, and often complains that her work doesn't look like anything in particular; I privately agree with that assessment.

Very privately.

Ali stood up and opened his arms for a hug. "I'll see you soon, *habibi*," he said. It's an Arabic endearment he reserves for Lily. He generally uses Italian ones with me. He thinks they make him sound sexy.

He's right.

Lily duly deposited at Mirela's house in the West End, Ali and I returned to the Race Point Inn, which was doing its usual brisk business. It was late June, the start of the tourist season, when Provincetown's population makes the switch from three thousand residents in the winter to eighty thousand in the summer. The inn's open year-round, and we're generally booked up completely from April to December. I've been part of the inn now, one way or another, for over fourteen years, and yet am still absorbing what that entails: people, people, and more people.

Ali disappeared into our residence, which is the penthouse on the top floor of the inn, and I went in search of Wendy, the inn's manager and—I could swear—magician. She soothed ruffled feathers, dealt with crises, handled difficult people, all the things I'm not terribly good at. We all have our areas of specialty.

Mine is murder.

***

That's not really true, of course; I haven't actually killed anybody yet, though I've come close a few times. In my fantasies, anyway. No; as Julie Agassi, the head of the Provincetown Police detective unit, tells it, if there's a dead body anywhere in town, I'm going to be the one to have found it. Or known about it. Or been somehow involved with it. And it's true that I seem to have a Jessica Fletcher/Miss Marple-level of amateur connection to crime.

It started one summer morning when I went to take an early dip in the Race Point's pool—at the time, I was employed as the inn's wedding coordinator—and found the body of my boss floating in the water with me. A thousand times *ick*, as well as a sorrow I've never really gotten over: Barry had been the kindest, gentlest man I'd ever known.

So of course I wanted to be part of bringing his killer to justice.

After that, it felt somehow natural for me to be on the scene of other crimes. Provincetown isn't very big, and my work brings me into contact with a tremendous number of people, so it's logical, really, that I'd have more success in figuring things out than would the State Police, dispatched from up-Cape to investigate homicides and not necessarily all that familiar with our little quirks down here.

And quirky doesn't even begin to describe Provincetown. The town is a vibrant art colony. It's also a gay-resort destination. And an old fishing village that still retains the remnants of the commercial fleet, along with the Portuguese families who worked it. Once upon a time, one of the whaling capitals of the world. And before that, the summer home of an indigenous population. All that history, all that mix makes for people who most decidedly do *not* do things by the book. Some outsiders find that disconcerting.

I find it… home.

Wendy was sitting in the empty restaurant drinking coffee and going over the evening's menu with Martin, the maître d'. "It doesn't matter; she says we have to take it off," he was saying.

I pulled up a chair. "Take what off?"

"The salmon *en croute*," said Martin. "She is not pleased with the quality of today's delivery."

Wendy was shaking her head. "Seriously? I don't get it. Everybody likes salmon," she objected. "Even people who don't like fish, like salmon. She's got it; for heaven's sake, what else does she want to do with it?"

Martin made a face; I could only imagine what "she" had said to do with it. *She* was, of course, Adrienne the diva chef, by whose graces we had earned and kept our Michelin rating. She also had absolutely no care for anybody's feelings; staff had been known to quit their first night of service because she'd completely terrorized them. My co-owner, Mike, seemed to be the only person who took her tantrums in stride. "It is not a local fish," Martin was saying, his French accent somehow making the remark more persuasive. "And she has two other piscatory dishes on the menu…"

Wendy snorted. "For heaven's sake," she said again, but she said it with resignation. We all knew the truth: what Adrienne the diva chef wanted, Adrienne the diva chef got. "I'm going to have to reprint the menus."

"Such is the nature of our curious enterprise," said Martin, shrugging; he knows which battles to fight. He turned to me. "Sydney? Was there something you needed?"

"I wanted to check in with Wendy about the TV crew," I said. We were being featured on one of the local-things-to-do, early-evening programs out of Boston, which was both a Good Thing—it helps to be known as a *Weekend Waypoints* destination—and also was going to be disruptive of staff and guests alike.

"Arriving tomorrow morning," she said, changing gears briskly and seemingly effortlessly. "Mike wants you to do the interview, did he tell you?"

"He did." Mike and I had become co-owners of the inn when its former owner gave up Provincetown for Amsterdam and his new love. Mike had been the manager, so he slipped easily into the role of keeping on top of the practical side of things, whereas once I gave up coordinating weddings, I tended more toward the public-relations side of ownership, attended business guild meetings, helped organize events, went off-Cape to conferences… and, apparently, did interviews for Boston television stations.

I also valued Wendy's impressive organizational skills. "Where do you suggest it will disrupt people the least? The interview, I mean? The part I'm doing?"

"You're doing the whole part," she corrected me. "You're going to have to stick with them, and take the producers to lunch here, I have a table for you at one o'clock." She pulled out her smartphone and started scrolling. "Juliet Mills and Bruce Peterson," she read. "And rooms thirty-four and eighteen will be empty and prepared for the cameras, but you have to be out of eighteen by lunchtime because we have an early arrival for it."

I raised my eyebrows ever so slightly. "Thirty-four? Do you think that's a good idea? You know they'll have done their homework." I could still hear Lily's voice saying she knew how to do research; there was absolutely no way television producers didn't.

It wasn't that thirty-four is a bad room—it's actually quite nice, with antique furnishings and a window overlooking the largest of our patios, the one with the arbor. It had been two years since Ali and I had stood on that patio exchanging wedding vows when we were interrupted by a man's body falling very nearly on top of us.

From room thirty-four.

"They requested it," said Wendy. "It adds a little pizzazz, knowing a murder happened here."

Two murders, in fact, if you counted the body in the pool years before that. My instinct was to downplay that particular facet of the Race Point's claims to fame. But Wendy leaned into it, and her decision had proved successful. There was even talk, sometimes, of a possible haunting. And people *liked* that. "Your call," I said, making a face.

"I've put together a schedule," Wendy went on, her voice brisk. Potential ghosts weren't playing into her agenda—for the day, at least. "They'll spend the morning shooting the inn, then after lunch they'll go down Commercial Street, do shots of the town. They call it B-roll. Back here for a wrap-up before dinner service starts. Nine of them in all: producers, director, the on-air talent, and cameras and sound."

"Okay." I knew better than to argue: Wendy knew what she was doing. Nothing could go wrong.

Which just goes to show how little I understand about fate, or life, or anything.

Chapter Two

It didn't go wrong all at once, and it didn't go wrong right away.

Ali was working in his office, one of the rooms in the penthouse apartment which had belonged to the previous owner and was now ours. He theoretically works out of Boston, but he put in a secure Wi-Fi connection with a *very* secure email server and so can stay in Provincetown most of the time when he's not in the field.

I don't ever go in his office. Ali is a special agent in Homeland Security's Center for Countering Human Trafficking, and even if I had clearance—which I don't—a whole lot of the time I don't want to know what he does, both because it sometimes puts him in danger and also because the little I do know about his work breaks my heart.

I decided to do something useful and was just putting a load of laundry in the machine when he came out for an orange juice. Ali isn't what you'd call a practicing Muslim—he doesn't even own a prayer rug—but he does abstain from alcohol and stimulants. I will never understand how anyone can face the world without at least two cups of morning coffee; but he does like his fruit juices. "Things okay downstairs?"

I pressed buttons and the washing machine started making mysterious noises. "Yeah. Wendy reminded me about the people from that show coming tomorrow." I trailed after him into the kitchen and leaned against a counter while he poured himself a glass. He held the bottle up toward me and I shook my head. "No, thanks."

He popped it back in the refrigerator. "Fame and fortune await," he predicted.

"Headaches await, more likely. They're going to film in room thirty-four."

He gave me the amused half-smile that can be either endearing or irritating, depending on my mood. "Living dangerously, are we?"

"They *requested* it," I said gloomily.

"Uh-huh." He drank for a moment, then set his glass down. "You're not forgetting I'm going up-Cape tomorrow, right?"

"Of course I didn't forget!" Of course I'd forgotten.

"Staying with Margo," he said encouragingly. Margo is our lawyer friend. Some years ago she'd represented Ali when he was, absurdly, suspected of having murdered somebody. (See! It's not just me that has murders follow them around!) She lives in Marstons Mills, a quaint Cape Cod village relatively close to the Sagamore Bridge that connects the Cape with the mainland, or what some people refer to as "civilization."

"I remember," I said, doubling down. When had he talked about it? "You have a—meeting, or something, in Hyannis."

"A training conference," he said.

I was close, anyway. "And it's a couple of days," I added. A safe bet; if it was only one day, he wouldn't be choosing to stay overnight.

"Very good." He had that amused look going again.

A terrible thought had occurred. "You and Margo are going to go to dinner at Bleu, aren't you?" No mistaking my tone now: accusatory. I can't help it—I love to eat, and I love to eat great food, and our own restaurant notwithstanding, Bleu is one of my favorite establishments on the Cape.

"Of course we're going to dinner at Bleu," he said.

"I hate you."

"Of course you hate me." He finished his drink and moved to put the glass in the sink. "Don't worry, you'll be so busy being a star on TV, you won't even notice I'm gone."

Oh, right. You had to remind me of that.

***

And so began my path to stardom.

The film crew arrived and created a stir right away because the on-air talent, as I learned the presenter was called, was apparently going to give Adrienne the diva chef a run for her money as Personality Most Likely to be Difficult. She had brought along a hair stylist and makeup person, not included in Wendy's calculations, and the crew pretty much filled the lobby and took over the inn.

Mike took one look at the melee and disappeared into his office, the door closing firmly and definitively behind him. *Thanks, partner.*

Wendy, predictably, took it all in stride. "No worries," she said calmly, and herded them all into the restaurant, which was closed until lunch; the Race Point has a less formal dining room where breakfast is served, so this was the only large space that should be devoid of guests, at least for the moment.

I stood at the back of the room, watching as equipment was removed from carrying cases and the talent complained about the lack of a proper dressing room. One of the producers—the woman, Juliet Mills—drifted over to stand beside me. She at least hadn't fussed with her appearance: blonde hair tied back in a ponytail, minimal makeup, jeans, and a t-shirt advertising Mystery Science Theater 3000. "We'll start with your interview," she said. "That way, we'll know what to emphasize when we do the walk-through."

I was watching the red-haired presenter. "Does she do this routine every time?" I asked. It didn't make sense: this was what they did, travel around New England to capture interesting places to recommend for viewers to visit. Certainly the Race Point Inn couldn't have been the first venue that hadn't supplied her with a dressing room. They did stories on *goat* farms, for heaven's sake.

Juliet laughed. "She's new," she said. "She'll get over herself. She used to do studio work exclusively, and sees this as a demotion."

"Lucky you."

"Right?" She watched the controlled chaos for a few moments, and then said, her voice carefully casual, "So, Sydney Riley. I hear you're something of a celebrity yourself. They say you're a regular crime-stopper out here."

"You've been talking to Detective Agassi," I said. Julie Agassi is the only person who complains about what she sees as my interference in police activity. "I don't actually do it on purpose." I frowned. "We're not going to talk about that in the interview, are we?"

"Don't worry," she said. "Your manager—Wendy?—told us what's off-limits. I'll respect that."

"Good." I relaxed slightly. The truth was, I was a little nervous about doing the interview—any interview. Despite my relative fame in a relatively small town, I really don't crave attention. And this wasn't a good time to be placed in the spotlight. I still have friends in Boston, and from them (and the local Boston news) I'd learned that my former husband had recently been having problems—marital problems, ethical problems, public problems, one old friend confiding that the Spotlight team from *The Boston Globe* was considering his hospital as an investigation target.

Our names had never been the same, but I'd be easy to find if anyone wanted to, and I very much didn't want to be part of any investigation involving Noah. Putting me on *Weekend Waypoints* felt a little like painting a target on me.

Plus, although since becoming part-owner of the inn I'd had to learn a lot about public speaking and public relations, and I'd gotten reasonably good at it, although it still didn't come naturally. My only asset was the years I'd spent teaching restless students at UMass; I'd learned how to keep people's interest.

Juliet sensed my malaise. "Don't worry, it's just a conversation," she said. "And we can edit out anything we need to."

"Good," I said again. *Breathe, Riley*, I told myself, and rallied. "Your job must be fun, going to all these different places?" Safer ground.

"Sometimes. And sometimes I wish I could just stay in the studio and get home every night for dinner at a decent time."

"I hadn't thought of that."

She shrugged. "No one does. Audiences never think about us having personal lives. We're not real people to them. Anyway, you're right. I like the work; I do get to meet a lot of interesting people. See things I wouldn't usually see." She smiled. "And this show, your show, is special to me. I love the Cape. My family used to come here on vacation when I was little. We rented the same cottage in Wellfleet every summer for years and years. I looked forward to it all through school. A week on the beach. Heaven."

"Heaven if you don't have to actually work while at the beach," I remarked.

"See? We have more in common than you think." She smiled again, her eyes on the other producer, Bruce, who was talking to the presenter. You could almost feel his frustration crossing the room in waves. "Actually, I get to come here twice this summer. We're doing a piece on the Wampanoag tribe, and we'll be filming the pow-wow this weekend. Do you ever go to that?"

I shook my head. "It seems a little—touristy," I confessed.

"Well, yeah, some of it is. But a lot of it isn't. The tribe does it for themselves, and for other native people who come. Having tourists there is just part of it."

I had never given it much thought before. The indigenous Mashpee Wampanoag tribe—the People of the First Light—still live on the Cape and Martha's Vineyard, though obviously in much smaller numbers than they had before the first European settlers arrived and, well, *stole* their land, incidentally wiping out something like eighty percent of the population with white people's diseases. Remaining tribal members had, after a protracted fight that took decades, received federal recognition, lands set aside as their reservation; they put on a several-days-long pow-wow in the summer. "Maybe I'll watch your show when you visit it," I said, trying for polite and noncommittal.

"Fine," said Juliet. She said it as though her mind had already moved elsewhere, and after a moment, she added, "Tell me about Provincetown. I mean, I see what the tourists see, that's all. When I was a kid, we never came all the way down here. Well, maybe for a whale watch, but that would have been it." She flashed me a glance. "So tell me the real story, not the one you'll be telling Stacey in a few minutes." She was smiling.

"Off the record?" I suggested. For all I knew, she might be recording our conversation, and I work at an inn—like it or not, I need the tourists, too.

"Pinky promise," Juliet said, unexpectedly, smiling, and we awkwardly touched fingertips.

I found I was liking this woman. "Okay." I took a deep breath. "It's changing, and it's changing fast. I mean, part of it's the same you see everywhere, money moving in, gentrification, all that. But it's pretty serious here. It's splitting the town apart."

She had stopped looking at the room and was focusing on me. "How?"

Another deep breath. It wasn't really a secret, anyway. "Wealthy people who want second and third homes, along with a handful of corporations, are pretty much buying up the town," I said. "And, yeah, okay, that happens everywhere. But in the process they're removing the lifeblood of P'town. There's one LLC in particular that's just bought up a whole lot of downtown space on Commercial Street, with plans to destroy existing buildings and build a super-marina and hotel; they've already forced out one art gallery—thirty working artists with no income, poof, all gone. They're not coming back; they can't afford to. We're the oldest art colony in North America, and we're losing artists. Artisans, too, all the craftspeople in Whaler's Wharf." I shook my head. "That's not just gentrification. That's a fundamental change in the town."

"The hotel will be in competition with the Race Point Inn," said Juliet. It wasn't a question.

"It will, but that's not the point." I sighed. "You have to understand—I'm not a normal inn owner; neither is Mike. We were *given* this inn. Literally: it was a gift. Before that, I was just the wedding planner, he was the manager—we were working people in this town, not the champagne elite that's buying it up and changing it. The working people—*they're* my tribe." I wondered how that word had popped up; probably because of the conversation about the Wampanoag. But it fit. And just as the Pamet and Nauset and Wampanoag tribes had their land taken from them, my own tribe here in town was now losing it to other invaders.

In a sense, it had a similar colonial impact. The Pilgrims were Calvinists, Puritans, who believed in their hearts they were doing something *good* for the indigenous population: bringing them their version of Christianity. And the people coming into town, now, saw themselves as making it beautiful and shiny, doing the current residents a favor. They weren't necessarily malicious—it was a lack of awareness of others' needs and lives.

But if they weren't malicious, they were all certainly condescending. Just as the Pilgrims were convinced of their own superiority to the native peoples, so too were the developers convinced of their own entitlement: each believed they were the chosen ones, and destroyed what they didn't understand.

Juliet was looking at me with some intent thoughts going through her head; I couldn't imagine what they were. "I want to hear more about that," she said, slowly and thoughtfully. "Maybe later? I'll buy you a drink?" She didn't wait for my response. "We're filming a friend of yours this afternoon," she said. "Stopping by the gallery. Mirela Petrovna, is that her name?"

"Now *she's* someone famous," I said. Mirela hated being interrupted, but even she couldn't afford to not use the summer months to promote her work. Two afternoons a week she sat in her gallery and answered questions about art and sold paintings. She'd welcome the interview, and ace it. Good luck to her, I thought.

Or, maybe, good luck to Juliet and company. Mirela can be quite dismissive if she thinks someone's being obtuse about her work. We often met up for a glass of wine at the end of her gallery days, when she was burned out from dealing with visitors. "How do I answer these questions? There is no answer to these questions. Why did I choose this shade of brown? Why is a circle on the floor? What kind of answer can I give to this nonsense?"

When she says things like that, I just sip my Côtes du Rhône and keep my opinions to myself, because I don't understand anything about her art, either, and could very well have myself thought of asking some of the questions that bother her the most.

Juliet Mills, however, seemed to be able to look after herself; I didn't suppose one got to be the producer of a popular and long-running television program by asking inane questions. She had gone back to watching the mysterious preparations her crew was doing. "Looks like they're close to ready," she said, and turned her attention back to me. "Where did your manager say we're recording your spot?"

"In the lounge," I said, gesturing toward the door. The Race Point has in fact several different places for guests to congregate; this was the smallest, with a sofa and a few chairs; it also had a door we could shut against prying eyes.

"Then let's go." She raised her voice. "Bruce! Stacey! Adam! Let's get moving!"

It took a ridiculously long time, from my point of view, to arrange us to the director's satisfaction, Stacey the presenter changing her chair twice for no particular reason, the lighting guy playing with screens and very hot lights, the sound guy interrupting to get us to do sound checks with the tiny microphones clipped to our clothing. And these people did this every day. Amazing.

I could feel sweat from the hot lights trickling down my neck and back, the inn's air conditioning being no match for this much light and heat.

Finally everything was set and cameras were rolling. The director signaled for quiet and Stacey suddenly came to life, bestowing an artificially bright smile on me and saying in a chirpy voice, "We're here in Provincetown at the Race Point Inn with Sydney Riley, the inn's co-owner. Sydney, what is it that makes this hotel special?"

I matched her smile; I can do artificial as well as the next person. "Well, I could answer that by telling you about everything we offer guests—we have two swimming pools, a Michelin-starred restaurant, forty-six rooms, a staff I'm particularly proud of, and more… but, honestly, what sets us apart is the ambience. I think we've managed to distill the essence of Provincetown, everything that's special about this town here at land's end." I paused, but she didn't say anything, so I went on.

"It's an art colony, as you know, Stacey, and we have a number of paintings here by renowned Provincetown artists, both past and present, right here at the inn. P'town is a gay resort, and we honor that by providing a venue for same-sex weddings and by participating in theme weeks and festivals such as Bear Week and Women's Week, and by supporting organizations such as the AIDS Support Group. And Provincetown's a former whaling capital and fishing village, and we sponsor talks by local historians and encourage guests to enjoy whale watches. And it's one of the most beautiful places in the world, and we encourage guests to explore the natural beauty of the Outer Cape."

"Why do you call it Land's End?"

I smiled. "If you go over to the ocean side, over in the National Seashore, if you look out to sea, the next landmass you'd encounter would be Portugal. No one comes here by accident; we're not on the way anywhere else. So anyone who lives here, *chose* to live here. We're called washashores, the people who weren't born here. Most of us couldn't imagine living anywhere else."

It was going okay. A few more questions, and she turned and addressed the camera directly, her voice continuing bright and chirpy. "And now we're going to take a tour of the inn. We'll let you see some of the rooms, and tempt you with some of the dishes from their famous restaurant. I don't know about you, but I'm ready to make a reservation at the Race Point Inn right away!"

Adam the director said, "and… cut!" and the lights went off and we were done.

Thankful the crew and the tour and everything else were now Wendy's responsibility, I fled. I'd have to connect again over lunch, but that was a couple of hours away, and the makeup they'd applied to my face was itching. There was plenty of paperwork waiting in my office, after all; for once, the boring forms seemed a refuge rather than a distraction.

But it had all gone rather well, on the whole, and lunch wouldn't be too bad—honestly, any day I get to sample Adrienne the diva chef's work is by definition a good day—and once again I thanked my lucky stars for Wendy's efficiency. The program was going to be positive, and it didn't hurt the inn's reputation to be featured on it. I found myself relaxing.

And then everything went south. Because Juliet Mills disappeared.

Chapter Three

No one seemed to know what had happened.

"It's not like her," Bruce, the other producer, was saying. He had already said it three times, and seemed baffled his mantra wasn't making her magically reappear.

We were all in my office—Bruce, Mike, and Wendy—and some part of my mind was off on a tangent, thinking that of all the situations they'd encountered and dealt with, this was one they clearly didn't know how to handle.

The crew had checked out the rooms (with, hopefully, no mention of room thirty-four's past guest), the bars, the pools, and Stacey had interviewed a few random guest volunteers; Juliet had gone outside with the cameraman and the director to scout a few locations for the after-lunch tour of the town. "I just went around the back of the building," the cameraman said; he was talking about Town Hall. "To see if I could get an interesting angle. That's all." He seemed to think Juliet's disappearance was somehow his fault. "I left her for maybe five minutes!"

Five minutes, I thought, was plenty of time for anyone to disappear into Provincetown's summer crowds. "Did you call her?"

"Of course I called her!" he yelped, wide-eyed. "It went straight to voicemail."

Mike, my co-owner, was practical as always. "She can't have gone far," he said soothingly. "Maybe she saw someone she knows?"

"I looked everywhere," the cameraman said. "She was standing by that stone thing. That's why I was in back, to get an angle on it for filming Stacey."

"That stone thing" was the AIDS memorial, inscribed with the names of all the men Provincetown lost during the epidemic. Back in the eighties and early nineties, there were far too many of them; there had been constant funerals, sometimes three or four in a week. But it still didn't make sense—the memorial wasn't tall enough to obscure anyone. "I swear I only looked away for a few minutes!"

"She can't be lost," Mike said again. He was right; the town is too small for that, and Town Hall is literally right down the street from the inn. "Like I said, maybe she met up with someone, or maybe she saw something interesting to film and wandered off to check it out."

"She wouldn't just wander off," said Bruce, and added, almost inevitably, "It's not like her!"

"We could speak to the police," said Wendy, problem-solving—and shifting the responsibility for finding Juliet to someone else, which seemed a good idea. "I mean, it's too soon to say she's definitely missing, but—"

Bruce cut across her words. "She's definitely missing!"

"Sydney can talk to Detective Sergeant Agassi," Wendy went on smoothly, her voice soothing. "At least they can all keep an eye out for her."

I nodded. "I'll call her." Julie wasn't going to thank me for it, but she was, after all, the detective. She had procedures. She'd know what to do.

But she didn't find Juliet. No one found Juliet. By the end of the day, the crew had packed up and left, the program stalled—"We'll put up the piece we did last year on Nantucket instead," Bruce said into the phone, presumably talking with someone back at the studio in Boston—and Julie was once again absolutely convinced I'd lost my mind.

It was Ali's turn to cook dinner, and I wandered into the kitchen and pulled myself up onto one of the counters to sit and watch him. He handed me a glass of Côtes du Rhône and got on with mixing lentils for the *mujaddara*, a dishcloth tossed over his shoulder à la Adrienne the diva chef but without the diva part. I cleared my throat. "Do you think she did it on purpose?"

He didn't look up. "People disappear for a lot of reasons," he said. Working as he does in human trafficking, he has some inside knowledge of disappearances.

I took a swallow of wine. "Maybe she was kidnapped," I said.

That got me a sharp glance. He knows kidnapping isn't as farfetched a concept for me as it is for most people. There had been a case a few years back, here in Provincetown—one that had only reminded me of another, earlier, more visceral one.

My sister. No; I wasn't going there.

"This woman's not an obvious target," Ali said reasonably. "It's a lot more likely she went off on her own for some personal reason."

"Maybe she got amnesia," I said. "Hit her head and doesn't remember who she is."

"Where are you *getting* these ideas? You're watching too many crime dramas. You know the most likely answer is the most obvious one."

"Thank you, Mr. Occam," I said, and lifted my glass in a mock salute.

He shrugged. "It's true," he said, setting the lentils on the stove.

"Bruce told me the cameraman said there was some kind of kerfuffle just before she went missing. Some woman yelling, or something. That could have something to do with it."

"Right," said Ali. "Because there are never kerfuffles in Provincetown in the summer."

He had me there. Summertime is tourist time—we call it the Silly Season—and a whole lot of visitors to our fair town don't remember their playground is someone else's home. This is where a lot of them come to let off steam. Or star in their own psychodramas; take your pick.

I decided to change subjects. "So," I said. "Margo."

"I'm not bringing you back anything from Bleu." He was caramelizing onions, steam dampening his black hair. He looked gorgeous. "I'm telling you that right now."

"Wouldn't want it out of context, anyway," I said. "What's the conference?"

"Training for new PATH volunteers." The People Against Trafficking Humans organization has a Cape Cod branch, another side to our little slice of heaven the tourists don't know about. It's a good group; they do outstanding work educating people about what to look out for, who might be a potential victim. On the Cape, there may be slightly less sex trafficking than in cities; but with all the serious money that's come on the scene over the past twenty years, there's been a rise in domestic-work slavery. After all, *someone* has to clean those big new mansions and hotels that keep being built.

Not to mention actually build them.

I liked it when Ali did things like trainings, because I didn't have to worry that he might not come home afterward. When he's doing undercover work, all bets are off. I have nightmares about one day finding *his* body.

I sighed, banishing the thought. "That smells wonderful, by the way," I said. I've tried in the past to make this ridiculously simple rice-onions-and-lentils dish, and it never comes out right. Ali always says you have to learn it from a Lebanese mother.

And he's a better cook than I am. The nights it's my turn to produce dinner, the kitchen never smells like this.

I went back to my original conversational thread. "I don't suppose *Weekend Waypoints* will ever be back to do a story on the inn now."

"It's not like we need more business," he said reasonably.

He was right: we were pretty much always at capacity, even in the off-season. Wendy had seen the show not so much for promotional purposes but more as another feather in our cap. "You don't suppose Wendy's working on her resume, do you?" I asked abruptly as the idea occurred to me.

"To go where?" he asked, shrugging, the question rhetorical. Wendy and her wife lived in town, and the Race Point didn't have any serious competition on the Cape as an excellent place to work. We had no problems attracting a never-ending flow of handsome young men to staff the front desk, to tend the bars and wait on tables. Wendy made a lot of money.

She also, to my mind, earned every penny of it.

I finished my wine and hopped down from the counter. "I'll set the table," I said, and we didn't talk about Juliet again.

***

Ali left early the next morning, and I went back to what I normally do, and the only reason I gave the matter any additional thought was because of Mirela. She showed up at cocktail time and was not happy. "Yesterday I was required to stay at the gallery all day!" She made it sound as if she'd been tortured to within an inch of her life.

"Did you sell anything?"

"That is not the point!" Which meant she had. Mirela doesn't need to hand-sell her work, but when she does, she's remarkably—almost magically—successful. Part of it's her talent, of course; but part of it's her persona. She's blonde and beautiful, with long legs and a flirtatious manner that's all the more powerful because it's completely natural. When you're with her, you feel you're in the presence of some kind of artistic royalty.

I shrugged. "Do you want a drink?"

"Only one?"

I smiled; I couldn't help it. "Come on."

There were a couple of empty stools at the tiki bar out by the pool and we settled in. The current handsome young bartender put a glass of Côtes du Rhône in front of me without asking. Mirela ordered a rum punch and caught me looking at her. "*What?*" she demanded.

"That's such a girly drink," I said, amused. Mirela doesn't have a signature cocktail; her selections change with her moods.

"I *am* a girl." She crossed her legs elegantly and surveyed the pool, filled as usual with gay men hanging out and talking. In the heat of the afternoon it was full of families with kids, but from now until dinnertime, male guests congregated there, mostly standing around in the shallow end discussing their plans for the evening.

"And you could also have called to tell me this program was canceled," Mirela complained. She was clearly enjoying the role of put-upon professional.

"Oddly enough, you weren't the first thing on my mind," I said.

She turned back to me. "What really happened?"

"I told you. The producer disappeared."

"People do not disappear," she said, blatantly ignoring what my husband did for a living. The bartender brought her drink; it was hard to tell if it was a cocktail or a waterlogged fruit salad.

"Apparently they do." I sighed. "The whole crew was pretty upset, but Ali thinks we're all overreacting. He thinks she wandered off somewhere."

"Perhaps she did, sunshine." Even after living for years in the States, Mirela still thinks "sunshine" is an endearment. I stopped trying to tell her otherwise long ago.

"I just think it's really strange," I said. "I can't imagine anyone who's the producer of an award-winning, really famous show is also the kind of person who just drops out like that."

She popped a chunk of pineapple into her mouth. "I see what is happening," she said.

"What?"

She smiled and drank some punch up through her straw. "Sydney Riley is looking for a mystery to solve."

"That's ridiculous," I said. It wasn't ridiculous. Thinking about Juliet Mills was making me twitchy. "It just doesn't feel right," I said.

"Hmm." We both sipped our drinks for a moment. "Ali's up-Cape for some kind of training thing," I said finally.

She nodded. Mirela often knows Ali's schedule better than I do; they're close friends, and she pays attention to her friends. "So it is a good time for you, then," she said. "You can solve a mystery while he is away."

"This isn't my mystery," I said. I didn't know if I was reminding her or reminding myself. "Meanwhile, he's taking Margo to dinner tonight at Bleu."

Mirela gave a hoot of laughter. "This is why you are in a bad mood," she said.

"I am *not* in a bad mood." I caught myself then, and grinned. "Okay, I'm in a bad mood."

"You can have dinner with us," she said. "Lily has invited a friend and they will eat and then play a game together on the computer. You will keep me company and forget about Ali."

"And a disappearing producer," I reminded her.

"And that."

Chapter Four

Ali called sometime after nine while I was watching my current favorite Nordic noir series streaming on MHz. "*Cara.* How was your day?" He sounded tired.

"It was a day." I used the remote to pause the show. "You don't have to tell me about your dinner, I'm not jealous anymore. *I* feasted on spaghetti and brownies."

He gave a snort of laughter. "Lily's brownies?"

"She thinks it's the height of fine cuisine," I said.

"Well, to be fair, they *are* pretty good."

"They are that for sure. How did Day One go?"

A sigh. "I'm going to have to stay up-Cape for a while. Something's come up. Not the training—that's fine, all good. But I've had the FBI here. There's been a disappearance that might be up my street rather than theirs."

"*Another* disappearance?" I got up and took my wine glass into the kitchen for a refill; this story was going to need more Côtes du Rhône. "Isn't that a little too coincidental?"

"I'd be surprised if there were a connection," he said, disappointingly. "Coincidences really do exist, *cara.* This one's in Mashpee, on Wampanoag land. In fact, it's a young Wampanoag woman that's missing."

I nearly dropped my glass. "Then it's *two* coincidences," I said. "Tell me what the chances of *that* happening are!"

"What are you talking about?"

I sat back down on the sofa and took a hefty swallow of wine. "Because Juliet Mills told me before *she* disappeared that she was getting ready to do a show on the Wampanoag," I said. "That has to be related!"

There was a long pause as he gave it some thought. "Doesn't have to be," he said at length, and he said it slowly and thoughtfully. "But you're right. There might be something to it."

"Might be?" I was all-in. Mirela was right—I did kind of like solving mysteries. Miss Marple, eat your heart out.

"*Might* be," he said firmly. "Don't get ahead of yourself. I'll look into it." Another pause. "There's one other thing, *cara*—"

His tone told me it was going to be something I wasn't going to like. "What?"

"It's Margo. She just got offered two weeks in Ireland. Someone canceled their reservation for a cottage in Dingle and she wants to go."

"Okay." I didn't see anything strange in that: Margo has dual citizenship thanks to her Irish grandparents, and she loves every inch of the Emerald Isle. An offer like that would have her packing her bags in three seconds flat.

"It's good for me," he said. "Since I have to stay on for a while anyway, I can stay here at her place." He took a breath. "And I thought, maybe you could use a change of scenery anyway, you might want to come up and stay here with me. Take a break from the crowds, get out of Dodge. It's not like the inn needs your constant presence."

Now I saw where this was going. "You're talking about cat-sitting," I said.

"It's been six months," he pointed out.

Six months, he meant, since Ibsen had died.

The cat I'd adopted and brought to Provincetown with me when I fled the breakup of my first marriage, the cat who'd been my emotional support through that first very tough winter, the cat who'd helped me move into my new life. He'd gotten old and then he'd gotten cancer, and I cried for about three days after taking him to Dr. Sadie to be eased into whatever next life he might have. I was solidly on board with the idea of a kitty heaven, because no one I knew had a more generous soul than Ibsen.

Damned entitled, too. He'd definitely had me wrapped around his little claw, and like most humans owned by cats, I lived to serve.

Wally, Margo's rescue cat, had little in common with Ibsen. When she brought him home, he'd immediately fled—through the fireplace and straight up her chimney, where he stayed for several weeks, descending secretly in the dead of night to use his litterbox and have a bite to eat. She'd sent me a picture of him she'd managed to take, sitting on some sort of inner brick shelf inside the chimney; we called him Saint Wally of the Grotto for some time after that.

He eventually got over his fears, and, in the time-hallowed way of cats, decided he was now in possession of the house and graciously permitted Margo to live there and wait on him. He even tolerated a few moments of petting before bringing out the teeth and claws.

Six months isn't a long time. My grief over losing Ibsen had moderated; it wasn't desperate and knife-edged anymore. But it was still there.

On the other hand, as I thought about it, the idea had appeal. It seemed at least possible that this particular mystery was centered in Mashpee—which was just one town over from Marstons Mills. And maybe Ibsen was giving me a nudge. I could live around Wally for a couple of weeks without breaking down, surely? It wasn't as if he looked like Ibsen, would remind me of my loss, right?

Ali was on the same wavelength. He said, tentatively, "It might be good for you to spend time with another cat, *cara*. Just an idea."

I shook the images of Ibsen out of my head and cleared my throat. "It's a great idea," I said firmly. "I'll just check in with Mike and Wendy, but I don't see why I couldn't."

"Yeah?" He sounded relieved. Ali and Ibsen had tolerated each other, since they both clearly loved me; but he hadn't really understood my anguish. There were no pets in the Hakim household when he was growing up; it wasn't a relationship he'd experienced or even fundamentally understood. And the howling depth of my grief when Ibsen died had left him bewildered. "Well, see what they say."

"I'm sure it will be fine." I was warming up to the idea. I strongly suspected I could convince Ali to take me to Bleu at least once while I was there.

Wally would probably ignore me anyway.

***

I didn't love the alacrity with which my co-owner, Mike, embraced the idea of my leaving for two weeks in the height of summer. "It'll be good for you."

"I know, but I was going to be designing the new flyers."

"You can do that from anywhere."

"It probably won't be long." Well, two weeks, to be exact, but who was counting?

"Sydney, just go. We have a manager. We don't have to be here all the time. Barry wasn't, and Glenn *certainly* wasn't, if you'll recall, and we did just fine without either of them. This place pretty much runs itself." The part about the inn running itself was a big lie, but whatever. "None of us is indispensable."

"*You* are," I said. Mike had been the Race Point Inn's manager for a whole lot of years before we inherited ownership, and he had vast historic knowledge of the place, which was useful more often than one might think. Plus he was just a really good guy. When the opioid epidemic spread through the Cape and claimed the life of someone he knew, he'd immediately made it his personal crusade. Every staff member had been trained to use naloxone should a guest overdose, and the inn hosted drug prevention programs; Mike himself volunteered in a drug treatment/education facility.

Not to mention the fact that, once upon a cold October night, Mike had saved my life. And he'd nearly killed himself doing so. I owed him no small debt.

Actually, when I stopped to think about it, it was amazing Mike ever even wanted anything to do with me, after the perils of our history together. Though the same, to be fair, could be said of many of the people close to me.

Curiosity around sudden death sometimes itself attracts death. It was a mantra I should recite every morning.

I took a deep breath. "Okay," I said. "I'm going."

"Good," said Mike.

"And you can reach me if—"

"I won't," said Mike.

"Oh, and I'll take the old flyers with me—"

Mike had had enough. "Go," he said, physically pushing me out of his office.

So now I had no excuse. I was going to go live with a cat, and see what puzzles my husband had found for me to solve. Well, not exactly for *me* to solve.

But for all of that, I knew I was going to try.

***

Getting from Provincetown to Marstons Mills doesn't sound too difficult. Fifty-five miles on a beautiful early-summer day. Part of the trouble—and let's not kid ourselves, there's always trouble—was in fact the very beauty of the day: once The Season begins officially on Memorial Day weekend, Cape Cod's roads are clogged. Second- and third-home owners. Visitors who come and fill our hotels and inns, who rent cottages by the bay. Day-trippers wanting respite from the city and the office. Going anywhere takes twice as long as it should, and never mind even *thinking* about making a left turn anywhere on the Cape between late May and early October.

And between Provincetown and Marstons Mills lies thirteen miles of a highway so reputably dangerous it's known, locally, as Suicide Alley. It's a stretch of road where headlights are *de rigueur* and alertness required. And it's invariably slow, which makes for the danger: there's no place along the entire stretch to pass, and the fact that some idiots still try to do so is why occasionally the road—the only road out of town, any town—is closed down with ambulances and fire trucks and police detouring drivers onto even narrower, winding roads that seem to end up far from one's destination.

I always put on my most soothing music when I'm on Suicide Alley.

Today it was no worse than usual. I bellowed happily along with some old favorites—Tom Petty, Jackson Browne, Stevie Nicks—and managed to not think ill of the driver in the car in front of me with Florida plates, who seemed to be paying as much attention to his phone as he was to the road.

Because we're Cape Cod and we do things weirdly differently here, Marstons Mills isn't even officially a town: it's a village that's part of the larger, sprawling town called Barnstable, not to be mistaken for Barnstable *County*, which encompasses the entire Cape.

Nearby Mashpee, on the other hand, *is* a town. Confused yet? (I still am.)

Margo's house is tucked away in a glen beside a kettle pond. It's a wonderful old house, filled with treasures from both her travels and her hobbies, with rooms that are oddly shaped, low lintels, wide floorboards. The early deeds were lost in a fire, but "it is believed," as Margo says, ever the careful lawyer, that it was built in 1780, though the beehive oven inside the fireplace argues it may have been earlier than that—they were losing too many wives to skirts going up in flames, and moved the ovens outside the fireplaces around 1750 or so.

She personally can trace its history to the early 1800s, when two Barnstable boys sailed on the whaling ship *Essex* out of Nantucket—the cannibal ship immortalized by Nathanial Philbrick and which served as the basis of Melville's *Moby-Dick*. One of the Barnstable boys was named Benjamin Wright, and he escaped into South America and so wasn't on the lifeboat where "it is alleged," says Margo, they ate the bodies of the other men who either died or were chosen to die, depending on what version of the story you were hearing. Wright was stranded for five years before making his way home, and when he returned, his father bought him Margo's house to live in. She'd in turn bought it two centuries later when she sort-of retired from her law practice in Boston. It is irregular and boxy and delightful, with nooks and crannies all over the place—along with, of course, that famous beehive oven.

Ali wasn't there when I arrived, but Margo still was, her bags literally packed and sitting by the door, while she herself was on the telephone rearranging appointments. She gestured me to come in, while saying to someone on the line, "Yes, I can do the twenty-eighth. That will help a lot. Yes. Okay. Thanks." She disconnected and turned to me, energy as always practically radiating off her. "Sydney Riley, as I live and breathe. Wally will be delighted."

"Wally will ignore me, more likely," I said, hugging her. "Ireland, here you come! Just make sure you come back, too."

She grinned. "We'll see about that," she said cheerfully. "I'm out of here. You remember the code for the door?"

"No," I said. "But Ali knows it, and I'm sure I have it written down somewhere."

She tipped her head to one side, birdlike, looking at me. "You really think there's something going on? With these people missing?"

"I think there's always something going on where people are missing," I said.

"Hmm. Pity the presenter isn't the one who disappeared. What's her name? Tracey? Stacey? The dumb redhead?"

"Hush your mouth," I said. "We don't say things like dumb redhead anymore."

"Then we shouldn't have people like her living out politically incorrect phrases," she said roundly. Margo doesn't suffer fools gladly. Or at all, come to think of it. "Never mind," she said, maneuvering through the narrow hallway to the door with her bags. "You'll figure it out, if there's anything to figure out. Wally probably won't make an appearance for you until he gets hungry. He disappeared once I brought out the suitcases."

"I'll try and charm him," I promised.

"Ha!" she snorted. "He only has eyes for Ali. But never mind, you try anyway."

I watched her drive away, nibbling at a hangnail as I pondered my next move. I fished out the business card I had from *Weekend Waypoints* and called Bruce the producer.

I was mildly surprised when he answered at once. "Peterson."

"Oh, hi—it's Sydney Riley. From Provincetown? I was just calling to see if Juliet, um—is back?"

"Sydney. Hi." His voice was flat.

"I guess that means she isn't," I said.

"Not a clue. You haven't seen her around town?" How did anyone manage to sound both hopeful and resigned at once?

"No," I said. "I'm not actually there at the moment. But I'm sure if she'd been seen, somebody would have said."

"Probably." It was all resignation, now. "We got her building concierge to give us the keys to her apartment—she lives in Back Bay, you know, and her neighborhood is very safe." *Okay, but she didn't disappear from Back Bay*, I thought. "Anyway, he gave us keys to check things out. Nothing was out of place that I could see, it looked exactly the same as it had last time I was there. A place for everything, and everything in its place, that's how she is. She's obsessive about everything, it's what makes her so good at her job. The apartment was spotless." He paused. "I heard you did this before—found someone who was missing."

"Once," I said cautiously. I didn't want to mention the person in question was already dead by the time he was found. "You should talk to the police."

"I did. Hang on." He covered the phone for a moment and I could hear him talking to someone else. "Okay, I'm back. Yeah, I talked to the police. Well, you saw that; your detective came and talked to us in Provincetown. And I told the Boston police, too. They said adults have a right to—disappear. As long as she hadn't committed a crime, she could go wherever she wanted. But that's ridiculous. Of course Juliet didn't commit a crime." He barely paused to take a breath. "And it isn't like her. I told them: it isn't like her."

Probably at length, if his reaction back in Provincetown was anything to go by. "Bruce," I said, hoping to forestall the inevitable, "Juliet told me you folks were planning on coming back down to the Cape next weekend and recording a segment about the Wampanoag. Um, the native tribe? It might be far-fetched to ask, but… well, were there any *problems* with that?"

"What kind of problems?" he asked, but didn't wait for an answer. "There weren't any problems, not that I know of, anyway. The program was originally Adam's thing, his idea, but Juliet was totally on board, so was the rest of the team. It's a good idea. I don't know why we never got around to doing it in the past, to tell the truth. They do a pow-wow, you know. The Wampanoag? She'd been in contact with—I don't know, some tribal leaders? To get permission? To interview? And she was psyched about it. She was looking *forward* to it."

I was still trying to remember who Adam was. The director, maybe. "Yeah, she told me," I said. I thought for a moment. "Do me a favor, Bruce? Let me know if you hear anything?"

"Like what?"

Ay, there was the rub; I had no idea. Thinking about this was like swimming in molasses. "I guess, anything about that program. Like whether she was raising any issues that might be political?" *Weekend Waypoints* was a travel-and-leisure show and as such avoided controversial subjects, which definitely included politics. But I had a feeling that distance might not have been possible here. And then again, I could be completely wrong and Juliet's disappearance had nothing to do with her work. *Breathe, Riley.* "And if you—hear from her, or anything?"

"So you'll help? Like you did that other time?"

I winced, remembering the body. Hopefully not. "I don't know what I can do, honestly. But I'll think about—what we can do."

"The police aren't going to help," he said. "You're all we've got." I heard an echo of *Star Wars* in his voice. *Help me, Obi-Wan Kenobi. You're my only hope.*

I was no Jedi master, but… "I'll think about it," I said again, and ended the call before he could tell me yet again that it wasn't like her.

If there was a connection—and I could be totally wrong, it was actually probable there wasn't one—then the Wampanoag were no doubt going to be less interested in the disappearance of a non-indigenous broadcaster than they were about the young woman who was missing from Mashpee, and deservedly so. But if the two were connected… well, I'd read the Tony Hillerman opus about mysteries that took place on the Navajo reservation. If the Navajo had a tribal police force, then there was a good chance other tribes did, too.

It took about two seconds flat for Siri to answer the question. The Mashpee Wampanoag did indeed have a tribal police force—as well as their own court system and a robust victim-service program. Too soon to contact them—they had their hands full with their own disappearance, and the last thing I wanted to do was tread somewhere I didn't belong.

But it would be worth a conversation with Ali for sure.

Chapter Five

I needed to learn more, and what I learned wasn't what I'd exactly call reassuring.

Wally was still nowhere to be found. I told him to be that way and installed myself with a glass of iced coffee and my MacBook in the beautiful three-seasons room Margo had added on to her house, capturing nature's air conditioning. Before I spoke to anyone, I had to have a little more data. Time to "ask the Google," as an elderly nun I knew had once described internet searches to me, bringing to mind an all-seeing, all-knowing creature not unlike Oz's wizard. I flipped open my laptop and punched in my query.

The Google delivered.

And far more than just a little data. Bewilderment segued seamlessly into shock. The United States as a whole was, I learned, experiencing a murdered and missing indigenous people crisis; President Biden had, during his term, even declared May fifth as a day of awareness.

I hadn't been aware of the day… or the scope of what it stood for.

"For decades," read the Bureau of Indian Affairs website, *"Native American and Alaska Native communities have struggled with high rates of assault, abduction, and murder of tribal members. Community advocates describe the crisis as a legacy of generations of government policies of forced removal, land seizures, and violence inflicted on Native peoples… reports indicate that there is no reliable count of how many Native women go missing or are killed each year."*

The more I read, the more nauseated I felt. While indigenous communities as a whole experienced racism and indeed racist *violence,* it was by far the women who bore the brunt of it. There was even an acronym for it: MMIW, missing and murdered indigenous women.

A few years back another young Wampanoag woman had gone missing; her body was recovered in Florida a month later, her abductor killed in a shootout before it could be ascertained where he'd taken her, much less why.

I was married to someone who investigated human trafficking. I could make a pretty good guess as to why.

Ali, consulted, took one look at all the websites I'd collected and said, "You'll make yourself crazy doing that, you know."

"Maybe I should," I said. "Apparently no-one else is." Which was a manifestly ridiculous—and completely unfair—statement to make to someone who was dedicating his life to helping these people, or at the very least to helping their families find justice if not peace.

I sighed. I know I overreact to things. I know I get upset and look for someone to blame. I generally am able to tell myself to breathe deeply and sort out what can and can't be done to improve a situation, but my first reactions tend to be intense. Panic. Fury. That sort of thing.

"Did you know," I said to Ali, "that in 2016 there were five thousand, seven hundred and twelve reports of missing American Indian and Alaska Native women and girls, but the federal missing-persons database only logged one hundred and sixteen cases?"

He was in the kitchen. "No," he said. "I didn't know that statistic offhand. Did you buy any bread when you went to the Stop & Shop?"

"I certainly did not buy any bread at the Stop & Shop." No one in their right mind would buy bread from a supermarket when in their very own inn there was an amazing bread-and-pastry chef.

"There's a loaf from Angus in the cupboard. I think he gave it to me to get me out of there." Both Angus in the morning and Adrienne the diva chef in the evening like having their space to themselves.

"Probably." I could hear cupboard doors opening and shutting. "There are a lot of reasons for that discrepancy."

"None of them good, I'll bet," I snapped.

He appeared in the doorway. "Do you want a sandwich?"

"Why not?" I sighed and closed the laptop. "It's just— infuriating, you know?"

"I know." He was back in the kitchen. "Minority populations are consistently undercounted and underserved. And often blamed for what happens to them."

Ali knew what he was talking about, if not through his job then through his family's experiences right after 9/11. Muslims got short shrift then for sure. Someone had unloaded a pile of feces on his parents' front lawn.

I stretched and wandered into the kitchen, which made the room very crowded; Margo couldn't even fit a table in it. "How was the conference today?"

"Good." He was assembling cheese and turkey slices. "Some of the people there didn't even know there's trafficking on the Cape."

"I didn't, either, before I knew you," I pointed out.

There's good reason to not know. It's a hidden crime. Vulnerable people make the best victims, and they're the least visible. Young women seduced by "boyfriends" who eventually become pimps. Undocumented residents willing to work the most punishing of jobs to avoid deportation. Healthy impoverished people seeing no way to put food on the table, butchered to sell their organs. Substance-dependent kids willing to do anything, go with anyone, for the next fix. Victims of past traumas looking for someone to be kind to them.

And a lot of it right under our eyes. Long ago I'd marveled at the layers of experiences any place holds; what is obvious to one person walking down a street is invisible to others. Even my own beloved Commercial Street held secrets, where various groups gathered, sought each other out, communicated through signs and expressions and words that were invisible to the rest of us, we who never see the connections being made because we don't belong to that particular clique or family or tribe. I had no doubt I'd seen, spoken to, interacted with trafficked individuals through my years of work in the tourism industry.

It made my heart hurt.

Ali—like a lot of men, I've noticed—is able to compartmentalize. He can just go somewhere else in his head when the pain gets insurmountable. No one could do what he does without that ability, I think.

He handed me a plate. "Orange juice?"

I wrinkled my nose and reached instead for my own new addiction, Fever-Tree Cucumber Tonic Water. We settled into the living room and I surprised myself by saying a brief prayer in my mind before eating. Sometimes prayer is the only recourse one has.

Ali left again after lunch, and I wandered aimlessly around the house. I needed a plan. I didn't know why I was so convinced I'd find the answers to either disappearance here, and I started second-guessing myself. Maybe I'd just been itching to get out of Province-town. Maybe Mirela was right and I didn't want a crime committed I couldn't be the one to solve. Maybe all these years of stumbling upon the right answer—and truth be told, luck had played a major part in my past ventures into detection—maybe they all had gone to my head. Or my ego.

Margo texted just as I was starting to wonder if Wally had found a way up the chimney again; I hadn't seen him since breakfast—a meal, he'd informed us in no uncertain terms, that was both late and inadequate. *Everything fine there?*

Absolutely, I texted back. No need to tell her yet that I thought maybe her cat hated me.

Forgot to tell you, I have a friend works for The Enterprise.

As in Star Trek?

Very funny. As in local paper. You might give him a call if you're serious about finding out about the girl who disappeared. He can fill you in.

I thought for a moment, and then texted back. *Why would he?*

I did him a favor recently. Name is Will Fortier. Ireland is beautiful even in the rain.

I smiled. *Don't forget to come home,* I texted. *Wally thinks I don't feed him enough.*

Wally thinks nobody feeds him enough. Don't fall for it.

One of my favorite internet memes is of an AI-generated cat seated at a grand piano. The caption reads: "My next song is about the complexities of trust and betrayal, and it's called Why Is My Bowl Still Empty, Janice?"

I wrote down the reporter's name and number, and gave him a call later in the afternoon. Voicemail. Feeling somewhat foolish, I introduced myself and said I was staying at Margo's house. "She suggested you might be able to tell me about the Wampanoag woman who disappeared," I said. He probably wouldn't get back to me, but it was better than doing nothing.

But the next day changed everything. Because the next day, there was a body.

***

It was in an appropriate place: a cemetery. And it wasn't an "it": it was Juliet Mills.

I would have been surprised if it had been anyone else.

She was lying beside a grave in the cemetery next to the Old Indian Meeting House, and looked as though she'd just curled up there and gone to sleep. This I learned from Margo's reporter friend, who called me with the news.

It must have been some phenomenal favor, I thought, *if he's taking time off from his story to call me.* "I know her," I said to him. "Well, I met her, anyway. She was doing a program on the Race Point Inn in P'town. That's where I work."

"Her colleague told me she went missing there," Will said. He hadn't wasted any time getting information; a neighbor had noticed the body and called the police barely two hours before. "What can you tell me about that?"

Fair enough. "Not much," I confessed. "Bruce Peterson probably told you everything." Bruce had to be the colleague he'd spoken to. "She seemed fine to me. Professional. We had an interview—well, the presenter interviewed me, not Juliet—and then she went with a couple other people to scope out some scenes of the town. And pretty much disappeared into thin air." I winced at my own cliché. "It isn't clear how… maybe it was her choice, no-one seems to know one way or the other."

"And it wasn't like her, I know," he said, an undercurrent of amusement threading his words. Bruce had apparently been repeating his mantra again.

I swallowed. "How was she—do they know what happened to her?"

"She was strangled." He had to have an absolutely stellar contact in the police to know *that* already. But I was imagining Juliet as I'd last seen her, brisk and efficient and at ease in her work. Not as a victim. Not as she would have been found, losing control of her bowels, her neck bruised. He interrupted the image. "Are you still there?"

"I'm here. Sorry." I took a deep breath. "Listen, I know you're busy, and I don't have any right to your time, but I'd be really grateful if you kept me in the loop about what you learn and—"

"You're kidding, right?" he interrupted. "Why do you think I called you?"

"Um… because Margo asked you to? Because you're polite?" *How should I know?*

"It was in the producer's pocket," he said obliquely. "Juliet Mills. Her ID, her phone, her keys, everything you'd expect, that was all in her purse next to her body. There was just the one thing in the pocket."

"What?" This conversation was making no sense.

"A note. There was a note." He paused. "It said, 'Now Sydney Riley will know what it feels like to be responsible for a death.'"

Chapter Six

No.

No.

I hadn't just heard that. I'd been standing looking out the living-room window while on the phone; my legs suddenly felt like they couldn't hold me up anymore, and I felt my way to one of Margo's deep cushioned chairs and sank into it.

"Are you still there? Sydney?" Will's voice was coming out of the phone but I couldn't pay attention to it; the room was gyrating madly around me, and there was a growing coldness in the pit of my stomach. I was aware of my heart hammering as though trying to free itself of my body.

This wasn't happening. This couldn't be happening.

"Please, no," I whispered, whether to God or the universe or Will, I had no idea. *Breathe, Riley*, I reminded myself. *Just breathe.* I tried that for a moment and finally punched the speakerphone option; I didn't want Will's voice that close to my ear. "Are you sure?"

Definitely one of the dumbest things I could have said, but thinking wasn't really my forte in that moment.

"Are you all right?" Okay, one of the dumbest things *he* could have said, too. We were even.

"No," I said. "I'm not." I took another breath. I didn't even know what to ask. "That's all it said?"

"That's what I heard. I didn't see it myself. Do you have a comment?"

Oh, damn. So that was where this was going; I should have realized. He was, after all, a reporter. "No comment," I said, automatically. *Anything you say can be used against you…*

They were probably looking for me. The State Police. In Massachusetts—with a few urban exceptions, like Boston—they're the ones who investigate homicides, and I'd already had more than one encounter with them. And just like Julie Agassi, they hadn't been overly pleased with my becoming part of their investigations. *Breathe, Riley.*

Will hadn't given up. "Okay, I get it," he said. "I can keep it off the record for now. Does it mean anything to you? Do you know anyone who—"

"No," I interrupted him. "I don't." But my mind was racing. Who, indeed? Had I unintentionally harmed some person in some way? If it elicited this kind of response, I'd probably know about it, wouldn't I? Or had someone from my past come back? And killed an innocent person just to get my attention?

How do you live with something like that?

Juliet, talking about her childhood summers on the Cape, smiling at the memory, not knowing that choosing to feature the Race Point Inn on *Weekend Waypoints* would lead to her death. Juliet, smart and quick and clearly loving her job. Juliet, dead, with a note from her killer in her pocket that named me responsible.

Nausea rolled over me, and I scrambled to my feet and ran to the bathroom to throw up, barely making it to the toilet in time. In the room behind me I could hear Will talking, but I couldn't make out the words. This wasn't happening. This couldn't be happening.

Just breathe.

I rinsed my mouth and splashed cold water on my face and returned to the living room. Will was still on the phone. "What am I supposed to do with that?" I asked. It wasn't a rhetorical question.

Will said, "I'm sorry. I guess I could have told you with more finesse."

"I wish you hadn't had to tell me at all." I wanted him to go away. I wanted this whole conversation to go away. I wanted Ali, I wanted the past: to curl up on my old Little Shop of Horrors sofa in my tiny former apartment with Ali and Ibsen and... there were tears pressing against my eyes and I dashed them away. *Feeling sorry for yourself, Riley? Maybe spare a little compassion for Juliet?*

"I'd like to talk with you more about this," said Will, perhaps belatedly realizing I was in no shape to continue the conversation. "Can we meet? Later today, maybe?"

If I'm not being interrogated by the State Police by then. I didn't say it.

He was still talking. "I could come see you at Margo's house," he said. "Keep it private."

Keep me away from other reporters, more likely. But he was right: this wasn't coffee-shop talk. "You know where she lives?" If he didn't, Margo wasn't going to thank me for giving him directions. Some years back, she'd written a book about a miscarriage of justice in Boston and as much as named the true killer, and since then had been very discreet about her whereabouts—*and* installed an extensive and expensive security system at her house.

He knew, anyway. "I have a couple of people I need to talk to," he said. "I could come over there... maybe eleven o'clock?"

"Sure." I felt dazed, suddenly exhausted. The initial adrenaline rush had drained; I had an intense metallic taste from it in my mouth. There was little point in saying no, and if I was going to cope with this at all I was going to need more information.

I sat in the same chair for a long time after the call disconnected. I was still feeling nauseated. Juliet had done nothing to set this in motion; it was me. Something I'd done. Something I'd said. Someone I'd hurt. It seemed a backwards way of looking at things, but I had to ask who would hate me so much they'd kill someone else, knowing that would be more powerful than just killing me.

Why couldn't you have just killed me?

I picked up the phone again and asked Siri to connect me to Ali; my hands had stopped shaking but it felt like too much of an effort to press anything. It went immediately to voicemail; he was busy, teaching or investigating or doing whatever it was he was doing. "Call me back," I said. I wasn't going to try to explain this in a message.

There was a sudden thud next to me: Wally had jumped up onto the arm of the chair, staring at me, tentatively reaching out a paw and feeling his way onto my lap, where he settled, purring. Cats are sensitive to emotions, even cats that aren't typically affectionate. It was what Ibsen would have done.

And then, because there was nothing else I could do, I burst into tears and sobbed and sobbed.

***

Ali called me back about twenty minutes later. I hadn't moved from the chair, not least of all because I had a nineteen-pound cat in my lap, but most of all because I just couldn't. "Can you come here?" I asked him.

"What's wrong?"

I'd thought I'd cried myself out, but apparently I hadn't. "Juliet Mills," I said through the sobs. "She's dead. Please—just come, okay?"

Ali knows my past connections with crime. He's lived with me through a significant number of them; knows the presence of a body isn't going to reduce me to a blubbering mess, even when I knew the person. I'd taken the murder of my former boss, Barry, in stride: with incredible sadness, yeah, but I'd stayed reasonably rational. "Give me a few minutes to sort something out here," he said.

"Hurry," I said.

When he got there, Wally abandoned me, affronted perhaps his efforts at comfort were being superseded. I probably wouldn't see him again until dinner. Ali knelt next to the chair and put his arms around me and I cried some more. He didn't say anything, just held me until I reached the hiccupping phase. Then he went to the kitchen and came back with a glass of orange juice. "Drink," he ordered.

"I can't."

"You need the sugar. Drink."

So I drank it and did actually feel slightly better. He'd pulled another chair close to mine and sat there, holding my hands in his. "So, tell me."

I drew in a very shaky breath. "Juliet Mills was strangled," I said. "There was a piece of paper in her pocket, and it said she was dead because Sydney Riley needs to know what it feels like to kill someone." Well, something like that, anyway.

"Who told you this?" He was calm, and maybe it was a good thing he dealt with terrible things all the time. That he was an investigator. *Just the facts, ma'am.*

I was going off the deep end here. "A reporter. He works for, I don't remember the name of it, some local paper. Somebody in the Mashpee police told him." Or maybe the Wampanoag tribal police; Juliet had been found, after all, on tribal lands at the Old Indian Meeting House.

Ali stroked the back of my hand with his thumb; I was still holding his hands too tightly for him to do anything else. "Okay," he said. "How did he know to call you?"

"*I'd* called *him*," I said, a little helplessly. I'd made it so easy. "Margo knows him, she gave me his number. She told me maybe he knew something about that missing girl, the Wampanoag woman." That part seemed to have happened years rather than hours ago. "So I left him a voicemail. When he called back, I thought he was just being polite, you know, doing it as a favor for Margo. But he knew about the note. He wanted me to comment."

"What did you say?"

"Nothing. I freaked out. Ali, seriously, what can I do? She's dead because of me!"

"Listen to me," he said. He pulled his hands away and touched my chin. "Look at me, *habibi*. She is not dead because of you. She is dead because of some terrible sick individual who killed her."

He'd used the endearment he usually reserved for Lily, a tender name for a little girl, and that was exactly what I felt like. Small and powerless and insignificant. "But—"

"No," he said, interrupting the thought. "You have to let that go."

"He's coming over here at eleven," I said. "The reporter."

"He knows where she lives?" He was surprised, too. "Do you think it's a good idea for you to be talking to him?"

"Better him than the Staties," I said defensively.

"Oh, you'll talk to them, too. And what you *don't* want, *cara*, is to be quoted in the next edition of the newspaper." He thought for a moment. "Let me make a call. I'll stay here with you."

"It's as much for me as for him," I said. "I need to find out—"

He'd been scrolling through something on his phone, and now he looked up. "No," he said sharply. "No, you don't. You can't be part of any of this. If you were a cop, you'd be taken off the case immediately."

"I'm not a cop, and I'm already part of it," I said. "It was my name on that note. It's because of me that—"

"Don't," he said again, and then his call connected and he walked off into the kitchen. I could hear him telling someone he wasn't returning immediately. I stayed where I was and did my best to keep the panic at bay. I'd thought telling Ali was going to make me feel better, and it hadn't. No instant solutions, no waving a magic wand to make it all go away. No putting Ali in the role of savior.

I was going to have to figure this out, and no-one else was going to be able to do it for me.

***

Will arrived promptly at eleven, and clearly knew his way around the house already. Curiouser and curiouser. This wasn't about romance—he was at best thirty, and Margo is a lesbian of a certain age—but there was some relationship there. I found I was thinking way too much about what it might be, as though dwelling on an innocuous puzzle would make the other, far less innocuous one, go away.

We sat in the big airy three-seasons room, Ali beside me on the couch, Will on one of the delicate wrought-iron chairs across from us. He was handsome in a young-Cape Cod kind of way, with a somewhat aspirational beard and thick black hair tied in a man-bun, earrings, and the hint of some tats beneath the checkered shirt. He'd taken Ali's presence there with no surprise; he already knew about my law-enforcement connection.

I hoped he also knew if he was going to get any information from me, he was going to have to give some up as well. He put his phone on the glass coffee table between us. "Okay if I record this?"

I nodded, and Ali said, "We're off the record until I'm sure this isn't going to come back on Sydney."

Will nodded; he'd been expecting that, too. "What we need to do," he said, "is think about anybody who might have it in for you."

"It could be anybody," I said helplessly. It felt too big a question to even begin to answer. I swallowed. *Breathe, Riley.*

Will asked, "What about your former husband? Was your divorce acrimonious?"

I glanced at Ali; we didn't talk much about my first marriage, mostly because there wasn't much to say about it. "It was unpleasant," I said. "But not—nasty, you know? He was—he still is—chief of emergency medicine at Metropolitan Medical. What happened was, he decided he'd rather be married to one of his ER nurses than me. And, anyway, it was a long time ago." I stopped to think how long, exactly. Remembered the telephone call saying he had fallen in love with someone else. The sinking realization that the house I loved almost as much as I loved Noah was *his* family home, not mine. The slow bewildering understanding that while I had been puttering along thinking everything was fine, Noah was experiencing a whole different reality.

I was teaching cinema studies out at UMass/Boston with nothing more weighty on my mind than a colleague's plea to adopt her cat that hadn't taken too well to her having a baby. After the call came, I ran away—literally—in Noah's Mercedes and somehow ended up in Provincetown. It was January, most of the town was closed, but the Race Point Inn wasn't and I wandered in and almost immediately lost my shit over everything, and the inn's owner, Barry, had offered me tissues and brandy and, eventually, a job if I wanted it.

I went back to the city and resigned from UMass, said yes to the cat, bought myself a second-hand Honda, and only looked back once, the day the divorce papers arrived. When was that? I did some quick counting in my head and said, finally, "Eighteen years ago, I think. And I haven't had any communication with him since then."

He'd done his homework. "Noah Whitcomb," he said, nodding. "He's been in the news lately."

"Nothing to do with me," I said defensively. "I only heard about it the way everybody else did, reading the news sites." And taking a couple of calls from curious friends.

"No," he agreed. "Nothing to do with you."

Ali said, "Sydney's been helpful to the police in putting some people in prison."

Will nodded; he knew. "Can you make a list?"

Wonderful. A list of people who hated me. Sounded like fun. "Probably," I said.

"And it will go first to the appropriate law enforcement agencies," Ali added smoothly.

Will didn't seem surprised. "I can wait," he said. I wondered if his friend would leak it to him. But in the meantime he had enough to write about… what was it Juliet had called me, back in Province-town? A *crime-stopper*: that was it. "You're going to write about all that, aren't you?" I asked. "Everything I've done in Provincetown." It wasn't really a question.

He gave me a quick smile. "Can't avoid it," he agreed.

There had been more than just the two murders at the Race Point Inn; now we were going to go public with a whole lot of stuff even Wendy was going to be hard-pressed to spin in a positive way. Details about people I'd thought I could forget. Details about their victims, too, who would never be able to rest.

It wasn't as if I'd exactly tried to hide my informal sleuthing; there wasn't anything untoward about it. But the thought of seeing it spread out on social media and in websites and opening it up to an ongoing online commentary—some of it no doubt nasty—was disheartening.

There was something in all this, too, about chickens coming home to roost.

"I do have some details I can share with you," said Will, almost diffidently. "Juliet Mills stayed at the MidCape Resort night before last."

"Alone?" asked Ali.

"Unknown," said Will. "It's spread out, lots of grounds, pine trees, you don't have to come and go in a lobby like some hotels. She checked in online and arrived late; a room key was left for her at the front desk, which wasn't staffed."

"So what happened between when she disappeared in Province-town and when she checked in late at the resort?" I wondered out loud. "That's a lot more time than it takes to just drive there, if she was going under her own steam."

"Did she have a car?" asked Will.

"No." I shook my head. "They all came together in a couple of vans, the production staff, the presenter, the director, the camera and sound guys. It seemed a pretty compact operation. But she could have gotten an Uber."

Will said, "There's another thing. The grave she was next to—well, on top of, really—was some tribal leader from the seventeenth century. Someone pretty revered by the tribe, even after all these years. The Wampanoag feel closer to their ancestors than most of the rest of us." Meaning elite white people. "It's going to be seen as desecrating the grave."

Super. With a little luck, I was going to be causing a diplomatic incident.

Chapter Seven

So there it was. The connection I'd fantasized about, now a neon flashing light.

"Maybe we're looking at this the wrong way," said Ali after Will left. "It's possible Juliet doesn't connect to your past. Someone could have planned to kill her, all along, and adding you in was a distraction. Could be as simple as someone who'd heard of you—and face it, Sydney, you're not exactly unknown around here—and they're trolling you. Or muddying the waters."

Though I needed his rationality, I found it irritating. "If you're trying to make me feel better, it's not working," I said.

"It's not necessarily about you, *cara*. You don't have any ties to the Wampanoag. She does. At least two: she was going to do a program about the tribe, and when she's killed she's left on a Wampanoag grave. That's a little more focused than looking for some random person in your past you've offended."

"Different lines of inquiry," I said.

"Better than freaking out because you think it's your fault."

But when I sat down and tried to create a list of people who could conceivably have it in for me, I found my hand was shaking. It was now the first week in July and hotter than I'd remembered July to ever have been—global warming, great, something else to worry about—and still I felt cold.

I'd have to start at the beginning. Bear Week in Provincetown. That was the week I'd met Ali, the week I went for an early-morning swim at the inn and discovered the inn's owner, Barry, floating face-down in the pool next to me. An image still as vibrant and shocking now as it had been all those years ago.

The handsome young man who had proven deadly to both Barry, the inn's owner, and nearly to me as well. I'd really, really liked him. I went to his trial, but only insofar as I was required to testify; I couldn't look at him in court. He had killed for gain, and yet I still liked him. It would make for a great mystery novel, actually: I understood that Agatha Christie often made the villain the nicest guy in the room.

I wrote the next name. I remembered it well. Ali had told me people were complicated; I didn't want people to be complicated. I wanted them to be clear. Just nice, or just mean. Good guys, or bad guys. But it's thinking like that which got us into our current moment. This murderer had used a knife—an unusual weapon, I learned, for a woman to choose. Maybe because we empathize too much and can too readily imagine the blade in our own flesh.

I'd had to testify at her trial, too. And I'd looked across the courtroom at her, and she seemed small and scared and it nearly broke my heart.

Really, most of these people had broken my heart. I didn't just read Agatha Christie; I read Chesterton, too, and his protagonist Father Brown always felt sad when dealing with crime and criminals; he always could envision how the situations they were in could happen to anyone, and wondered, often, if the rest of us might not have made the same decision under similar circumstances.

A humanist crime-stopper, Father Brown.

Then there was the time at the Provincetown International Film Festival… Mike's former husband had been back in town, and I'd organized a wedding for two movie stars. I'd had to testify against someone then, too, but fortunately for me he was just as nasty in court as he'd been when he was trying to kill me. No guilt there.

I'd lost a beloved neighbor during one hot Portuguese Festival, and in the process solved a decades-long cold case along with two newer ones, though not before Ali got shot and I'd taken another unintentional dip in the harbor. But that killer had been elderly already when they took her away in handcuffs; she probably wasn't alive anymore.

I was just stretching and thinking about making some coffee when my phone buzzed, and the absolutely unwelcome photograph of my mother appeared on the screen. Because apparently I didn't have enough to worry about; let's pop in a little family drama and make it *really* interesting. The cherry on top. "Hi, Ma."

"Is that you? Or is that a recording?"

"It's me, Ma."

"I'm surprised you picked up. You never pick up," said my mother, going as always directly for the jugular. And patently untrue: I do sometimes answer, but she just seems to have a knack for calling at the absolute worst time, and I have a knack of "forgetting" to call her back.

"I'm here now," I said. "What is it?"

"What is it? Why? I need a reason to call my daughter now?"

Breathe, Riley. "Ma. You never call without a reason." *And you can't have it both ways.*

She wanted to be crystal-clear about how miffed she was. "Maybe if you called me sometimes, I wouldn't have to be planning my calls around your schedule and we could just chat, like normal people do."

My mother can get into an argument faster than anyone. She could probably on a good day argue with herself. "Ma, I'm here now, what do you want?"

"Don't take a tone with me, Sydney Riley." This woman will be on her deathbed and accuse me of taking a tone. Maybe she'd enjoy the drama so much she'd forget to die.

Somehow she managed to drag herself around to the point. "Now, I know it's your famous *season*," (I could feel the air-quotes around the word) "and you can't leave your inn for more than five minutes, but my friend Grace's granddaughter just got engaged, and I told her you'd be happy to take a call and give her some tips for planning the wedding."

Oh, you did, did you? Somehow, though, the predictability of my mother's life being bizarrely centered around weddings was a relief. I didn't have to think about dead bodies when I was thinking about weddings.

Well, most of the time, anyway.

I think my own wedding had been a disappointment to her for a number of reasons, not least of which was the body crashing into our ceremony; it had pretty much taken center stage and deprived her of the importance she (and her many upper-class friends) assigned to being the mother of the bride. I'd spent the last two years assuring her that sometime we'd have a big renewal-of-vows ceremony.

Maybe sometime in the year 2999.

I cleared my throat. "Ma, I'm a little busy right now. And there are people who do this professionally. They're called wedding planners."

Okay, maybe sometimes I do take a tone.

"You're always too busy. And *you're* a wedding planner."

"Not anymore," I said. "I have to pay one, just like everybody else."

She didn't pick up on the hint. "In fact, I told Grace they could have the wedding at your inn. Isn't that a good idea?"

It was a terrible idea. What poor bride wanted her grandmother and her grandmother's cronies planning her event? "When is this supposed to happen?"

"Well, that's part of what she needs you for. To work out the timing. Grace says she doesn't even know where to begin. Some people only get married once, you know. They don't have your kind of experience."

That's me, a Scarlet Woman on my—gasp!—*second marriage*. My mother conveniently forgets it was Noah who'd left me—and that she'd started trying to match me up with various friends' various offspring before the ink was even dry on the divorce decree. "Ma, why don't we let this person make her own decisions about her own wedding?"

The absurdity of the conversation was starting to get to me. I shouldn't have been surprised; sooner or later, the absurdity of any conversation with my mother gets to me. I don't know why she has such a fixation on weddings; hers, from everything I could tell, had been lavish—not by Indian three-day-seven-hundred-guests-standards lavish, but pretty impressive all the same.

"Grace says she doesn't know the first thing. Sydney, aren't you supposed to be helping people?"

Yes. I'm supposed to be helping people. In particular those whose deaths I didn't cause. "Ma, I'm not even home right now. And—I can't think about it right now, either." If she had been someone else's mother, she'd have heard the note of desperation in my voice, thought to ask me what was wrong, offered some maternal warmth. Instead, what she said was, "You're not home? Why aren't you home?"

I sighed. "It's a long story, Ma." There was absolutely no way I was getting into it. "I'm looking after my friend Margo's cat while she's in Ireland."

"What's she doing in Ireland?"

Disconnecting from stupid conversations. "Probably relaxing and enjoying herself," I said. "It's a vacation. So I'm not even at the inn, I can't check dates or anything like that. And I wouldn't be able to even if I was there, because it's not my job. If your friend's granddaughter wants to, she can call the Race Point, we have a great manager and a great events planner and I'm sure they could help her. If she even wants to get married on the Cape."

"Why wouldn't she want to get married on the Cape?" And round and round we go. Some days, I really *really* hope I was a thoroughly obnoxious two-year-old.

If so, she was getting more than her share of revenge.

Revenge. And the word brought me back to the present. My present.

As soon as I managed to extricate myself from my mother, I picked up my notebook and frowned at the half-finished list. Okay… who else?

I closed my eyes and saw it: my brilliant beautiful Jamaican doctor, Thea, and me, tied up together at the top of the Pilgrim Monument. Can't ever forget *that*. The white nationalists intent on starting a race war, and one of them a state trooper. It couldn't be him, surely: I had some vague knowledge cops don't fare well in prison. I added the name to the list.

There was one name I didn't need to add—the person who had threatened Lily, back when she was a baby. Mirela had taken care of that. It was adjudicated as self-defense; Mirela had a good lawyer.

Margo, of course.

Who was I forgetting? The years blended seamlessly, marked by festivities and theme weeks and the long bleak windy winters. I had to do better. I had to remember someone who had hated me enough to do—this.

I thought for a long moment before adding another name to the list. One of Provincetown's beloved town employees. And me, swimming furiously, trying to survive in Provincetown Harbor's frigid water. I'd testified against him, too.

When I put them all together like this, it seemed I'd spent more time in Barnstable County Superior Court than I'd imagined. Each time it was chilling. And each time when I later heard the jury's verdict, I'd felt gratitude wash over me. I was alive, Ali was alive, Mirela was alive, Mike was alive. When you considered all the times we'd each come close to becoming very un-alive, there was a lot to be thankful for.

I believe my guardian angel must be up for some sort of heavenly award; over the years, I'd kept him/her/them/it working a whole lot of overtime.

I roused myself. No time now for metaphysics. Or pronoun preferences. Who else?

The kidnapping of Victor, the owner of the Dolphin Fleet, our whale-watching boats. And how I'd been triggered, remembering my own sister's kidnapping—we hadn't learned yet what had happened to her, but she was suddenly there with me, and my memories of her disappearance kept surfacing. Victor resurfaced too, sadly; he was dead before anyone got to him.

I'd done therapy from time to time, in college, during my divorce, at various points since then, but even there I'd never talked about Alexandra. Never opened that door. Never revisited myself as the little eight-year-old girl sitting on the front steps sobbing, with the young FBI agent urging her to *breathe… just breathe… you're going to be all right, honey… just breathe…*

I hadn't been able to save my sister, and I wasn't able to save Victor, either; but I did help the authorities arrest the murderer, and yeah, I'd testified there, too.

On the plus side, I'd once *almost* been able to figure out who pulled off the famous Isabella Stewart Gardner heist, which would have been nice; I learned a great deal about the economics of the art world, and eventually I'd testified against the person who'd tallied three deaths before finally being taken into custody.

And then there was my wedding, and the body hurtling out of room thirty-four, disrupting everything quite effectively, and the least likely individual—whose motives I understood better than anyone else's—was sent off to prison as well. Last name on the list.

So what did I do now? Follow up on where they all had ended up, like doing some kind of demented class-reunion research? It was a long shot, but I didn't have anything I could consider a short shot, either.

Had anyone been released? Had their conviction overturned? That could be a place to start. I wondered if Ali would have any ethical problems with finding out.

"It's not an ethical problem," he said later. He'd popped back over to his training event and returned to the house in time to find me furiously scribbling names. "It's a practical one. That's all on record, the information is public, your friend Will probably knows how to access it."

"But you could do it faster," I countered. "Through your contacts."

He shook his head. "I'm not investigating Juliet's murder. I don't have access to that kind of data."

"What happened to inter-agency cooperation?" I demanded. I'd done my part, and I wanted to keep the momentum going.

"Let's just see what the police say," he countered reasonably. "You need more information before you can hypothesize."

"They haven't even spoken to me yet," I said.

The doorbell rang. We looked at each other, and Ali shrugged. "They're about to," he said.

Chapter Eight

They weren't in full trooper jodhpurs-and-polished-boots uniform—the investigative unit wears khakis and dark blue polo shirts; but the very tidiness of the outfit still screams "cop" even before you get to the fact that they were wearing sidearms.

Law enforcement just *loves* their sidearms.

It wasn't the same two I'd had dealings with in the past. I was trying to work out whether this was a good thing or not when Ali let them in. *He* wasn't wearing his sidearm, but they recognized him as part of the fraternity anyway; maybe they had some sort of internal radar that picks up on stuff like that.

Or maybe they'd just done their research and found out who I was married to.

We sat down again in the three-seasons room, which was starting to feel more like an interview area than a pleasant getaway space. I wondered briefly in passing if it would ever get back to just being a nice room.

"Detective Lieutenant Whitney," the woman said to me. She didn't offer her hand to shake. "This is Detective Sergeant Franklin," and a nod to the guy next to her. Their names were as white as they were. "We have some questions for you."

Join the club, I thought. "Okay."

"You're aware of the homicide we're investigating." It wasn't a question; I nodded. "Good. And now it seems you've had some time to think about it." *Some time to think about it? What does that mean? Not pleased, are you, that Will beat you to my door?*

At least she didn't go in for the trooper-speak that makes every conversation sound like a written report; she actually used contractions. Maybe she was just trying to put me at ease. Though on reflection, probably not: when dealing with the public, the last thing a homicide cop wants people to feel is comfortable.

I said, truthfully, "I have no idea why someone killed Juliet Mills, and I have no idea what that note was referring to."

She nodded; she'd been expecting my response. "Most people would say that," she agreed. "But I think you're a special case. And I'll be frank with you, Sydney, I absolutely think you do have *some* idea."

I looked at Ali, a little helplessly, but he wasn't interrupting. I remembered what he'd said to Will, and latched on to that. "Okay, yes, I get it: some people have gone to prison," I admitted. "That's true. But I didn't put them there. The district attorney did."

"It wasn't the district attorney's name on that paper."

I shivered at her tone. "People get things wrong," I said quickly. "They make connections where there aren't any. It might be— anybody." I took a breath. "There was that time—I don't remember when it was—that guy who tried to kill the president because he wanted to impress some actress? Do you remember? It could be something like that. Someone making a connection that isn't even there." I was floundering, and everyone in the room knew it.

Franklin put in his two cents. "You knew Juliet Mills," he said. "Did you have any conversations with her about your past involvement with law enforcement?" His phrasing made it sound like I'd been the one arrested.

Well, in Ali's case, that was true.

"I didn't *know* her," I said. "I *met* her. Just that once. And the only thing that even remotely connected to—me—in any way, was she said I had a reputation. But it was just in the course of conversation, you know? I mean, we also talked about her vacations on the Cape when she was a kid. And about the Wampanoag pow-wow. And Provincetown, generally. And a lot about the Race Point Inn itself. It was… just passing the time chatting, while they were setting up my interview." I was talking too much.

He ignored most of the floundering and zeroed in on the least comfortable aspect of the conversation. "Your reputation? What was that about?"

I took a deep breath. I didn't want to say the word, it was too cringeworthy. "She said I had a reputation as a… a crime-stopper." There. It was out. *Breathe, Riley. Just breathe.* "She said it like I was famous, or something. But I'm not. Not really. I told her she should go talk to Mirela. Um, Mirela Petrovna. I said she's really the famous one."

Whitney checked her notes on a small tablet computer; I hadn't even noticed her pulling it out, nor did I see where she could have pulled it from. "The artist," she said.

"Right. She's famous. I thought she'd be more interesting to the audience than anything I could say."

"You wanted to deflect Juliet Mills's interest in you?"

"It was just a *conversation*," I said again; even I could hear the desperation in my voice. "We were chatting. That's all. It's not like she was thinking of doing a program on me, or Mirela, or anything. Just chatting."

"I see." She didn't say anything else, just kept looking at me. Seconds ticked by. I recognized the technique; silence makes most people uncomfortable and they'll talk just to end it. I wasn't falling for it.

Until I did.

I might have given it sixty seconds; probably less. I said, in a rush, "Listen, I know you have to investigate this and believe me when I say I wish you all the success in the world. Juliet didn't deserve to die. And if I had anything to do with it, with her getting killed, then it's something I'll carry inside me for the rest of my life." Understatement. "But also—and I'm not just saying this to get out of anything—that note could have been a—" oh, God, I was going to use the expression "—red herring, right? I mean, someone could have written it to make your investigation go one way, and it has nothing to do with reality. That's at least possible, isn't it?"

I'd seen the quick glance between the detectives when I said *red herring;* it was all a little too much Miss Marple. The inexperienced amateur sleuth strikes again. *Stop talking, Riley.*

Whitney looked at me about three beats longer than the question deserved. "We are," she said austerely, "investigating every possible option. But let's stay with you for now. Do you have a list of people the *district attorney* sent to prison" (nice little sarcasm there) "with your assistance?"

I took a deep breath. "I've been putting one together," I admitted.

"Which," said Ali, "Sydney will of course make available to you."

I shot him a look. *Thanks a lot, husband.* But he was right; I was going to have to give it to them sooner or later, and sooner would at least give me some grounds for saying I'd cooperated.

"That would be helpful," said Whitney, and waited.

I blew out a sigh. "I'm still working on it," I said.

I wasn't still working on it. I was feeling stubbornly resentful and not inclined to help. Massachusetts has a laudably high solve-rate for homicides—I'd read somewhere it was ninety-four percent, which if true is pretty spectacular—but there are times when they get it wrong, too. And I had a feeling that if they got this one wrong, it was going to come back to bite me.

And all anyone had to do was look at the Karen Read case to know not every cop in the Commonwealth is working toward the greater good. Margo could point to the Eddie O'Brien case under that category, too; her book was an indictment of politics guiding the hand of the law. And people paying for it with their lives; Eddie had lived in prison much longer than he had lived out of it.

Whitney wasn't interested. "Then let's start with what you have." She settled her backside more firmly into her chair. The message was clear: she wasn't going anywhere until I delivered.

I allowed myself one more theatrical sigh and got up and fetched my notebook from the dining table where I'd been working on it. "Here."

Franklin took it from me, flipped it open, and gave it a cursory glance; he nodded to Whitney, and she stood up. "Thank you for your cooperation, ma'am."

Ali stood up too. "I'll see you out," he said. I didn't know if he was helping me or wanted a quick word with the detectives on his own, and I didn't even try to figure it out. I was suddenly feeling exhausted.

Because there were a lot of names on that list. And if this particular "line of inquiry" was the right one, it meant something I'd never had occasion to think about—that there was a sizable number of people who could want me dead. Or, worse, want me alive and in pain.

But which one was it?

***

Ali said, "You could have been more cooperative."

I hadn't moved. "You could have been more helpful," I said.

"Sydney, there are times when it's better to just let other people do their jobs."

"What does that even mean? You're taking their side?"

"We're all on the same side," he said. He sounded frustrated. He probably felt caught between being my husband and being a cop, and if this were any other situation I might have felt some compassion for his conflict, but I was tired and scared and was again absurdly fighting back tears. He was the guardian of so many people; I just wanted him to be mine. I just wanted him to keep the bad things away. "Maybe you should go home," he said.

"*What?*"

"I'll stay on, look after Wally," he said. "I have work to do here. But there's nothing you can do, not without getting in the way of the police—don't!" he added, as I opened my mouth to speak. "They'll find out who killed Juliet. You're too personally involved. Go back to the inn, try to relax, and deal with real life for a while. There's nothing you can do here."

"I'll leave if you promise me you'll investigate it, too."

He shook his head. "*Cara*, it's not my department. It's not even my agency. There's no indication that Juliet was going to be trafficked. And I do have a real case to look into."

"I'm not a real case." I knew I was whining, and I hated myself for it.

"You," he said, sitting beside me on the couch and taking my hands in his, "are very much alive, and if I have anything to do with it, you'll stay that way. There's a young woman out there somewhere who may or may not be alive, and if she is, I need to find her and shut down whoever is responsible for her disappearance."

Put it that way... I took a deep breath. "You're right." Somewhere, there was a very scared and very vulnerable girl who needed Ali a whole lot more than I did. *Get a grip, Riley.*

"And the truth is, *cara*, there's no guarantee that note was the end of things," he said, opening up a whole new terrifying arena for thought. "Whoever this person is, they might have other plans for you. Think about it. You're here, mostly alone, in an isolated house with no one around keeping an eye on you. Anything could happen. I'd feel a lot better if you were back in P'town with Mike and Mirela and a whole bunch of people who care about you."

He was right, again. Margo's house is as safe as she could make it, knowing there was someone somewhere out there who wished her harm—she was still, years after the book's publication, getting threats; but with the current parade of people stopping by to interview me, that safety must have been slipping a little. There was no question but that the Race Point Inn was a better place for me to be. Really.

But they'd found Juliet in P'town. Whoever they were. They'd gotten to her in the middle of a brilliant bright summer day in a place teeming with tourists. Maybe when stuff like this happened, there *were* no safe spaces.

"I'll think about it," I said at last.

"*Cara*—"

"I'll think about it," I repeated. "I really will." I looked at him and managed a smile. "And you have places to be. Go on."

"You'll think about it," he said. "Okay. Why don't we go out to dinner tonight, and if you decide to go home, you can leave first thing in the morning."

"Okay," I agreed. I didn't feel much like celebrating, but I also didn't feel much like cooking. I actually didn't feel much like *eating,* either, but going through the motions had served me well in the past. Fake it until you make it sort of thing.

He was looking indecisive, and I made a shooing motion with my hands. "Go on. I can't think with you in the room. And you have work."

"Text me if you leave the house," he said.

"I will."

"I'll pick you up at six."

"Okay."

I sat for a long time after he left, letting my feelings settle, trying to look at things as a reasonable adult.

I'd given the cops my notebook. With a sigh, I went back into Margo's study and found some paper, and slowly reconstituted the list.

And then I called Will Fortier.

Chapter Nine

In the end, I didn't go back to Provincetown.

Will was pleased to hear from me. "So, have you come up with a name?"

"I've come up with too many names," I said. "And I have no idea how to narrow it down." I paused. "I thought maybe you could help."

"Maybe." He wasn't very good at concealing the eagerness in his voice. For the first time, I considered what this story, or series of stories, meant for him. Someone as professional—and young—as Will Fortier wasn't going to be happy spending his career working for a local newspaper. I was his stepping-stone to bigger and better things.

Okay, fine; I planned to take full advantage of it. "What about Juliet Mills?" I asked. "Have *you* come up with anything?"

He chuckled. "A little quid pro quo," he said. "I can appreciate that."

"Well?"

"Okay." He thought about it for a moment. "Are you up for a field trip?"

Anything to get out of the house and my endless ruminations. "Sure."

"Meet me at the Old Indian Meeting House," he said. "Um— tomorrow morning? Around ten?"

I didn't try to hide my disappointment. "Not now?"

"Tomorrow," he said firmly. "Ten o'clock."

Ali wasn't happy with my decision. He knew better than to suggest dinner at Bleu; what we both needed was plain comfort food, not escargots, so we headed over to Marshland in nearby Sandwich, the home of pot roast and meatloaf and chicken parm. I ordered a large glass of wine as soon as we were seated; it wasn't Côtes du Rhône and I didn't care.

"I can't keep you safe here," he complained.

"It's not your job to keep me safe," I said. "I appreciate that you want to, don't get me wrong, but it's not up to you." I sighed. "Ali— I'd go crazy at home." Never mind that right now I'd feel on the edge of insanity anywhere, but maybe even more so at Nuthouse-by-the-Sea, which was what the Race Point Inn often felt like in the summer. "I won't do anything stupid. I won't take risks. But you have to understand—this is too personal. I need to know."

He was looking out the window, looking at his food, looking anywhere but at me. After twelve years together, I was pretty sure I could read his mind, know what he was thinking. What he wanted to do was to protect me. What he also wanted was to respect me and my decisions. Total conflict. I loved him a lot for both those considerations.

I knew he'd finally come down on the latter, and he'd support me in any way he could… *and* that if anything bad did happen to me, he'd find it extremely difficult to live with.

So I had to make sure nothing bad happened. Which was actually fine with me, that being my preference as well.

Still, we were both clearly uncomfortable. Back at Margo's house, Ali went into Margo's study to "do some work," but mostly, I suspected, to get away from me. I sat in the living room with my laptop and—surprisingly—Wally, who was starting to get behind the notion that if you can't be with the one you love, you can love the one you're with.

By the time we went to bed we were chilly and polite to each other, extra-careful around manners (no, you can have the bathroom first; no, please, you go ahead) and both of us, I think, relieved the day was over. We each needed the other in all the currently wrong ways: me to feel that Ali was backing me up, Ali to talk me out of being stubborn and reckless. We were both probably right.

And I had a bad feeling it was just the beginning.

***

The Old Indian Meeting House was built in 1684, Mashpee being the first and largest of the of the "praying Indian" towns to embrace Christianity.

"Praying Indians?" I asked Will. It sounded way too colonial and racist for comfort. "Seriously?"

"Some people think it's a major reason the tribe survived," he said. We were waiting outside the door; Derek Collins, the current chairman of the Mashpee Wampanoag and a member of the tribal historic preservation board, was going to give us a tour. "It meant they got a lot of support from the Puritans, who were running things by then."

It still didn't feel right to me, though if I were going to make any progress deciphering why Juliet had been murdered here, then I should probably start wrapping my head around one or two uncomfortable concepts. "Do they still have church services here?"

He was scrolling through something on his phone and nodded. "Church, community center, all that," he said.

It was my first look at where they'd found Juliet's body. The police tape was still up in the cemetery, and he saw me gazing across at it. "Jurisdictional chaos," he commented. "It's in Mashpee, so the Mashpee police take an interest. It's on tribal grounds, so the tribal police would normally take the lead—theoretically, anyway. But also because it's a homicide on federally protected land, the FBI is involved." And the only reason Ali and his agency weren't also involved was that Juliet had been murdered, not trafficked. *Cheer up, Riley, maybe it will still come to that.*

I shivered; I'd noticed—you couldn't help but notice—the sign on the driveway leading to the Meeting House: "Reservation Boundary Marker," it read; "authorized access only." *We're not in Kansas anymore.*

"Anyway," Will said, going back to scrolling, "it will be interesting to see who ends up with the ball."

As "the ball" was referring to the investigation of a very real death of a very real person, I wasn't all that interested in whatever alphabet agency took the lead, just so long as they ended up with the right result. For Juliet, and maybe for me. "The State Police interviewed me yesterday," I said.

That got his attention. "Who?"

"A lieutenant called Whitney and her sidekick," I said. For the life of me, I couldn't remember his name.

"What did you tell them?"

I snorted. "Tell them? I didn't tell them anything. That's because I don't know anything. But I gave them the list." My desperate notebook scribblings had taken on a life of their own: The List. "I made you a copy," I added.

"Text it to me."

I nodded; I'd scan it when I got back to Margo's house.

"Here's Derek," he said. "Leave the list out of it for now, okay?"

"I'd like to leave it out of my *life*," I said fervently.

So we got the tour. Derek was tall and clearly spent significant time working out, with glossy hair in a ponytail and a beaded necklace and several earrings. We sat on pews in the stark sanctuary that comprised the Meeting House. We learned about the materials used to build it, back when trees on the Cape were old and tall and broad; we learned about the construction method (post-and-beam, if anyone is interested); we learned how it had fallen into ruin and was rebuilt in the early two-thousands.

"But you have to put it in context," Derek said. "This church was built only seventy years after Captain Thomas Hunt kidnapped twenty young Wampanoag men from Patuxet and seven more from Nauset. He sold them in Spain as slaves."

Trafficking. There it was.

Derek was still talking. "And not long after that was the Great Dying."

Will wasn't taking notes; he knew this already. I could vaguely recollect seeing something about it up at the Provincetown Museum. "European diseases," I said, remembering.

Derek nodded. "We don't know which one it was, exactly," he said. "But in just three years, some catastrophic plague killed tens of thousands of native people up and down the New England coast. It weakened our nation in every way you can imagine, politically and economically. And especially militarily."

"Almost as if it were intentional," I said.

He gave me a sharp look. "It worked," he said. "The tribes were decimated." He'd told this story a hundred times before, I thought, and yet the pain was still there, his voice positively shimmering with it. This was real, and present, and immediate to him. "In 1661, Chief

Massasoit died, and his son Wamsutta succeeded him. But Wamsutta was arrested by the English." He glanced at me, quickly. "And then he died during questioning."

A pause so we could imagine exactly what kind of questioning ended that way. "His brother Metacom became chief, and by then no-one thought the English were our friends. So Metacom launched a war—a last-ditch effort to avoid recognizing English authority and stop English settlement on our land. That war is named for him—his English name was Philip—and lasted only fourteen months, right up to when they killed him. Him, and countless other Wampanoag."

"And yet they built this church less than twenty years later," I said, wondering if my math could be right; it wasn't very long. I couldn't imagine what kind of peace had been negotiated when the invaders had killed most of the population. The people from whom I'd descended had a lot to answer for. I thought of my parents' home in New Hampshire, and wondered what tribe had lived in their Stepford-Wives town first.

Derek gave me a look. "We survived," he said, and it was there in those two stark words: centuries of oppression, centuries of determination to stay alive.

Will said, almost diffidently, "The grave where Juliet Mills's body was found... does that have any special meaning?" He was looking at his phone, and I wondered if anyone still used the once-ubiquitous reporter's notebooks. He already knew the answer, but I didn't say anything. He was going somewhere with this. "Amos Thatcher?"

"All the graves have special meaning," Derek said. He wasn't going to make anything easy for us. I couldn't say I blamed him.

Will was undeterred. "Who was Amos Thatcher?" he asked.

"A tribal elder. Very much respected. After the war, he was instrumental in negotiating with the English to designate Mashpee a praying town, which is what gave it some limited legal and political protections." One of his shoulders twitched, slightly. "It didn't stop them from continuing to sell men into slavery in the Caribbean, and enslaving women and children right here in New England."

Trafficking. Again.

Will said, "And you lost more land in the meantime."

The other man's dark eyes rested on him for a moment. "It's always been about land," he said. "We never thought about land ownership until the Europeans came. It's still not a concept we're comfortable with. It's not part of our culture. We caretake the land, we don't own it." He paused. "Finally the colonists designated Mashpee a reservation, but it didn't stop them from encroaching."

He gave a bleak ghost of a smile. "We had everything they wanted: wood, and fish, and game. But especially fish, shellfish. Do you know that today there's only one acre of the reservation with direct access to the water? Everything else is landlocked, and all the old paths are blocked by private developers, or fences, or overgrown brush. Our access is supposedly legally protected, but that doesn't stop non-indigenous people in their big houses with their big fences from accusing us of trespassing on *their* land. And our kids have to see that, see them yelling at us. It's an odd way to grow up."

Will was clicking his phone, dutifully taking notes. I was thinking of the Race Point Inn, and all of Provincetown, also now populated, at least in the summer, by a new set of invaders, people with money and several-million-dollar homes. I was thinking of the history spiel we gave visitors, glossing over the fact we'd built on unceded land— in our case, that of the Pamet people (who had disappeared entirely, though some had found refuge with the Wampanoag)—and moving on to the whalers and the Portuguese fishing families and the bohemian art colony and all the other, prettier things. Maybe it was time, I thought, for the inn, at least, to revise that bit of storytelling.

I said, tentatively, "But a lot of places and people are now including land acknowledgments in their work. Isn't that a step in the right direction?" I knew the Wellfleet Harbor Actors Theatre did; it was on their website. There were probably others.

Derek gave me an odd smile. "Tell me this," he said, not ungently. "If someone steals your purse, and announces they've stolen your purse, but still doesn't give it back, is that announcement a good or helpful gesture?" he asked. "What it does is make them feel good that at least they've had the humility to say they stole it, and that they acknowledged your loss. It shows they're *sensitive*." He sketched air-quotes around the last word, then shrugged. "They don't understand this isn't about land ownership—it's about stewardship and broken promises."

I hadn't thought of that; I actually had thought it was rather brave of WHAT to include the land acknowledgment upfront. I hadn't seen it as performative. And I was pretty sure they didn't *mean* for it to be performative, either.

We apparently had a lot to learn.

He let it go and brought us back to the subject at hand. "You have to understand, this isn't just a matter of that poor woman's death. For us, this is yet another desecration of our past."

And another layer of meaning, which I was sure had been deliberate on the murderer's part. But which layer held the key to finding out who had done it?

I had no connection to the Wampanoag.

Or hadn't until now.

Chapter Ten

We weren't done with our field trip.

"Hungry?" Will asked after we left Derek at the Meeting House.

"Always."

He took me to a place called Oneil's Kitchen, and I couldn't help but notice the poster on a telephone pole outside the restaurant: *Have you seen this woman?* it asked, with a photo of a beautiful young indigenous woman and a number to call. After I noticed that, I couldn't un-see her.

I ordered a belated breakfast and was rewarded with the best banana bread I'd ever eaten.

Will knew the owner—Oneil himself, a big Jamaican guy with an even bigger smile—and they talked together for a moment while I thought about what it would feel like to have someone move into your front yard and then claim you couldn't stay there anymore because they were building a bigger house than the one you've lived in for generations, that your home didn't count, and your presence was no longer required.

"What I don't understand," I said when Will came back to the table, "is how Mashpee is an indigenous reservation but is also a town where clearly a lot of non-natives live." In fact, Mashpee had struck me as pretty similar to other Cape Cod towns, complete with the usual suspects—Dunkin' Donuts, CVS, even Walmart—and *that* wasn't even beginning to consider Mashpee Commons, essentially an outdoor shopping mall designed to look like Ye Olde Quaint New England Village and filled with even more national chain stores, along with little pretentious boutiques.

And Bleu.

"Not all of the town is part of the reservation," he said easily. He waited while his hamburger and my omelet were served, and continued while putting a prodigious amount of ketchup on his fries. "Okay. Land Holdings 101. There are various types of land holdings involved with tribal nations. The most common is something called a federal-trust land. What that means is, the federal government holds the legal title to the land on behalf of the tribe. Then the tribe can exercise its sovereignty over the territory." He paused, thinking. "It's rooted in something called the Doctrine of Discovery, if I'm remembering that right."

"Sounds official."

"Yeah, well, that's how land grabs work. By sounding official." He ate a French fry and went on. "A lot of indigenous people in the US and Canada want it rescinded. But it's totally made up. It didn't even start here. I think it was sometime in the twelfth century that some pope said if European Christians wanted to colonize non-Christian lands, then they could. They'd *discovered* them, after all." His turn to use air-quotes. "Essentially, the tribes have occupancy rights, but radical title? That goes to the white dudes."

"I'm almost sorry I asked," I said. "So what does that have to do with Mashpee?"

He grinned and ate his hamburger for a moment. "Thing is, you're thinking of native reservations out West," he said. "Wampanoag land isn't all in one place. It's all over Mashpee, sure, but it's spread out. About sixty acres around the tribal council offices, another ten in conservation land, and then there's the museum, the Meeting House, the burial ground... it all adds up."

That made more sense than trying to untangle the roles of each government entity involved. And I'd seen the boundary markers. "I still think," I said, "if I were Wampanoag, I'd resent like hell having other people run my town."

He looked amused. "Do you *think*?"

I knew how it felt, though to a smaller degree, seeing the Instagram posts of Provincetown's new elites sharing how amazing their lives were, each one trying to outdo the others with the sheer wonderfulness of what they did and who they saw, the latter definitely not including anyone who'd lived in Provincetown for more than ten years or wasn't a multi-millionaire. I could imagine that if Instagram had existed back in the day, the English colonists' posts would look very much like theirs. They'd feature selfies with the people who were important to them—definitely not the Wampanoag.

"All right, all right," I said, pushing my empty plate away. "I get it."

And then he finally told me about the girl.

***

Her legal name was Skye Taylor, but her real name, her Wampanoag name, was Sokanon. She'd graduated last year from Mashpee Middle-Senior High School but had also taken classes in an advanced history program at Nauset Regional High (and there it was: another native tribe that didn't exist anymore; the Cape was dotted with towns named for the people the town displaced—or worse). She was taking a gap year, helping her parents out in the small convenience store they owned on Main Street while taking a couple of classes at Cape Cod Community College, known locally as the Four Cs. She wanted to be an archaeologist.

Will brought up a photo on his phone and passed it across to me, the same photo from the flyer posted outside. She was lovely, with long shining black hair and a smile that could illuminate a major metropolitan area. She was going to be one of the dancers at the upcoming pow-wow.

Until she disappeared.

Questioned by the tribal police, her parents had seen nothing particularly amiss in the days before she'd gone missing. Yes, she had been seeing someone, but she'd always had boyfriends, she was such a pretty girl. They didn't know who the current one was; she'd told them it was no-one they knew; someone new to the area, they thought. Of course that last bit had given the police a whole array of flashing red warning lights, but her parents hadn't seen it that way— she was friendly, she was always making new friends.

"She didn't show up for work, which they say wasn't like her," said Will, unconsciously echoing Bruce Peterson's lament about Juliet.

"What about her friends?" I asked, passing his phone back to him. "They must have been questioned." If she was like most other seventeen-year-olds, the friends would know more about her daily life than did her parents.

"That's where it did get interesting," said Will. He scrolled for a moment to find his notes. "Kathy Taylor—that's her cousin, also her best friend—met the guy. And as your husband could tell you, he ticks all the boxes. White guy. Older—Kathy thought he was in his late twenties, early thirties—lives maybe in Hyannis, maybe in Boston, she thought. Met Skye at the Four Cs. Gave her gifts, jewelry mostly. Expensive stuff she didn't show her parents."

"Grooming," I said, my stomach sinking. This wasn't good.

"Grooming," Will confirmed. "Took her up to Boston a couple of times. When they were in the city, he introduced her to another girl around her age, maybe a little older, wanted them to bond. He said it was his sister. Skye believed him."

I was starting to feel more than slightly nauseated. "Textbook."

He nodded. "Yep. Tribal police didn't have to go looking for Kathy; she was the one raised the alarm, went straight over to tell them. Said she'd tried to talk Skye out of seeing him, but Skye wasn't having any of it. Kathy told her a secret boyfriend wasn't a good idea."

I could nearly hear the conversation in my head. *If you really love him, then be proud of him! Introduce him to your family, to your people. Let us get to know him. What you're doing here, it just seems you're sneaking around.*

What do you know about it? He's more sophisticated than anyone around here! He took me to the Museum of Fine Arts! He's a real man, not like the boys our age.

Do you even hear *yourself?*

The problem with growing up in a small community—and I expected it went double when your community was your tribe—is that everyone knows everyone else, and knows everything about each other. Family histories, local scandals. Even Provincetown, at least for those who weren't washashores, was still like that.

I knew a little about it myself, having spent my angsty teenaged years in the Stepford-Wives town of Bedford, New Hampshire. Everyone there knew you when you were a kid, knew every misstep you'd ever made. And you've long ago exhausted dating anyone remotely interesting in the small circle of available love-possibilities.

Which made small-town girls very vulnerable indeed.

"Did you talk to the parents?" I asked. Juliet's murder was still fresh; Skye had disappeared several days ago, so Will had had time to look into it.

He nodded. "Couple in their fifties. The father's name is Amos Taylor. He was part of the tribe's aquaculture business, harvesting oysters. You know about that?"

I shook my head. "I don't know much about any of this," I confessed.

"It's called the First Light Shellfish Farm. It's been there a long time, actually, since 2009. Gives the tribe income, employment, but especially it improves the water quality of Popponesset Bay. Anyway, long story short, Amos worked there until his arthritis got too bad. That's when him and Christine, that's his wife, opened the convenience store." He took a deep breath. "I'd call them naïve," he said judiciously. "Skye's their only child, and they think the world of her. At first, they were just bewildered, you know? Seemed to think she'd gone off with friends from the Four Cs. But even *they* know, now, that it's more than that. Well, the FBI interviewed them, and I'd guess that by now your husband has, too. Now they're still bewildered, but they're scared, too."

I couldn't even imagine what they were going through, seeing a Pandora's box of possibilities opening up, and none of them good.

Will finished his soda. "You ready? I can drop you back at your car."

I nodded.

"Send me that list," he reminded me. "You have any more ideas about it?"

The names kept circling around my brain. People I hadn't thought about in years. "I think at least two of them are probably dead," I said slowly. "One was a Statie who'd gone to the dark side, and cops don't last long in prison, do they? And one of them was really old, she's probably dead now, too."

"Leaving how many?"

Good question. The names were still ricocheting along all my nerves. "Nine?" I guessed. "If this is really what we're dealing with, then it's nine."

"And you testified against all of them?"

I made a helpless gesture with my hands. At least, that was what I was feeling. "I wasn't the only witness," I said. "Not for any of them."

"But an important one."

I dismissed the thought because it scared me so much. "Maybe someone else who was at their trials, someone who felt they'd been railroaded? A friend, a family member, someone who just saw me as a busybody?" I took a deep breath. "That widens the circle quite a lot."

"Trial transcripts are public information," he said. "We could look them up."

"I can't think of anything I'd like less." I caught his look. "I know, I know… but it's hard to go back over all that. It made sense when I was—"

"—investigating," he supplied.

"Trying to help out," I said firmly. *Sydney Riley, crime-stopper extraordinaire.*

Except... I hadn't actually ever stopped any crimes. I'm pretty sure anyone who's deep enough in the anger or panic or whatever to consider murder isn't going to be put off by the presence of a fulltime inn-owner and part-time mystery-solver in the immediate vicinity. *Oh, gosh, I really want to kill that guy, but better not, Sydney Riley's around.*

The cozy-mystery fiction genre is filled with amateur sleuths whose regular occupations or hobbies enable them to solve crimes, often in wildly improbable ways. There's one series in which a pair of Siamese cats outthink humans and point the way to a solution. Another one assembles Great Minds in a crochet club. There are witchcraft covens, baristas and bartenders, librarians, booksellers—in fact, there's a whole subsection of retailers selling everything from scones to antiques to Christmas trees—all of them finding murders interrupting their everyday pursuits and solving said murders with unexpected finesse.

I am not unaware most people would add me to that list, were I a fictional character. I get it that no-one in the real world takes any of these amateurs very seriously—*if* such a coterie of unskilled, untrained, and very informal amateur detectives even exists, which I very much doubt. And the truth is that when I stepped back from the list I'd made, I could see myself in their midst.

I realized then that I'd never given more than a moment's thought to what happened to people after they were convicted and sentenced. Well, that isn't entirely true: I fretted about one of them, because she had someone dependent on her, and I did follow up to be sure Social Services was looking after him. But that was the full extent of my post-trial involvement. I went about my own merry way, working at the inn, taking long walks in Beech Forest, flirting with my husband, sharing drinks with Mirela, generally living what the internet influencers would call my best life.

While, meantime, people were sitting behind bars. And perhaps fixating on me. Planning my demise—or worse. I shivered at the thought.

What we humans don't do well, or at least don't do naturally, is anticipate consequences. We make decisions and choices based on available information and—if I'm being completely honest—on emotions. If something feels good, or feels right, we don't look much further than the act. Airline pilots (I'd recently developed a curious interest in aviation, a story for another time) have to go through special training to step away from emotions in times of crisis. They call it PIOSEE: Problem, Information, Options, Select, Execute, Evaluate. It's a structured decision-making process they use methodically to address challenges during flight.

The rest of us? We don't usually take more than one of those steps. We do things out of a whole host of emotions; we do things because we're reactive rather than proactive; we do things because the immediate consequence is one we want, but we don't generally look farther down that road.

And then those damned chickens appear, awkwardly winging their way home to roost.

I pulled my attention back to Will. "I don't suppose," I said slowly, "I ever thought about what would happen to people once they were off my radar."

"Not many people do," he acknowledged. He was thinking along the same lines, anyway. "Object permanence isn't always our strongest suit, as humans." He paused. "The thing to ask yourself is whether you'd have done anything differently if you *had* thought about it."

"Probably not," I acknowledged, and sighed. Some of the people on The List had tried to kill me, or kill someone I loved. They'd all made some seriously bad choices, even those with good motives. They were most assuredly Bad Guys, and I hadn't wanted them polluting my life any more than they already had.

I'd had nightmares, of course. Nights of insomnia. But those were all about what had occurred, or what I was afraid might occur.

Nothing about any of them as... people. No; I'd definitely never thought twice about their future life experience.

We pulled up outside the church where with Derek's blessing I'd left my car. "Send me your list," said Will. "And let me know if anything happens."

"Like me getting killed?" I asked flippantly.

He looked at me for a beat or two longer than the remark deserved. "Take care," was all he said.

I sat behind the wheel of my car—my second Civic, the Little Green Car having given up the ghost; this one I called the Grey Goose—and stared at the Old Indian Meeting House. Sitting on tribal land. Wondering what the connection was. I still wasn't seeing it.

I was going to have to, though, and fairly quickly.

***

Even Margo's well-hidden and well-protected property now felt vulnerable, dangerous. I pressed the numbers on the keypad and let myself in, locking the door behind me. It felt all wrong. In Provincetown, I never locked doors; I even routinely left my keys in the car, mostly because otherwise I'd always be misplacing them, but also simply because I could. It felt strange to be thinking about that now.

More immediate problems surfaced: Wally wasn't in his grotto, he wasn't anywhere to be seen in his usual spots; it took me a good five or six minutes to locate him under Margo's bed, and when I did—mostly due to hearing a series of sneezes—it was clear something was amiss. He was hunched over, his eyes with that inward-focused look I recognized from Ibsen when he started feeling unwell.

That day had ended in euthanasia.

I texted Margo, having no idea what time it was in Ireland and praying she wasn't asleep. *Hey, don't want to worry you, but Wally's not looking good. Who's your vet?*

While I waited for her to get back to me, I tried to coax him out. He wasn't having any of it. Treats, food, nothing. I lay on the floor beside the bed and talked to him, steadily, softly, trying to be reassuring. "You're going to be okay," I assured him, though I wasn't really feeling it.

He spared me a disparaging glance and another series of sneezes before going back to looking worried, focused on nothing I had access to.

I gave Margo another ten minutes and made a decision, calling my own vet Dr. Sadie's office in P'town. "Yes, you should probably bring him in."

Great. Tremendous. I went in search of a cat-carrier and wondered how much violence he could do to me when I tried to extricate him from under the bed.

It took twenty minutes and could have been done more efficiently had I been wearing a full suit of armor, but I managed. Wally shook himself out of his torpor to take up yowling instead. I didn't know if that was a good or bad sign. Ibsen was the only cat I'd ever lived with, and he was blessedly healthy pretty much right up to the end. I did what I could to stop my bleeding, went through the whole locking-up process again, and we set off down Suicide Alley. There was nothing wrong with Wally's lungs; he yowled for the full hour and a quarter it took me to get him to Dr. Sadie's.

He stopped when we got to the waiting room and started looking scared instead. I checked us in, then sat with the carrier on my knees, still murmuring encouragement.

There were two other people there with us, both middle-aged women, one with a very tiny dog on a leash and the other with something that moved mysteriously around inside a small-animal carrier; they obviously knew each other and in fact looked vaguely familiar to me—which was standard fare for Provincetown, full-time residents all more or less know each other at least by sight. I settled in and absurdly stroked the outside of the cat-carrier: I knew what would happen if I put my hand inside and tried to stroke Wally himself instead.

"It was a shock, seeing her, for sure," one of the women was saying to the other. "After what happened, I thought she'd stay away for good."

The other woman was nodding. "I hated it when she left," she said. "It took me forever to find a doctor I liked as much as her."

"I know, right?" There was a pause. "I've always wondered if we shouldn't have done something."

"Like what?"

"I don't know. Made her feel safer here."

"Listen, she had the whole Jamaican community here. If she didn't feel safe, she didn't feel safe. If they couldn't do it, we couldn't."

Their conversation was starting to displace the anxiety over Wally in my consciousness. I had a feeling I knew who they were talking about.

The first woman shrugged. "I still don't see why," she said. "It's not like we have a lot of white supremacists in this town."

"They're afraid we'll turn them all gay," said her friend in agreement. They shared a chuckle over that.

I cleared my throat. "Sorry to interrupt, but are you talking about Thea Madison?"

They both looked startled. "Dr. Madison," one of them said, nodding.

"She's back in P'town?" She couldn't be, I thought.

The woman with the dog nodded in turn. "I saw her at the Stop & Shop," she said. "Was she your primary, too?"

"She was," I said, a little disconcerted. Thea was back? And hadn't called me? What was up with that?

Another hot summer. Carnival Week, and I'd just met Thea. She was working Urgent Care at the clinic, and I'd cut my hand. Even in her scrubs, she'd looked beautiful. She and her girlfriend, Emma, had settled in Provincetown and wanted to get married. During the Carnival parade. On the Race Point Inn float.

That was, of course, before the float exploded. Tensions had been running high that summer, and we were lucky no-one was killed or even badly injured when the device went off.

They'd gotten married anyway, at the inn… and it was Thea who'd been taken with me by some white supremacists, tied up together at the top of the Pilgrim Monument, with someone who wished us very ill indeed.

I don't know about you, but I found nearly dying with someone gives you a certain bond together.

Thea stayed on in town for a while after her newly minted wife also tried to kill us (along with Ali, Julie Agassi, and Ali's sister Karen, who was then Boston's police commissioner; Emma didn't do things by halves), but maybe it all got to be too much for her. Too many memories. She left the Octagon House in the West End where they'd lived together and I'd heard from her occasionally… though not recently. It made sense: she had a new life somewhere, and I was part of the life she'd wanted to forget. I missed her; we'd become friends.

And now she was back.

I sat with Wally on my lap and thought about that. Emma had been sent to a federal prison somewhere in the South—Alabama? Florida? I couldn't remember. But what I did remember was it was medium security, as apparently there aren't any high-security prisons for women in the federal corrections system. And I'd briefly—very briefly—wondered if that would be secure enough.

Now I wondered if she was still there.

Could *Emma* be behind the note left in Juliet Mills's pocket? She was on The List, but I'd flicked over her name: Emma was Filipina, and tiny; I'd have been surprised if she weighed over a hundred pounds. I couldn't see her dragging bodies around.

But the timing couldn't be ignored. Thea back on the Cape in time for Juliet to be killed. Sometimes, I told myself, a coincidence can just be a coincidence.

But sometimes it isn't.

Chapter Eleven

Wally was fine.

Or would be soon, anyway: Dr. Sadie diagnosed an upper respiratory infection. "It's the cat equivalent of a cold," she said cheerfully. The vet tech took him, loudly protesting, into the back room for some IV hydration and antibiotics. He looked at me balefully when they returned and we popped him back in the carrier. I know cats: it was going to be a while before he'd forgive me.

It felt absurd to be in Provincetown and not stop by the inn, or see Mirela, but I wasn't going to torture this animal any further than I'd already done, so we got back into the Grey Goose and hit the road back up to Marstons Mills. Released from the carrier, Wally dove back under the bed, and I left him to it.

I carried a glass of iced coffee and a new notebook into the dining room along with The List, Reconstituted, and belatedly texted it over to Will. Then I settled in to think.

Emma had been radicalized through her own experiences and by groups around her that promised what all cults and terrorist organizations promise: a better life, a better world. Death to enemies. Starting over.

Not just starting over in their own lives, but forcing *society* to start over.

What had happened in Mashpee didn't seem to suit Emma's style. This was a small gesture, a personal one. Nothing had been blown up; Anthrax hadn't been released; there was no suicide vest.

Ali called as I was doodling stars and triangles on the page around the question: *Emma?* "Hi, sweetheart. How's it going?" I glanced at my watch; five-thirty. Time to think about dinner. I had no idea whose turn it was.

"Checking to see you and Wally are okay." When I'd texted I was taking Wally to P'town, I could imagine the relief he'd felt when he texted back: *Why not just stay there? Bring Wally to our place.*

"He has a cold and probably will never speak to me again," I said. "We're back at Margo's." Just in case he'd had his hopes up.

"I figured you were." He sounded resigned. "I'll be there in about half an hour. Shall I bring pizza?"

"Good idea," I agreed. I was starting to have the sneaking suspicion I relied just a little too much on having great food available to me all the time at the Race Point Inn. And I've never been a stellar cook.

No, Riley: you've never been an adequate *cook.*

"You locked the doors, right?"

"Yes," I said, forcing indignation into my voice. Had I? Quick change of subject. "Hey, I heard someone saw Thea Madison at the Stop & Shop. In Provincetown."

"Thea? Haven't heard that name in a while." There was a pause, and I could sense where his thoughts were going. *Emma.* "I'll be there in half an hour," he said again.

"I'll be here. Bye."

The pizza was some sort of special with lots of stuff piled on it; I got two bottles of the Fever-Tree from the refrigerator and we settled in to eat. Ali looked tired; there were shadows under his eyes. "How's it going?" I asked again.

"I'm going to Boston tomorrow," he said.

"You think she's there, don't you? Skye Taylor."

He was unsurprised I knew her name. "I think she's there," he agreed, which was a lot more than he usually shared with me. Then again, I'd never been associated, even this peripherally, with his work.

I thought about Skye, about her goals and her dreams. "Will says she wanted to be an archaeologist."

That got a response. "She *wants* to be an archaeologist," he said sharply. "Present tense. And she will be, if I have anything to say about it." He paused, a slice of pizza dangling somewhat absurdly from his hand. "And Sydney, seriously, don't get involved. I can't stop you from doing what you do about Juliet, I wish I could, but I know you. I know it's personal to you, and I can't really blame you. But don't get involved with Skye. We'll find her." He took a breath. "And if the two are connected, then it's all the more reason for you to—"

"—for me to find out," I said, interrupting. I could feel the tears starting up again, the sense of free-falling into something big and dark, the fear. "If someone's out for revenge, don't say they wouldn't stoop to kidnapping, or trafficking, or whatever's going on—for heaven's sake, they've already killed someone!"

"All the more reason for you to stay out of it!"

I stared at him. "You've never reacted like this before," I said slowly. That was scaring me more than my own thoughts.

He blew out his breath in frustration and tossed the slice of pizza back into the box. "Listen. You've gotten in people's way before," he said. "You've stumbled into situations and we've made the best of them, and do you know what? You're lucky you're not dead. You should be dead. Every time something happened, you should have died. Drowned in the harbor. Shot in an art gallery. Blown up at Carnival."

"I get it!" I snapped. Didn't really need a tour of all the near-misses.

"But you don't! You never do! Listen to yourself. You have a fucking *list* of people who wish you harm, doesn't that tell you anything? That's not normal. You've gotten away with it because the murders you've been involved with were personal. People who were trying to find personal solutions to personal problems." He shook his head. "But the people I deal with, Sydney? They're organized, and they're armed, and they will *crush* anyone in their way because it's their *business*. They ruin people's lives because it's their *business*. It's not personal. And you're trying to make it personal."

There was a long silence. I was trying really, really hard not to cry. *Breathe, Riley.* "My name was on that note," I said, and even I could hear the shakiness in my voice. "That's as personal as it gets, Ali."

"So you and your pet reporter think you can crack the case? Pull a Hercule Poirot and assemble everyone in a genteel drawing room somewhere and unmask the killer, maybe even find the girl?" He shook his head and stood up. "Don't you think that maybe that's the intention here? Get you involved, out in the open? You had some safety in P'town. The community loves you, cares about you. You're noticed, and because of that you're protected. But up-Cape? Why not just hold up a sign that says, *victim here?*"

"It's not that bad." It really was that bad.

"There's a better than even chance these two cases aren't connected," he said. "You want to connect them. Okay, sit around with Mirela at the bar and play puzzle-games with them. Write a mystery novel. Do something that isn't dangerous. Because real life is a lot messier than you're trying to make it, and it's going to catch up with you, and I might not be there when it does."

That stung; on more than one occasion it had been Ali who'd kept me off death's doorstep for a little while longer.

He moved to the door, jerked it open. "I have work to do."

"Where are you going?"

"Sydney, I wouldn't tell you even if I could."

***

I wandered aimlessly around the house, alternately blaming myself and blaming Ali for the argument. Tried to watch Netflix and gave up, as every show I clicked on—even the fictional ones—seemed to be about crime in some way or another. Why wasn't I the kind of person who watched reality competition programs? I could do with a little Gordon Ramsay swearing at some hapless chef right now.

My phone buzzed just as I was working myself up into a froth about being alone in the house. A Boston number; I hesitated for a moment but then thought, *Hey, if it's a telemarketer or a scam it would be a nice way to get rid of some of this anxiety.* "Sydney Riley."

I froze as I recognized the voice, even after all these years. "Hi, Sydney, haven't spoken to you in a while."

Noah.

Breathe, Riley.

"How did you get this number?" I demanded. But I already knew.

"Your mother," he said.

Thanks, Ma. "What do you want?" I had enough to worry about, I hadn't expected a different kind of ghost invading my life. Especially not this one.

He asked, "Have you seen the news about the hospital?"

"It's hard to miss it," I said dryly, and took another deep breath. "Again: what do you want?"

"I wanted to give you a heads-up. It's gotten a little out of hand, and—well, the thing is, you're going to be subpoenaed."

Another court appearance; way to make my day. "Why?"

A sigh. Poor beleaguered ex-husband. "It's one of my cases," he said. "Legal cases, I mean. You know I'm going to trial?"

"I'd heard something to that effect."

"Listen, I know we didn't part amicably, and I'm sorry about that. But I really need you now. And I'd appreciate it if—"

"No," I said. "Whatever it is, no."

"I know you don't owe me any favors." *Understatement of the century*, I thought. "Okay. Fair enough. I get it, you never want to hear from me again. But here's the thing." He paused. "If you'll do this favor, this one thing, for me, I'll give you the house. Free and clear. No strings attached: it's yours."

I lost my breath entirely. The house in North Cambridge, with its fanlight and rose garden, its polished wood that glowed in late-afternoon sunlight, its carved staircase, its fireplaces and floor-to-ceiling bookcases. I had loved that house. I hadn't tortured myself imagining him with his new wife, but I *had* tortured myself imagining someone else living in that house. It was the one thing that, years on, I still missed. And now he was offering it to me.

What the hell does he want in exchange?

He gave me a moment to think about it, no doubt following my thoughts. "I don't have much to salvage of my life," he said. "I'll never work in a hospital again, probably never even practice medicine again, once this all shakes out. It's really bad. But I think—my lawyer thinks—I can stay out of prison."

"If I lie in court." That was the only place this could be going.

"I have the papers on the house drawn up," he said. "Got them last month, in fact. I've been thinking about doing it for a while, about signing it over to you."

That was when I made the connection. And immediately dismissed it. There was no way Noah would have killed Juliet, left me that note. I didn't think much of him as a human being, but he'd always been an outstanding doctor. Not only that, he was an *emergency* doctor, making life-and-death decisions every day, saving injured people half the medical world would give up on. Saving people was personal for Noah.

He'd even taken an oath never to cause harm. And murdering someone? Strangling them? That pretty much fell into the "causing harm" category. He'd always been distraught whenever someone died in the ER, whenever he lost one—that was how he phrased it, as losing something, not someone. Like a tennis match. A game of darts.

Plus, he didn't spend time on the Cape, he had no connection to my life here. And whoever had killed Juliet had really hated me; Noah had, presumably, moved on. Had *chosen* to move on.

"Tell me this," I said. "Do you blame me for what happened? For the divorce?"

"Sydney, you have to admit, you were difficult to live with."

I lost it for a moment. "*I* was difficult to live with? *You* were away all the time, and when you were home, you were exhausted. How many times did we have to change plans at the last minute? How many dinner parties did I go to alone, because you had to stay at the hospital? Or go in to supervise some tricky case?" I stopped. This was ridiculous. I took a long, deep breath. "I don't think you can blame me, when you were the one having sex with someone else!"

"If you ever had wanted to have sex with me, I wouldn't have had to start seeing Alice," he said.

"Are you *serious*? *I* made you unfaithful?"

"I just think you could have made more of an effort," he said.

We'd never had this conversation before. I hadn't wanted to hear any of it. I'd felt cold fury at the time; hadn't wanted to hear his excuses. I'd screamed and raged and never asked him the question.

Talk about chickens coming home to roost.

And now he was dangling the house, his family home, where generations of doctors and surgeons had grown up. The house I had loved, where I'd expected to spend the rest of my life. Dangled it in front of me, all for one little lie. Like all the myriad, never-ending little lies he'd told me. I took a deep breath and steadied myself. "I will never, ever do anything for you," I said. "It's all over. I have a life here, Noah. I'm married. I'm happy."

"Owning an inn, instead of owning the house you love? Is that really what you want? Don't you remember how much you loved it?"

"No," I said reflexively, and then caught on to what he'd said. "How do you know I own an inn?" I demanded. If that was down to my mother, I might have to debate strangling *her*.

But another thought was hovering over me, dark, too close to be ignored. "Wait," I said. "Have you been to the Cape recently, Noah?"

"Alice and I went there every year," he said, a short phrase that was going to take a lot of unwrapping. Where, exactly, on the Cape? A sudden frisson grabbed me, a swoosh of wind over my shoulder. Had they been in Provincetown? Had they stayed at the Race Point? Could I have ever come close to bumping into them?

The cold feeling in the pit of my stomach intensified. I'd been stalked once—thank God, only the once—and the same feeling was spreading through my body: the fear, the anger, the sense of futility. I know cops do this better, now, but at the time when I sat in the police station and showed them proof of a stalker, the officer had just looked up and said, "It's a compliment, though, isn't it? That someone could get so obsessed with you?"

I came close to leaping over the desk and decking him.

That situation had resolved itself—it was back when I was in college—but our bodies never let go of the feelings, of the terrible sense of being watched, being followed, someone else incorporating our lives into theirs without our ever knowing it, or why. Making us an integral part of their story. Our bodies remember.

Noah was giving me very strong stalker vibes.

And then, as my brain finally kicked in (*thanks, brain*), I heard what he'd actually said. "You went?" I asked. "Not anymore?"

"Alice is dead," he said, his voice flat. "You see why I need you, Sydney."

I was seeing a little more than that. "She would have testified for you," I said. "She would have been willing to lie for you. And now you need someone else to step in."

I was still thinking this was about the malpractice scandal. Maybe he needed her to say he hadn't gotten some medication dosage wrong, he hadn't cut in the wrong place, whatever it was that had sent the whole emergency department into a tailspin and the Spotlight reporters sharpening their pencils.

But then I caught my breath. This was something else. If he was asking me to testify, then it wasn't about the medical scandal; I wasn't an ER nurse, I'd never actually seen him in his professional role outside of the night we'd met.

My vision went blurry for a moment as I thought about it. Thought about asking it. Thought about not asking it. Probably a bad idea. Not my first. I asked it anyway. "Did you kill her, Noah?"

"No. Of course not! How can you ask that? I loved her."

"What happened? How did she die?" And I think I already knew it wasn't going to be cancer or a car crash or old age.

"I'm not supposed to talk about the investigation," he said stiffly. He was getting impatient. "You want to make me suffer, Syd? Is that what this is about? Hurt me like I hurt you?"

He knew I hated him calling me Syd, although to be fair, for a time in college my online username had been a very tongue-in-cheek *Syd-Vicious*. Still, it was a funny way to ask for a favor. "What happened to her?"

He let out a sigh of frustration. "That doesn't matter, all I'm asking you for—"

"I want to know, first," I said. I really didn't want to know. I wanted nothing to do with him. "What were you doing on the Cape? Where were you?" Stalking is generally an individual pursuit; I couldn't imagine his wife accompanying him on that particular series of outings.

I could feel another flicker of impatience, even through the phone. Noah wasn't used to this kind of conversation. His position—and the adulation that went with it—meant he seldom had to face difficult questions. He was a doctor: everything he did was precise, well thought-out, loaded with facts and differential diagnoses and arrogance. I wasn't falling in line like I was supposed to. "It had nothing to do with you," he said.

"Just like everything else you've ever wanted not having anything to do with me." I was sounding waspish and I didn't care.

"It wasn't personal, don't you get that?"

"No? Your wife just had a longing to vacation in the same place your ex-wife lived and worked?"

"There you go again. It's not always about you."

"No, you're right; in your world, it's never about anyone but *you*." I took a breath. I found I was trembling. "How did she die, Noah?"

I'd gotten to him; he was shouting now. "She committed suicide. All right? Are you happy?"

Happy, no; but it was beginning to make sense. "They think it wasn't a suicide," I said slowly. "They think you did it. That's why you need me in court." Another idea was floating on the periphery of my anger. "She did it here, didn't she? In your favorite *vacation place*? You want me to give you an alibi."

"It's going to help us both," he said, and his voice had turned low, dangerous. "She died on the same night Juliet Mills was killed. So I'm giving you an alibi, too."

"Don't be ridiculous," I said. "I'm not a suspect." No wonder the Staties had asked me about my first marriage; they knew about this, that Noah and Alice had been around, that Alice's suicide was suspicious. Cape Cod was experiencing a sudden uptick in unexplained deaths, and I was involved, to one extent or another, in all of them.

I was thinking, a little wildly, that Noah had even better contacts than Will. There had been an obituary for Juliet in *The Boston Globe*. It hadn't offered any details.

"I'd double-check that if I were you." He was trying to sound menacing.

And then, just like that, I was done. I really didn't want to know. Provincetown, the Cape… this was my home now, and had been for over fourteen years. I didn't want to imagine Noah here, too. The sense of being stalked was starting to feel asphyxiating. And I'd had enough. "Noah, it doesn't matter. I'll deal with my life, you deal with yours." The image of the beautiful house in North Cambridge was still there, but receding, a shimmering jewel from my past, briefly remembered. That was all. "I won't commit perjury for you, and you can keep your damned house. I don't need it, and I don't need you. Please don't call me again." And just to make sure, I clicked off the call before he could come up with something else with which to engage me.

Margo's house was feeling a lot less secure, the shadows ominous, the protection it afforded nothing but a wishful thought.

I tried to push it out of my mind, the cold claw of fear and something else that hearing Noah's voice again after all these years had formed inside me, but I was spooked and couldn't stay away from it.

And then the other shoe dropped. He'd drawn up the paperwork to transfer the house's title to me weeks ago, but Alice was only a few days dead. He'd already decided, weeks ago, that he was going to try and use me as an alibi.

He knew she was going to die.

***

I went to bed when it was clear Ali wasn't coming back, but woke up twice in the night, reacting to various unfamiliar sounds and frankly scared out of my wits, imagining shadows coalescing into people emerging from the bushes, intent on killing me. I wondered if Margo's house, old and mysterious, had a ghost or two lurking in the attic, shimmering translucently by the ancient fireplace.

I would have welcomed a ghost, to be honest. Ghosts don't carry weapons.

I remembered some lines from a long-ago poem. *Airy ghosts/That work no harm, do terrify us more/Than men in steel with bloody purposes.* Personally, they both scared the hell out of me.

Wally contributed to the mood, once by rubbing against my ankles while I was in mid-stride heading to the bathroom, and thus effectuating a little attempted murder on his own, and once by insinuating himself silently on the pillow next to me so that when I opened my eyes I was gazing across at those opaque unblinking slightly scary ones.

I finally gave up around five o'clock and made myself a coffee and took it into the big three-seasons room. Margo has a small Zen fountain there, and the trickling water along with the bird chorus greeting the day felt soothing. And I could really use soothing right about then.

And of course because Ali had explicitly told me to stay away from thinking about Skye, I started thinking about Skye.

Follow the money. I couldn't remember who had first told me that, but it worked more often than not. While some of the people I'd encountered in the past had been motivated by things other than monetary gain—hello again, Emma—the adage mostly held true. Greed was at the base of most crimes, whether it was greed for money or for power or for someone's affections.

And trafficking people is always about money. Ali had been clear about that, at least: it's their business.

Kidnapping a person is about gain: you hold them for ransom, and when everything goes well, the ransom is paid and the kidnappee returned. Didn't usually go to plan, of course: and that was where things went terribly wrong and people ended up dead.

It was still after all these years unclear whether my sister Alexandra, ten years older than me, had been trafficked or held for ransom; it seemed to have been an unholy combination of the two. She'd been lured out of our safe upper-class New Hampshire neighborhood with the promise of modeling contracts. And she was eighteen—old enough to not be a child, old enough that her disappearance could be accepted as voluntary.

She had great cheekbones, they'd told her.

They took one look at our parents' financials, though, and pivoted, doing the whole nine yards you see on TV, sending a photo of Alex holding a dated newspaper and offering us the option of paying for her return. That was what had finally interested the police and the FBI in her situation.

That it had all gone horribly wrong and Alexandra had ended up dead wasn't their fault, it hadn't been anybody's fault, not really, because at the end of the day kidnapping is a precarious endeavor, and rarely has a happy ending. Too many things could go wrong.

Too many things had gone wrong.

This wasn't the same, of course. My father hadn't worked in a convenience store; he had the means to pay for Alex's release. That was what was so cruel: he was going to pay. Skye's family had nothing: they'd re-mortgaged their house to open the convenience shop, which was, according to Will (my "pet reporter"—that still stung), just barely staying afloat. And a would-be kidnapper couldn't extract money from the tribe: the Wampanoag had nothing.

Or…wait. I frowned and grabbed my laptop. The three hundred twenty acres finally returned to the Mashpee Wampanoag hadn't all been in Mashpee itself: something slightly over half of the reservation wasn't even on the Cape, but up on the mainland, in Taunton.

And that was where the money was.

After decades of protracted negotiations, court cases, and general—let's call it what it is—racism, the tribe was recognized by the federal government and granted permission to construct a casino. There had been a lot of fits and starts, but finally they broke ground on the First Light Resort and Gaming Casino. To date only a welcome center had been constructed, with the opportunity for visitors to learn about the Wampanoag, to view artifacts in a mini-museum, and to sample some fifty slot machines. The plans called for a full-on resort and casino along the lines of the Pequot tribe's Foxwoods Resort and the Mohegan Sun in Connecticut.

And no one but Donald Trump has ever lost money owning a casino.

It didn't track, though. Skye had been missing for five days; well enough time for any monetary demands to have been made, if not to her parents, then certainly to the tribal council. And even I had to admit I was conflating kidnapping with trafficking with something approaching wild abandon; just because it had happened with Alexandra didn't mean it was happening here, or was even a thing.

But following the money has never been a bad idea. The money in trafficking was painfully obvious: Skye was beautiful, young, vibrant.

Just how vibrant she'd stay after a few months working for her new "boyfriend" was anyone's guess.

Which brought me back to Ali. I was angry with him, sure, but I had enough self-awareness to recognize it was really only because he was right—these were deep waters about which I knew next to nothing.

Stick to what you know, Riley. And one thing I did know was my own past, my own experiences. Deep breath. If Thea was in Provincetown, and if she was there because of something that had happened the last time she'd been in town—a lot of "ifs", granted—then I needed to think about what had happened.

Carnival parade. And a bunch of neo-Nazis targeting a very liberal enclave.

I'd thought they'd been there because of P'town's current incarnation as a gay resort town, a safe space for gay and trans and other queer people; but now I wondered. Would it be expecting too much of their limited historical perspective to wonder if these champions of white men might have also considered the Cape's earlier past? Indigenous people were also brown people. And, let's face it, if you're keeping a *racial* scoresheet, Provincetown's story was a triumph for the white man, even today; our diversity doesn't have anything to do with the color of our skin.

I didn't need Derek to tell me this part; I recited it often enough myself to visitors at the inn. After a lengthy and altogether awful crossing of the North Atlantic in November of 1620, the *Mayflower*—way off-course—finally anchored in what is now Provincetown Harbor. What would come to be known as the Mayflower Compact was written and signed here; and here the ship stayed for five weeks before giving up and heading to shelter in what was now Plymouth.

The caretakers of the land were the Pamet Wampanoag, who initially greeted the Pilgrims with openness, not having any idea what the Europeans' notion of conquest and land ownership would bring to them, nor how centuries of so-called history would interpret it. The "first Thanksgiving" may sound like a heartwarming tale, but when measured against reality, it loses a lot of its allure.

My own favorite story is of how the Pamet cultivated corn, which they stored in the ground at harvest time so they could continue to eat through the Cape's fierce winters. The Pilgrims "found" the corn, stole it, and thanked God for the bounty that helped them survive those first miserable months.

A story any self-respecting neo-Nazi would surely find heart-warming.

Was it a connection? Were they really and truly back and wanting their revenge on me, seeing leaving a body in an Old Indian Burying Ground as a way of flipping the bird at anyone who dared to stand up to white usurpers?

It would help to know if any of the tribal members had experienced that level of racism recently. Someone had to be keeping an eye on that sort of thing.

I pulled out my phone and texted Will. Then, hesitantly, I texted Ali as well. *Sorry for being so difficult. I hope you're okay. Talk to me when you can.* I paused, then added, *I love you.*

Of course, I wasn't doing myself—or Ali—any favors here by switching my attention away from the probable trafficking situation. Last time I checked, the white nationalist movement in the United States was even better armed than any traffickers taking care of business.

Maybe I wouldn't text him that part.

Chapter Twelve

"Breakfast is on me," I announced when I met Will for a second time at Oneil's Kitchen.

He blinked. "You breakfast rather late," he said.

"Make it lunch, then," I said, gesturing lavishly. "Or both. I don't care." As long as I could have more of that amazing banana bread.

We ordered our food, and he got down to business. "Okay. First of all, I can't find anybody you've put in prison who's out now."

"I didn't put anybody in prison."

"Figure of speech," he said. He sounded irritated.

"You looked up everybody on The List? In twenty-four hours?"

"I'm a reporter," he reminded me. "It's what I do. Besides, it's all public record."

I sighed; of course it wasn't going to be that easy. The only glimmer of light was that the State Police were dealing with the same results. "Tell me," I said.

He had his phone out again. "The O'Lalor guy," he said, and I saw him at once, young and oh-so-stereotypically gay; he'd been great fun. Up until the moment he wasn't. "Still with us here in Massachusetts, over at Souza-Baranowski in Shirley." He glanced up. "He was doing pretty well until he had some contraband smuggled in; it sent him to supermax."

From whence no-one escapes. And I also couldn't imagine the flippant smart-ass adorable young man surviving there for any significant time. "Okay."

Our food arrived and I found I had no appetite for it.

"Taisie Murray," Will said between bites of the inevitable hamburger. "She's still at the women's prison in Framingham."

She must be more resentful than most, I thought: she'd killed the wrong person by accident. Imagine living out a prison sentence knowing the person you wanted dead was still walking around in the world, free, having the life you didn't have anymore. "Okay," I said again.

"You were right about the old woman, by the way," he went on. "Died when they couldn't contain Covid in the population. A lot of people died then, but she was one of the first—older, compromised immune system."

I didn't want to talk about Covid. I'd lost people I cared about then, too; we all had. "Who else?" I made myself take a bite of the scrumptious banana bread. It tasted like ashes in my mouth.

"Another one of them died, too," Will said. "Kai Bennett? He was in Walpole. Don't know what happened to him; could have been Covid too. I can find out. And Carlson's up at the supermax, too, actually—he got involved in some racial thing, killed a couple of Black dudes in prison. He isn't going anywhere."

The List was getting decimated, and I still hadn't heard the name I was waiting for. I let Will eat for a moment in peace. This wasn't going anywhere. What if we'd been wrong, what if this had nothing to do with my past, and I'd spooked myself for nothing? Then where did we go? I could hear Ali's voice. *Leave it to the professionals.*

I decided to cut to the chase. "What about Emma?" I asked. "Emma Abadiano?"

He looked startled. "Why her?"

"Just a feeling," I said inaccurately, then relented. "She was super-scary. She—she bought into the whole race-war thing. She had some PTSD from—stuff—in her past, and she thought the world was going in the wrong direction. She'd aligned herself with some skinheads. She didn't just want to kill me, she wanted to kill a whole lot of people." If she'd written that note, it wouldn't have had just my name on it. "I just—I got a little triggered because I heard her wife is back in P'town." It sounded more than a little lame in retrospect.

Will waited a moment, but I didn't say anything else. "Abadiano's at Hazelton. In West Virginia," he said.

Well, that's that, Riley. Some super-sleuth you are. "Okay," I said.

He was still studying me. "She upsets you," he said.

"She shot my husband," I said defensively. "Yeah, you could say she upsets me."

He nodded and consulted his phone again. "Donnelly," he read. "He's going nowhere, he had prior convictions. Three strikes and you're out. Hyde's still in after he went after your colleague. And Harrison got herself into a minimum-security camp and has been a super-model prisoner. Took over where Martha Stewart left off. Designs things."

"That tracks," I agreed.

"She'll get out for sure, but she isn't now. O'Connell—"

"I know about her," I said. She was the only one of the lot I felt distressed about.

"And that's it. None of them is stalking you." *No; just my ex-husband.*

Will picked up his hamburger again.

I let him enjoy it in peace and sat for a moment thinking about staring at a blank wall. Finally I roused myself. "We've got nothing," I said gloomily.

"We know who it isn't," he pointed out.

"Them and the rest of the world's population."

***

The only other thing I could think of doing was going to require a little finesse.

Back at Margo's house, I threw The List away and focused instead on Juliet. She was the one, after all, with whom I had an undeniable connection.

And to focus on Juliet I had to learn more about Juliet. If the note in her pocket was left out of our calculations, if maybe that was somehow an add-on (*do the compartmentalization thing, Riley*) then she had to have crossed someone in a pretty significant way to get herself strangled.

Okay, then: personal or professional life?

I didn't know anything about her personal life, other than she'd spent summers on the Cape as a child. There could be something there, but it would take some work to unearth it: she'd very much struck me as someone without secrets, without anything to hide.

Of course, I've been wrong before.

And while we all at some time or another absolutely want to kill someone we work with, we generally don't follow through—well, there is that whole going-to-prison thing, which for most of us works as a pretty strong deterrent.

But nothing in her professional life screamed murder, either. She wasn't an investigative reporter: she produced a much-loved, much-watched, feel-good show. She hadn't brought down any titans of industry; she hadn't revealed the identities of pedophiles or people living double lives or even income-tax cheaters.

She told people where to go on vacation.

I tried applying the pilots' PIOSEE format, but I still needed the Options part of it. So I opened my laptop and asked The Google. Her name was there—let's face it, these days, everyone's name is there, the privacy ship not only has sailed but has had time to circumnavigate the globe several times over—but the first few entries didn't tell me anything useful. There were photos taken at some sort of awards ceremony, the kind only people who are deeply involved in an organization go to. She'd apparently done a couple of triathlons, which was pretty impressive. She'd made a speech at some kind of fundraiser for getting tech equipment into schools in disadvantaged areas.

Yep: that's the kind of person you'd set out to kill.

I found the jewel buried on page five of the search results (no-one but obsessive-compulsives like me ever gets as far as page five, even in pre-AI days; now even page one has fierce competition). It was only peripherally about Juliet: she was at a wedding. Her sister Eloise was marrying one Rick Thatcher.

Rick Thatcher was Mashpee Wampanoag.

I sat and stared at the wedding pictures. Eloise, practically shimmering with joy; Rick, proud and handsome and wearing a conventional tuxedo, a ponytail down his back. Exchanging rings; leaving a church; cutting the multi-tiered cake. Nothing untoward. Juliet looked as happy as everyone else there.

Another connection for sure—but what did it mean?

I looked for references to Eloise Mills Thatcher, and found a few. Like her sister, she had a clear sense of civic duty: she'd served on the city council in Taunton for several years, volunteered at the local animal shelter, and did a few five-kilometer runs for various charities.

Then I looked up her husband, and hit pay dirt.

***

It took a minute, because he'd been peripherally involved in a scandal, and most of the results latched on to the more important people in the affair.

"What happened," I said to Mirela on the phone, wanting to talk it out with somebody who had a little more distance than I did, "is the tribe was looking for federal recognition. It was a long, protracted fight."

"Why?" asked Mirela.

"It was complicated," I admitted. I was reading from notes Derek had emailed me. "They first went to court in 1976, but they had to convince a non-native jury that they qualified as a tribe. *They* knew they were, of course, but over time—that is, since the 1600s— they'd intermarried with European- and African-Americans, and that played against them. Something about purity and continuity, I don't know the details." I took a breath. "Anyway, the application dragged on for literally decades, and then we get to the most recent iteration, when the tribe's chairman was this guy named Glenn Marshall. And it turns out he was pretty corrupt. He was convicted of making illegal campaign contributions and embezzling almost four hundred thousand dollars from the tribe." I took a deep breath. "And there were a lot of issues at play, but eventually it became about the casino." *Follow the money.*

"Because there were investors." It wasn't a question; Mirela is a gifted artist, but she knows about money, too, mainly because she makes so much of it.

"Big-time investors," I agreed. "And lobbyists, too: they hired Jack Abramoff's firm, which as everyone knows turned out to be totally corrupt." Even *I* had heard of Jack Abramoff, and I don't exactly have my ear to the ground when it comes to economic and financial news. "So he's sentenced, and the next tribal leader, Cedric Cromwell, does this whole song-and-dance about how awful it was and how moving forward he was going to make sure there was transparency and integrity. That's what he said: transparency and integrity. So the tribe never—wait, let me read it to you—so they *never again experience this type of betrayal.*"

"Oh, yes?" said Mirela. "I believe I see where this is going, sunshine."

"Bear with me," I said. "So then Massachusetts legalizes casinos and the plans for a Wampanoag casino move forward, with Cromwell at the helm. They jump through a lot of hoops—"

"Hoops?"

"Challenges," I said. "From the federal government, the state, the locals in Taunton. And he takes them all on. To the tribe, Cromwell is a hero."

"Until he is not," said Mirela.

"Until he's not," I agreed. "Turns out, Cromwell was working hand-in-glove with this guy DeQuattro, who owned an architect-and-design firm. To build the casino, you know? And he extorted a whole lot of money from DeQuattro, but not just that, he stole from the *tribe* as well."

"This is transparency and integrity?" asked Mirela.

"Exactly. Cromwell was removed from his position as soon as he was indicted, and he was found guilty and sentenced, but the damage was done. Again the tribe had to express their 'disappointment' in their leadership's integrity. That's how the press release phrased it, as disappointment."

"But it is better now," Mirela said. "The casino is on track, no? You said they started."

"I think a whole lot of other things are going wrong, but that's not my point," I said. "The point is, Rick Thatcher is connected to the Cromwell affair. He wasn't indicted and he doesn't take bribes as far as I can tell, but he's working—now, not ten years ago—on the investor side of the process. And they need more investment to move to the next phase of the casino project."

"And you are interested in Rick Thatcher?" Mirela asked, as usual singling out the thread holding my disjointed storytelling together.

"He," I said triumphantly, "is married to Juliet Mills's sister."

There was a long pause as she thought about it. "You think Juliet Mills was involved in some way," she said.

"It's too much of a coincidence," I said. "Listen, Mirela: she talked to me about spending summers on the Cape when she was a kid, she talked about covering the pow-wow for *Weekend Waypoints*, but she never mentioned she was *connected*."

"Perhaps she was not," said Mirela judiciously. "You spoke with her for only five minutes. She would not tell her life story to you."

"She had to be doing some research for the program," I insisted. "And she had to have seen her brother-in-law's name come up. In fact, she knew he was part of the tribe; how could she not?"

"Perhaps," Mirela said again, and I could hear the skepticism in her voice.

"Seriously," I said. "You're as bad as Ali."

"And Ali is correct. You sometimes chase bright shining objects, sunshine. You are like a cat."

Bright shining objects? "You know how to kick a girl when she's down," I complained. "And it's shiny, by the way, not shining." I couldn't resist the correction. I couldn't resist the correction. Mirela's

English is excellent—bar her inability (or refusal) to use contractions—but whether she chooses to expand her vocabulary or not depends largely on her mood. I'd tried for years to tell her "sunshine" is more sarcasm than compliment, and had finally given up. But sometimes I can't help myself. "Okay, but listen. What if Juliet did do more research on the tribe, just as prep for the program? And what if she looked into the casino project and saw Rick's name there? What if he's also involved in some shady deals? After Glenn Marshall and Cedric Cromwell, they were two for two so far. So what if he was in on it, or maybe picked up where they left off? He wouldn't want any journalists looking at things too closely." I took a breath. "What if Eloise told him what Juliet was doing, and he wanted to silence her?"

"Who is Eloise?"

"The sister," I said.

"I see." She paused. "But there is no connection between this person—Rick?—and you. He could not have written that note. He would not know who you are."

I felt deflated. "Okay, not yet," I said. "But it's a viable hypothesis, all the same. Give me a break here, Mirela, I just learned he exists. He could have already heard of me. Not to be too much of a braggart, but I *am* famous in certain circles."

"In certain circles," she repeated. I didn't know if she was agreeing or assimilating a new expression into her vocabulary.

"It's a line of inquiry," I said. "Something to think about."

"You think about it," she said. "I am going to the pool."

Chapter Thirteen

So now I had another name and another motive. Definitely a line of inquiry—and one that kept me off Ali's turf. Well, technically not his turf; we might accidentally find ourselves in the same circles, but working to very different ends. All good.

It turned out Rick Thatcher wasn't just a guy who happened to be good with numbers; his work on behalf of the tribe was actually a volunteer endeavor. Professionally speaking, he was a psychotherapist, with an office in Boston's very expensive Back Bay, to which he apparently commuted from Taunton. A bit of a drive—but what did I know, I got to live in the same building where I worked, so anything would seem long to me.

His areas of specialization included something called multicultural counseling, which was, apparently, "consciously processing biases, addressing multicultural and intersectional identities that affect the client and impact their experience, creating an open and respectful dialogue."

The things the internet knows. I was frankly afraid to Google myself.

I thought about telling Will. He seemed pretty good at getting answers—well, if he wasn't, he'd have to pursue a different career goal. I even picked up the phone to call him.

And put it down again. I was becoming a little tired of reacting—reacting to Juliet's disappearance, to her death, to the note. Reacting to Ali. Reacting to Will. Reacting—God help me—to Noah. Maybe I should drum up a little of that crime-stopper energy and do something on my own.

Probably a bad idea. But I'm kind of known for those, too.

The answer, I decided, wasn't in Mashpee or Taunton; it was in Boston. Juliet lived in Boston. She worked in Boston. As did Rick; his office was there. All roads seemed to be leading to Boston.

I should be in Boston.

I thought about it for a few minutes. That could be tricky, for several reasons. First and foremost, there was Wally, getting over his cold and requiring not just companionship—which he could apparently take or leave—but mainly for the critical bit about providing meals and cleaning litter.

I always think of Boston as being impossibly far away, but that's only because I live out at Land's End—everything seems far away when you include the calculation that to get anywhere you first have to leave the Cape, and Provincetown's at the very tip. But from Marstons Mills it was immediately more accessible.

Didn't mean I could leave Wally alone to fend for himself.

Another issue was my husband. As far as I knew, Ali was in Boston today, no doubt in his cool air-conditioned office in the Federal Building. He'd made it pretty clear he didn't want me involved in his investigation… and that was exactly what it was going to look like if I followed him up to the city.

Finally, and frankly the least disturbing bit but perhaps an issue, was my own past. Not as in The List kind of past; as in my own life. I'd lived in either Boston or Cambridge for a lot of years before becoming a washashore on the Cape. I'd been happy there for most of that time (we'll leave out the part about my then-husband dumping me—via a phone call, no less—and the rage and despair and depression that life event had brought on); and I wasn't at all sure I wanted to deal with the nostalgia.

That was the least of my problems, I told myself. *Snap out of it, Riley.* I'd been in Boston plenty of times over the past ten years or so; it's where we go when we need an infusion of culture. We go for the museums, the theatre, the restaurants. We go to walk around ethnically and racially diverse city streets, eat exotic foods. It's not a big deal.

But I was feeling more vulnerable than I think I ever had, and that's never a good starting point. I couldn't get that note out of my mind, the venom behind the words, the implication I'd done something awful. Responsibility for a death?

How do you live with that?

And I couldn't help but think it wasn't over. That kind of—passion, I guess you'd say—was a driving force. You see it in obsessives of every kind. The fixation on something that causes an anxiety so overpowering it has to be relieved by acting.

The best thing for me was to do something about it. And I felt somehow I was being pointed north—to Boston.

I could handle challenges two and three. Wally was going to have to survive a few hours without me.

***

I called Bruce Peterson, and to my surprise he picked up; he must have seen my name on his phone, and if I were him, I'd be the last person he'd want to speak to. "It's Sydney Riley," I said anyway, because I was a little surprised he'd take my call at all. I wouldn't have blamed him for blaming me.

"Hello, Sydney," he said. He sounded exhausted, and it occurred to me that while I'd been fretting about having nothing to do, he'd probably had a lot of extra work to fill his time. I didn't know how

TV shows worked, but if they needed two producers, then they needed two producers. And one of them was absent. "What can I do for you?"

Put it like that… I cleared my throat. "Bruce, this probably sounds a little weird, but I'd like to come to the studio and have a look around. Maybe talk to a few people. And—well, I know the police have probably done that already, but I think you understand why I have a—a personal interest in helping find who killed Juliet."

I found I was crossing my fingers, holding my breath, but again he surprised me. "I'd like that," he said.

"Okay." I hadn't been expecting that reaction, was readying a host of arguments with which to persuade him. Time to regroup. "Okay. That's great. Thank you. Are you—um, there, in the studio, yourself?" For all I knew, he might be off doing a show about whitewater rafting in Maine.

"Yeah, there aren't any more shoots this week. We're in planning mode."

"Oh, good. Um, I mean, thanks. Would tomorrow work for you?"

"Fine." He sounded resigned, like he couldn't summon the energy for anything else. I couldn't say I blamed him. "I'll let the front desk know to expect you."

Okay. So if I fed Wally and serviced his litterbox (who says cats don't have it good?) early, I could be in Boston—well, in time for the morning commute, but I could handle that. Wally would have to spend a day alone; I was pretty sure he'd survive.

And then I called Ali.

I wasn't exactly expecting him to take the call, but I was still a little panicked when I got his voicemail. Not for him per se—Boston was hardly being "in the field," that mysterious place that took him away for weeks at a time—but for us. Well, probably for just me. We'd left at the end of a pretty heated argument, and I couldn't remember a time when he'd voluntarily chosen to not communicate with me. He had to be really angry.

Or maybe really scared.

Breathe, Riley. I had to figure out what my next move was. I looked up Rick's information again and briefly considered presenting myself to him as a potential patient, but decided that wasn't my best option.

Not yet, anyway.

I called Ali three more times throughout the afternoon and got his voicemail every time, and finally gave it up, the coldness in my stomach spreading further as the day went on. It was time to clear my mind—and my heart, if I could manage it.

So I did the only sensible thing and took myself off to a solitary and absolutely fabulous dinner sitting at the bar at Bleu.

***

Wally was pleased with my early rising the next morning: the sooner breakfast could be served, the happier he was. He finished eating and embarked on an extensive grooming session, and I spent some time dithering about what to wear. A small consideration, granted, but sometimes it's easier to fixate on what we have agency over when everything else is running chaotically out of control.

I settled on Hot-Weather Tidy: tied my long hair up into something approximating a chignon, put on a demure cotton skirt and a simple short-sleeved button-down shirt, and called it an outfit. I was on the road by eight o'clock.

Like most cities, Boston's population growth has outpaced its ability to handle said population. Beginning in the 1990s, an ambitious project was undertaken to ease traffic congestion, reimagining the city's transportation infrastructure. It was known as the Central Artery/Tunnel Project.

We who lived through it knew it as the Big Dig.

It lasted for a decade and a half, with even more than the usual time and money overruns, and was a massive headache: anytime you wanted to get anywhere, you found yourself thwarted by yet another new street closure or rerouting; we called it "being Digged." The result was pretty spectacular, but these days there were still massive traffic backups on all the roads leading into the city from the "bedroom" communities surrounding it. And that was discounting roadworks and accidents.

I slowed to a crawl around Hingham and made it to the station out on Soldiers Field Road by ten, which wasn't bad, all things considered.

The middle-aged woman at the front desk knew I was coming, checked my ID, and called up someone on her telephone; shortly thereafter someone who looked about Skye Taylor's age appeared to escort me to my destination. A metal detector and an elevator later I found myself deposited in front of an unprepossessing door simply marked *Weekend Waypoints*, where my guide left me.

The corridor was alive with activity, people—many of them young women carrying clipboards—walking briskly around and carrying on conversations with their earbuds. I knocked on the door a few times and then just went in. It was a large room with the expected computer stations in the center and an immense whiteboard with colorful lists and diagrams and what looked like a word cloud at one end, and a couple of glass-sided smaller offices off on the right.

The first person I recognized was the director I'd met briefly in Provincetown. He caught sight of me across one of the desks and came over. "Sydney Riley, right?"

I couldn't for the life of me remember his name. "Yes. Good to see you again."

He nodded with the merest trace of a smile that indicated he knew exactly what I was thinking. "It's Adam Bennett," he reminded me. "We met at your inn. You're looking for Bruce, right? He's expecting you. Come on, I'll show you in."

In one of the smaller side offices, Bruce was at a computer, frowning. He looked up, distracted. "Sydney. Right. Come on in."

I was a little shocked. He had visibly aged in just a few days. His face had a gray tint, and there were bags under his eyes I hadn't noticed before. The additional workload had taken its toll, but there was a lot more to it than that. For the first time, I wondered what his relationship with Juliet had actually been.

"I'll just close the door," said Adam from behind me.

"Thanks," Bruce said and gestured me toward a chair. "Have a seat."

I sat primly on the edge of the chair. I'd prepared some questions to ask, but my mind was blank, given the transformation I was seeing. "Are you all right?"

Stupid question.

He nodded, though, as if the inquiry were normal. "Yeah. Just not sleeping much."

"I can understand that. I keep hearing noises in the night."

He nodded again. "She's haunting me, too."

That wasn't what I'd meant, but it was clearly and pretty understandably what his issue was. "You were close," I said.

He gave me a pained look. "We've worked together for fifteen years," he said. "Everybody else on the team has come and gone, no-one's the same as the crew we started out with, but me and Juliet, we stayed. The show's a roaring success, and that's completely down to Juliet." He looked away, out into the bustling central office. "I don't know what to do without her."

The eternal cry of the grieving, and there was Ibsen, suddenly tugging at my heart. No, I wasn't going to compare the loss of my cat to the loss of his friend and colleague. I took a deep breath. "We have to find out what happened to her," I said.

He brought his gaze back to me. "How?" he asked, his voice listless.

This wasn't the same Bruce who'd implored me to help. Had he given up? It wouldn't be completely surprising: grief is exhausting.

But he was no good to me like this. "Listen," I said. "Somewhere, sometime, she encountered someone who wished her harm. All we have to do is find when that happened, how that happened, and we'll know who did it." *Yeah, Sydney, it really is that easy.*

"The police are trying."

"The police," I said firmly, "didn't know her. You did. It's your insights we need." I was almost convincing myself. Mostly I wanted to pull him out of whatever dark place he'd been living in. "Why don't you show me around here for a start? Show me her desk. Tell me how she interacted with people."

"It's not much."

"It's a start," I said again. I leaned forward. "Bruce. This wasn't like her, to disappear, you said so yourself. And no-one ever asks to get murdered." He recoiled at the word and I cursed myself for using it. "We can do this," I said, a little desperately.

He looked at me. "You're here because of that note," he said. "That's why you care."

"Does it matter?" I asked. "Of course I care because of the note. But I also care because that's what people do, or should do, in the world. We should all care."

The platitude, surprisingly, reached him. "Okay," he said, and stood up. "I'll introduce you around, and we can go through her desk."

"We can do this," I told him, sounding as confident as I could.

But even I was beginning to wonder.

Chapter Fourteen

I wasn't going to remember everyone's name, and it didn't matter. What mattered was asking them all some of the questions I'd come up with the night before, sitting up late alone in Margo's house, listening to vague unidentifiable noises that all made me jump.

No-one had noticed anything "different" about Juliet in the days before she went to Provincetown. She hadn't been worried about anything—or, if she had, it hadn't shown. She hadn't confided in anyone, "but she wouldn't," said the cameraman, whose name I still didn't catch. "We don't socialize much." He caught my look and shrugged. "It's not a power thing," he explained. "Juliet wasn't like that. It's just an age difference."

Now that he mentioned it, everyone in the room was a lot younger than Bruce or me. Maybe early to mid-twenties, I thought, and most of them on the younger side of that range. Bruce was closer to my age. Like a lot of people, I am firm in the belief that I don't age much—you're only as old as you feel, right?—but my (cough, cough) forty-plus years on the planet probably speak for themselves. Even the director, Adam, was at best thirty, probably younger.

Juliet had a routine, and she'd kept to it. She arrived at the station early. "It's the only time for her to get peace and quiet," explained one young woman earnestly; I had no idea what she did. "We all roll in after ten, and after that, it's pandemonium!"

It was a well-controlled and well-choreographed pandemonium, I thought. The place was humming, but with work.

"She'd make a pot of coffee and go through her inbox and do some reading," offered a kid who looked to be about twelve. He had an English accent.

"And she always listened to music!" the young woman added, nodding. "She didn't use earbuds or headphones; she'd put it on a speaker in her office and close the door so she wouldn't bother anybody. She was old-school." Nods all around; this constituted, to them, unusual behavior.

I started to ask what music, but dismissed it as irrelevant and just as quickly changed course again. Who knew what details might help? "What did she listen to?"

Glances all around; they didn't know or they didn't want to say. The English kid said, "Well, like we said, old-school. Like—" and here he looked around a little wildly for help.

"Jackson Browne," said the earnest young woman. The answer was quick and efficient; these people were about information, and she smoothly took the question on as her current assignment. "And Led Zeppelin. And Dan Fogelberg." There was a slight titter at that one from the back of the room. "And—um—Creedence Clearwater Revival."

"Tori Amos," suggested the director, Adam.

Old-school for even Juliet's age, I thought, but realized some of the same names lurked in my own playlists.

It didn't help, not really; but it gave me a chance to get these kids relaxed enough to answer some other questions. "I like Tori Amos," I said lightly.

Their eyes told me they weren't surprised. Maybe I should start using some kind of anti-aging skin routine at night.

Enough about me. "What was she like to work for?"

That elicited a crossfire of glances; the question was unexpected. Bruce, leaning his backside on one of the desks, said, "No one here thinks of working *for* either Juliet or me. We work as a team. We're responsible to the executive producer—" here a series of groans "— But she doesn't have much to do with us on a day-to-day basis."

"Leaves us alone," affirmed Adam.

"Just as well," said the earnest girl.

"How does that work, doing programs as a team?" Any longer down this line of inquiry, I thought, and I was going to get a tutorial on Business Management 101.

Bruce pointed to a large conference table at the far end of the room. "We all sit around there, and anybody can suggest a place, or a program," he said. "We all come in with ideas. We talk it all out, whether we'd ever done anything on the place before, what it had to offer, who might have some special insights. Then, when we have about a dozen possibilities we all agree are feasible, we put them up on the board and vote on them."

"You *vote*?" Somehow I hadn't pictured television being so democratic.

"Usually the team member who came up with the idea talks a little about it, but yeah, then we vote. Everyone's got a voice in everything we do."

"Except Stacey," said a young Black man who was sitting on another desk, running some Buddhist beads through his fingers. The remark got smiles all around. "She does what we tell her to do."

Bruce said to me, "Stacey's got great camera presence, and our viewers seem to like her, but she doesn't like to be involved in the nitty-gritty stuff." Translation, I thought: Stacey wasn't one of the station's Great Minds.

The Great Minds assembled, however, were more than enough to go on with.

"So who came up with Cape Cod? I asked.

Everybody immediately swiveled to look at the whiteboard, which had nothing about Cape Cod written on it. Their visualization seemed to work, though, because the earnest one, who I now thought maybe was called Cally, said a little diffidently, "That was Juliet, wasn't it?"

"She put it up *last* year," said the Black man; I thought his name was Fred. "But then, remember, there was that program in Maine we decided to cover instead."

"Oh, right." She giggled. "A TV program about a TV program."

"What was that?" I asked.

Cally—that *was* her name, right?—said, "This educational channel was doing one of those reality-show events, but it was serious, not one of the mean ones where people get voted off the show. They constructed a whole medieval castle on one of the uninhabited islands off the Maine coast, and people went to live there for a couple of months. You know, in the roles they might have had in the Middle Ages. And the crew filmed them getting used to medieval life. They'd share their reactions with these little cameras hidden in cupboards. You know, like they were confiding to the things, talk about how hard it all was. They called it Medieval House—you know, like the PBS shows *Frontier House* and *Colonial House*." She stopped, looked around. "*What?*" she demanded. "It was a good premise, and we got positive feedback—through the roof, actually—on the show."

"Stacey didn't like it," said Fred. "She only got about two minutes of airtime."

"That's because she wouldn't put on any of the costumes," someone else responded, and a few people laughed.

It all sounded pretty interesting, but it wasn't what I was after. I remembered Mirela saying I chase *bright shining things*. Not this time. "So who came up with the Race Point Inn show?" I asked. "And the one on the Wampanoag pow-wow?"

These people were clearly not ego-driven; they seemed to think whoever suggested any story was less important than the story itself. Professionals. But that humility wasn't helpful. "Was it the same person?"

"I think it was Jennie came up with the Race Point Inn," said Bruce tentatively. "Wasn't it?"

Cally caught me looking around the room. "Oh, she isn't here," she said. "Maternity leave. It could have been her."

"I suggested the pow-wow," said Adam the director. "Well, not just that one. I had a list. There's been a lot of recent public interest in indigenous peoples, so we wanted to do something to highlight some of the ones in New England. There was the pow-wow on the Cape, and another with the Abenaki in Vermont, and one in New Hampshire, the Koasek Abenaki, and the Redhawks in New Jersey."

"I remember!" squealed the English kid. "And there was that one we eighty-sixed because none of us could pronounce the tribe's name."

"The Wollomonuppoag," said Fred, quietly and probably correctly. "Attleboro."

"How did you decide on the Wampanoag?" I asked.

"Closest," said Bruce briefly. "Plus, the Cape's always a desirable location. Juliet championed it, I think. She loved the Cape."

There was a moment of silence. "I still think we should have gone to Vermont," said Adam.

I had a feeling Juliet did, too, now. "Okay," I said, sighing out my frustration. "So it's not like anyone set her up to go there."

They all gaped at me. "It doesn't work that way," said Cally finally.

So the murder couldn't have been pre-planned, or at least not pre-planned too far in advance. Unless its locale was irrelevant; the same thing might have happened at any indigenous burying ground, any pow-wow.

But then my name wouldn't have figured into it.

"I think," said Fred, "we'd already put Provincetown on the calendar, to do a show at your inn, and we saw the pow-wow was coming up near there…"

"That's it!" exclaimed the English kid. He seemed to be taking every idea as a major revelation. "Remember? We were going to do them together? Move the hotel thing right up to the day the pow-wow started, put two shows in the can with less effort."

That sounded like a reasonable plan. "Why didn't you?"

"It was Juliet," said Bruce unexpectedly. "She said she needed a few days in-between."

"So we had to traipse all the way back to Boston, and now we have to go down to the Cape again in Fourth of July traffic to catch the pow-wow." A note of discord from a short fat kid who hadn't spoken yet. There was a ripple of agreement through the room. Apparently everyone had wanted to stay over.

"Do you know why Juliet didn't want to do it that way?" I asked.

"She wanted to see someone," said Bruce. "At least, I think so. Who knows?" They clearly hadn't followed this line of reasoning.

"Her sister," said Cally, nodding. "She wanted to see her sister. I think she'd just had a baby, or something."

Eloise, I thought. I'd had a feeling she was going to pop up again somewhere. "And Juliet couldn't wait until after the pow-wow?"

"It wasn't a baby," said Fred, giving the prayer beads a final twist around his wrist. "It's Jennie had the baby. It had something to do with the story. She said she needed to check and make sure it would be okay."

What? "Okay for you to do the story? Or to check whether her sister was okay?" I asked.

He shrugged. "She was worried about something," he said, and caught Bruce's eye. "Nothing important," he said. "Nothing that would have got her killed. And maybe worry is too strong a word. It was some family thing, but she thought it might affect the shooting script. You know how she was, every last t crossed and every last i dotted."

"Did you know anything about this?" I asked Bruce.

He shook his head. "The Cape programs were primarily hers," he said. "I'll be honest—I wasn't really paying attention. I have a couple of programs coming up, and I was focused on them. I was kind of along for the ride on the Cape stories."

I looked around the room, and everyone looked back at me. No furtive glances, no sense of anything held back.

But before Juliet went to the pow-wow, she had to check in with her sister, who was married to a tribal member who might or might not be involved in something illegal.

It would make for one hell of a mystery novel, I thought.

***

The Romper Room gang got back to work, and Bruce showed me around the studios. Interesting stuff I managed not to lose my mind over, Mirela's *shining things* remark still stinging. I had a purpose.

Didn't mean I could fulfill it.

We ended up in Juliet's office, the mirror image of Bruce's but with some softer touches: fresh flowers on the desk—now drooping a little—a good Impressionist print on the wall, sofa and chairs in pastel colors. "We've already looked in her desk," Bruce said. "I did, and the police did."

"Did they take anything away with them?" I asked. No sense looking for something that wasn't going to be there.

"Her Mac," he said, and that was why the room looked odd: no computer on the desk. "I didn't see anything else. They didn't let me stay when they were in here."

I sat down behind the desk and tried to see the world through Juliet's eyes. Had something happened here that connected her to me? "What else did they do? The police?" I was imagining Detective Lieutenant Whitney and her sidekick pawing through Juliet's life. It wasn't an appealing image.

"It was the BPD," said Bruce unexpectedly, as though reading my thoughts. Great: the city police had entered the chat. If nothing else, we'd have one hell of an acronym stew when this was over. "Nothing. They looked, and they made a mess. I had to put everything back after they left. Like they were searching for drugs or something." He sounded affronted.

You don't produce a top-rated show in a competitive media environment when you're high. I didn't have any concerns about that.

I started opening drawers. Not much there, of course; no-one keeps papers in their desks anymore, it's all digital. But in the spirit of leaving no stone unturned, I kept at it.

She liked a certain brand of lavender skin moisturizer; little packets of it were scattered all through the shallow middle drawer, along with some lavender sachets. A couple tins of wintergreen ZYN nicotine pouches. A small sewing kit, identical as far as I could tell to the one my mother kept in her purse for what she called emergencies. A gorgeous fountain pen; I made a mental note to see if mine still worked. *Focus, Riley.*

There was a set of walkie-talkies in one of the deeper drawers, pushed way to the back; probably cell phones had obviated the need for them, but it's hard to throw electronics away—my own desk drawers contain mysterious cables and adaptors that had once connected to *something*. Some pads of paper, blank; I even held them to the light to see if any writing was revealed, ghostlike, to see what she'd scribbled. Nothing. A book on time management, signed by the author; it looked like it hadn't been opened, though I flipped through the pages to be sure.

A journal, the ultra-pretty ones you find in gift shops that no-one wants to write in; Juliet had filled two pages with notes about a man she'd been seeing, but the date on the page was three years old. Some coins. This was getting ridiculous.

What are you doing, Riley?

I shut the drawers; there wasn't anything there. Then an idea wormed its way into my head. "You have researchers here at the station, right?"

Bruce looked startled. "We're all researchers," he said. "Everyone at *Waypoints*."

"Okay, I know, but really good ones? Um—not just where's the next pretty place to record a show?"

He straightened. "We're as thorough as the news teams," he said stiffly.

But are you? "Okay. I believe you. Will you look into something for me? Um—discreetly?"

"Is it illegal?"

"Probably not."

He gave me a look. "Sydney, listen—"

"No, wait, it's about Juliet. I could probably do it, but you'll do it better and faster. You want to find out what happened, don't you? You want to know why?"

"What I don't want," he said, "is the news teams doing a segment on *us*."

"They won't," I said, hoping it was true.

He looked at me for a long time before rapping on the glass wall separating the office from the bigger room. Everyone looked up. He pointed to someone and then made a come-hither gesture.

The earnest girl called Cally got up, notebook in hand—see, some people still use them—and stuck her head in. "You want me?"

"Come in," said Bruce. He still sounded exasperated. "Close the door behind you."

She settled into one of the hard client chairs facing the desk. "What do you need?"

"I want you to look into something," he said, and gestured to me. "Sydney needs some research."

She transferred her gaze to me. "How can I help?"

I took a deep breath. "Look into someone called Rick Thatcher," I said. There was no reaction; the name didn't mean anything to either of them. "He lives in Taunton, but he has an office in Boston, in Back Bay. He's some kind of shrink."

She was taking notes and nodded. "What do you want to know?"

I paused. What *did* I want to know? "He's a member of the Mashpee Wampanoag tribe," I said, and felt rather than saw their interest quicken. "There was a scandal a few years ago—well, more than one, actually—"

Cally cut me off. "I know about it," she said, nodding. "I brought it up as a programming option, but it didn't fit in with *Waypoints*. One of the other shows covered it, though."

Bruce hadn't sat down; he was leaning against the glass wall, one foot balancing against it, stroking his beard. "Remind me," he said to her.

"That whole mess, remember?" she said. "After they spent—oh, decades—applying for federal recognition, and they finally got it, and there were a lot of rights that came with it. Sometime in 2017 or 2018, I can't remember, the first Trump administration took the status away, but then the tribe managed to get it back again. And then come to find out, the tribal councilman who was working the hardest on getting recognition, he was also at the same time fleecing the tribe."

"Glenn Marshall," I said.

"Fact," she agreed. "Glenn Marshall. So they fired him, and the next guy did exactly the same thing."

"Cedric Cromwell," I said.

"Fact," she said again, nodding. "They both went to prison, but I think they're probably both out by now. Their sentences weren't all that long."

For a moment I got distracted. Had one of the two men been in the same facility as any of the names on The List? That hadn't occurred to me before.

Bruce interrupted my thoughts. "So what's the problem?"

Cally looked at me expectantly.

"All the embezzlement had to do with building a casino in Taunton," I said. "Lots of money, lots of opposition. It got ugly."

She nodded. "But they've started building," she said. "There's a casino welcome center, though it looks like it's run out of a shipping container or a double-wide. I think they're still looking for investments."

"They are," I confirmed. "The thing is, this guy—Rick Thatcher—he was involved, at least with Cromwell; I don't know about Marshall. I just don't know *how* involved, and that would be good to find out. Maybe he's a good guy, and this is a waste of time. But if he's not…" My voice trailed off and I touched the desk in front of me. *I'm sorry, Juliet.* I took a deep breath. "He's a psychotherapist here in Boston, but he lives in Taunton—that's Mashpee Wampanoag land, where the casino's being built—and he's something to do with handling the investors." Now for the bad news. "He's Juliet Mills' brother-in-law," I said. "And if he thought you were doing a piece on the casino—"

"He'd kill his own sister to stop it?" Bruce's voice was incredulous.

"Sister-in-law," I corrected. "And I don't know anything about him, so maybe we can't rule that out, but maybe it was just a matter of wanting to postpone the show."

"Why?" asked Cally. "We weren't going to uncover anything nefarious. It's a fluff piece about the pow-wow, and maybe ask a few questions for viewers to understand what it means to the tribe. Lots of color, dancers and drummers, indigenous beadwork for sale. Perfect for us."

"Do you think everyone saw it that way?"

Bruce pushed himself off the glass wall, grabbed a chair, and spun it around, sitting on it backwards. "We keep our prospecting in-house," he said. "In that room, there. No-one knew we were working on it." He held up a hand. "And if you're going to accuse one of my team—"

"I'm not," I said hastily. "But seriously, no-one knew? Juliet told me about it in a room full of people. You said it yourself, you do fluff pieces. No reason for people not to talk about it, especially if it was already in the works. What if there was something in it that could be incriminating? Even maybe something you yourselves wouldn't be aware of?"

Cally shook her head. "The timeline doesn't fit," she said. "Sure, we're recording it this year, but the segment won't air until next year, about a month before the next pow-wow. Viewers don't want to see what they missed, they want to see what's coming up."

"Wait," I said. "You said you're recording it? The show's still on?"

They both stared at me. "Of course it is," said Bruce. "Everything's in place."

"As a tribute to Juliet?"

"As our job," said Bruce.

Chapter Fifteen

I went to Juliet's apartment alone.

The *Weekend Waypoints* team had had about enough disruption from me, I figured, so I left as they were wandering about with energy drinks and sandwiches. Bruce had a meeting with the invisible executive producer—"Oh, God, Her Majesty beckons. Wonder what I've done now"—so he simply offered me the keys to Juliet's place; he hadn't returned them to the building manger, he said. "Just— leave it nice, okay? I know she's not going back, but she'd hate to know it was a mess."

His concern was touching, though I suspected the police had not held the same delicate sensibilities. I've seen police searches conducted: they're fast and thorough and leave the place looking like a tornado's been through.

Juliet's apartment was in an old house in Back Bay that literally overlooked the Boston Common, just where it starts going up Beacon Hill, not too far from the State House. I didn't know what kind of money people made in television, but *Weekend Waypoints* hadn't paid for this place. This was generational wealth.

It was bright and cheerful, sun streaming in through the windows fronting Beacon Street. She'd liked color, had Juliet: there were heaps of it everywhere, cushions on the sofa, warm jewel tones in the rugs, a woven tapestry scattering flowers on one wall. I found myself catching my breath, listening for another presence in the apartment; but if Juliet had haunted her home, she was long gone now. I wondered briefly who inherited.

Inheritance being an excellent motive for murder.

To my mind, the motive is almost always greed—greed for money, greed for power, greed for status, greed for a relationship; but greed for an inheritance is a good one. Maybe someone didn't want to wait.

Oh, right, and they just happened to knock her off on Wampanoag land and happened to put my name in her pocket. That's Olympic-level stretching, Riley.

I sighed. It would have been a nice alternative.

Someone had been there since the police searched the place; it had been tidied. I wondered who was in Juliet's life besides her colleagues; why hadn't I thought to ask? That was elementary, one of the first things one queries. I hadn't.

Then again, no one had pointed to me as being the motive for a murder before. Maybe I could be forgiven a lapse in protocol. Besides, I told myself, Will would probably know.

In the meantime, I was clearly late to this party, but I might as well learn what I could.

I stood in the doorway to her bedroom, irresolute. There was a scent lingering in the air, the same lavender as the sachets in her desk, and I breathed it in and wondered what her life here was like. A double bed, but that didn't mean anything; even most people who lived alone had at least double beds these days, more likely queens. A stack of books was on one of the nightstands, and I scanned the titles; we'd had similar tastes in fiction, it would seem. Doerr's *All The Light We Cannot See*; Rooney's *Intermezzo*; Makkai's *The Great Believers*. The closet was filled mostly with work clothes, brighter colors than I wore, but still all very understated. Not a lot of tchotchkes around—everything was elegant, unpretentious, a bit like Juliet herself. If this apartment was anything to go by, she could afford the best, but kept it simple.

I had a feeling I would have liked Juliet Mills very much, and remembered her possibly thinking the same about me. We'd agreed to meet for a drink on the day she disappeared, after all.

The second bedroom was for work. Piles of books on the desk which, again, was missing a computer, though there was space for a laptop. Here was paper: scrawled notes in the same truly terrible handwriting; a couple of printouts about the Wampanoag; a brochure on Martha's Vineyard. Nothing saying *Meet me at midnight at the Old Indian Burial Ground.* I sighed and flicked through the stack and almost missed it.

I was looking for papers, for words I could recognize, so I didn't immediately understand what I was looking at. That probably had been what happened when the police searched the apartment.

But once I saw it, it was all I could see.

The envelope was stuck to the back of a folder by some sticky residue, and if the cops had seen it, they'd clearly discounted it. I looked inside: there was something about ten inches long, tiny purple and white cylindrical beads held together in a pattern I couldn't recognize as representational of anything. Somewhere from the depths of my mind—probably from some trivia game or other—the word *wampum* floated into my head. I pulled out my phone and took some photos of it.

Beadwork. Wampanoag beadwork.

Also inside the envelope was a scrap of paper that just said, "from Rick."

***

I left two more voicemails for Ali. It was ridiculous; he was clearly not going to return my calls, and the more messages I left, the sillier I felt. Actually, what I felt was that I was sixteen years old and romantically pursuing someone who had absolutely no interest in me.

I thought about just showing up at Rick Thatcher's office and confronting him about the wampum, but on reflection that would probably place me firmly in the Crazy Lady section of the bus and might even involve the police, so I sat on the riverbank of the Charles for a long time, eating a belated lunch and watching the Harvard and MIT crews glide by, fast and apparently effortless. There were small sailboats from the various clubs staggering around in the river, and slowly the sounds of traffic and people receded and I almost—almost—forgot why I was there.

By the time I reclaimed my car from the exorbitantly expensive garage where I'd left it, I was feeling like I could breathe again. Cally would find something. Or Will would find something. I wasn't in this alone.

The drive back to the Cape was everything I expected, but I felt an odd sense of relief when I crossed the bridge. Things were settling in my head: whatever Juliet had been doing, it connected to the tribe and to the pow-wow, now only two days away. And it wasn't too much of a stretch to think it connected to the disappearance of a Wampanoag girl. I'd replaced my earlier wild guesswork with some understanding of at least some of the underlying dynamics.

One thing was clear: I was going to have to go to the pow-wow.

Margo's house seemed undisturbed, and Wally was pleased to see me, actually rubbing around my ankles. Or maybe that was another attempt to kill me. You never knew, with cats. I changed into shorts and a t-shirt and called Will. Voicemail.

I was becoming seriously tired of getting people's voicemail.

Too soon to check in with Cally, and I wasn't going to add yet another call to Ali. I wished I were the sort of person who could take off for a healthy run and pound the anxiety out of my body, but bicycling up and down Commercial Street in Provincetown is about the extent of my summer exercise routine, and I settled for a cold drink in the three-seasons room. I opened my MacBook and began idly looking up what I could find about wampum.

The List was still sitting on the table, mocking me.

I ignored it.

***

Wally came and curled up next to me as though it were the most natural thing. He still had a few sneezes in him, but the scared, inward-focused look was gone. Kudos to Dr. Sadie and her crew.

I had maybe found a clue, and I had no idea what to do with it. And it occurred to me that if so much of the mystery around Juliet's death—not to mention Skye's disappearance—centered around the Wampanoag tribe, then I'd probably been spending way too much time talking to white people.

And Will Fortier was my entry point there. He knew them, or at least some of them. I didn't like my chances of walking into the tribal office building and asking whomever might be staffing the front desk about some of my theories.

Not, of course, that I had a whole lot of theories.

I sighed and picked up my notebook and flipped resolutely past The List. What did I have?

I started a new list of names, starting with my new favorite option: *Rick Thatcher*. I thought about it a moment longer and added *Eloise Thatcher*, she was, after all, the connective tissue between Juliet and the Wampanoag. Feeling somewhat foolish, I wrote *Mr. X*, the guy who'd apparently been grooming Skye for trafficking. Was that really all I had?

I tossed the notebook down in frustration and turned to the cat. "Cocktail time," I announced. I gave him his dinner, poured myself a glass of Côtes du Rhône, and stood for a long time looking out the window at the lush green garden beyond. Too many names; not enough names.

I texted Will and asked if he could reconnect me with Derek. I rifled through Margo's CD collection, taking a page from Juliet's book by playing the CD through an old-fashioned speaker: Billy Joel's *The Stranger*. The music filled the house, and the shadows lengthened; I wasn't accustomed to being in a place with so many tall trees—on the Outer Cape, they're all stunted and twisted by the wind. Here they managed to stand upright, which meant they blocked out more light; the sky above was still blue, but evening was wrapping itself around the house already.

There was something unsettling about the whole thing. The house felt most isolated and scary at night. I didn't want it to be night, not yet; I didn't want to think of danger and darkness and the people who might be interested in doing me harm, which now potentially included my former husband. Or the person who might want to do Margo harm; that murder, decades old, was still alive in someone's mind.

Margo's client, Eddie O'Brien, had appealed his conviction to the Innocence Project. He'd been fifteen when the events occurred, and most courts nowadays accept acts of violence committed before a child's brain has grown and matured should not be punished in the same way as other crimes; many incarcerated for that sort of crime had already been released. Not Eddie; he would never admit to doing something he hadn't. The person who killed Eddie's best friend's mother was still out there, and Margo could name him.

Knives. He had stabbed a woman to death and made sure someone else got the blame. I'd read somewhere people who kill more than once tend to stick to the same method, and I shivered thinking about it.

And now every sound seemed threatening. Even the music. *The Stranger* is about the hidden secrets people keep from each other, but to me it had become ominous, personal: there was a stranger out there, possibly looking for me. *Some are satin, some are steel...*

I texted Mirela and asked if she and Lily wanted to come hang out with me in Marstons Mills. I didn't mean it: she wouldn't come, anyway, and putting a child deliberately in danger wasn't part of my plan; I just wanted the comfort of communication. I'm someone who spends most of her time surrounded by people, and the isolation and silence of this house were starting to spook me.

I ate a yogurt in lieu of dinner, walking around the house, peering out of windows. Billy wanted to know *Did you ever let your lover see the stranger in yourself?*

I don't love taking drugs. Alcohol—and alcohol in moderation—is as far as I go these days. But with the night wrapping itself around the house, with the myriad small noises creatures make in the dark as they either settle in for the night or prepare themselves for hunting, I finally gave up and took out the Ambien.

I hadn't been in bed for five minutes when I heard—I was sure I was hearing—someone fumbling with the keypad on the front door. *It's him*, I thought wildly; Margo's suspect. I had a list of people who possibly might want to kill me; Margo had a list of one who absolutely did. *It's him, he's found the place...*

The door opened; floorboards were creaking. I looked around the bedroom in some panic: what was here I could use to defend myself? I scrambled out of the bed and put it between me and the bedroom door, armed rather foolishly with the coffee cup I had placed on the nightstand that morning and hadn't bothered to move. Probably couldn't hit him with it, anyway, pitching not being anywhere in my roster of skills.

Someone was in the house.

Pity Wally isn't an attack cat, I thought, clutching the cup, my heart beating wildly, my senses sharpening: the room's shadows were cast in bright relief, I could sense as well as hear the footsteps approaching.

And then the voice, soft and inquiring. "*Cara?* Are you awake?"

It was Ali.

Chapter Sixteen

I went to throw myself into his arms—well, that was the intention, anyway—but tripped on something and sprawled out on the floor at the foot of the bed instead.

"I see," he said, reaching down to help me up. "Falling for me all over again."

Oh, right. I did that just to hand you a line. "Where have you been?" I demanded. "I've been leaving you messages." I scrambled up and sat on the edge of the bed with as much dignity as I could muster. I could have been a cat: *I totally meant to do that.*

He sat down next to me. "Work," he said, and then relented. "And I was angry with you."

I bit back all the things I wanted to say, which were precisely what my mother would say—that alone stopped any recriminations. I was not, but not, going to be That Person. "Are you all right?" I asked instead.

He sat down on the bed next to me and took one of my hands in his. "I'm all right," he said.

I didn't ask where he'd been staying. I didn't tell him what getting his voicemail over and over again felt like. "Did you find her?"

He was stroking my hand slowly with his thumb; I didn't think he was even aware of it. "Almost," he said.

"What does that mean?"

He shrugged. "Found where she was being held," he said. "She was gone, and this other young woman was there—cleaning, she said. It was a nice apartment, no-one would have noticed anything wrong unless Skye had been putting up a fight. Which she hadn't."

"Who was on the lease?" Okay, so he would have thought of that, but I was still orienting myself to his presence.

"Guy who's out in LA," Ali said. "He sublets it a lot, especially in the summertime. Neighbors say the current tenant is white, mid-thirties, polite. His wife—they assumed it was his wife—never went out, stayed in the apartment most of the time. But nice, too. She took in packages when people in the building were at work, that kind of thing. They'd only been there for a few weeks."

"Skye? Were they pretending to be married?" And why *would* she?

He shook his head. "Nope. We showed her picture around, no-one'd seen her. They were pretty clear about that—and you have to admit, she's memorable. We took the cleaner in: she was the one they said was living there, they thought she was the wife. White, in her late twenties, unremarkable in that neighborhood. Had a lawyer waiting for us by the time we got her back to the Federal Building."

"That was quick."

"Yeah. She was involved. I had the tribal police show her picture to Kathy Taylor, she said it might have been the woman Skye met when the guy took her to Boston. Skye showed her a photo of them once on her phone, but at the time Kathy wasn't really paying attention, just wanted Skye to come to her senses."

He was probably telling me more than he should have—Ali's always been good with work/home boundaries, but maybe he was feeling he owed me something—and I wasn't about to stop him. "So Skye's gone," I said. "Where? Do you think he knew you were coming?" A thought flashed through my mind. "You don't think she's—dead, do you?"

"I think," said Ali slowly, "maybe this wasn't about trafficking. I can't prove it. But I'm pretty good at seeing the pattern when there's trafficking, and this just isn't it."

"Then—why? There were no ransom demands, were there?"

I felt rather than saw him shake his head. "I don't know," he said. "But I think she's back on the Cape. Someone bought two bus tickets for Boston South Station to Sagamore. I'm waiting to get a name. The bus company requires a credit card, getting a ticket is all through an app now."

I thought for a moment. Ali is smart: he knew how to totally engage me… *and* postpone any recriminations about his disappearance and the argument that had preceded it. I knew what he was doing, but I let it happen. I was relieved things were back to whatever passes for normal in our lives. And from Sagamore it's just as easy to get to Taunton as it is to get to Mashpee. "Then there has to be another reason," I said. "Not kidnapping, because there's been no ransom. And you're saying it's apparently not trafficking, either. So it's something else."

"Ah, *cara*, we think as one. I'm working on it."

I thought briefly that he was back because of the investigation, not because he missed me or wanted to make amends, but dismissed it and didn't say anything; I'd had time to think about what my involvement in crime over the years had meant to him. He'd been so angry because he felt so helpless.

I cleared my throat. "I was in Boston, too," I said. "Just for the day. I went to see where Juliet worked, at *Weekend Waypoints*." I took a deep breath. "Turns out, her sister is married to a Wampanoag, someone who's been involved with getting the tribe federal recognition."

He was interested. "You found a connection?"

"Not yet. But I'm sure it's there. Someone from the research staff is looking into it. They all really liked her, by the way."

"Someone didn't."

"I know." I sighed. "It's like, the answer is there." Floating just beyond reach. "We just need to find the connections."

"Not tonight," he said firmly. "We'll have to sleep on it."

"Sleep?" I asked. "Really?"

"Well, eventually, yes. Let's go to bed."

***

We were two days away from the pow-wow. I didn't know why I was so convinced something was going to happen then, but it felt like a deadline of sorts.

Ali took himself off somewhere after breakfast, and I checked my phone: I'd somehow missed a message from Will, returning my call. He picked up almost immediately. "Sydney, hi, what's the news?"

"Not much," I said. "Can you help me? I'd like to talk to Derek again—or someone from the tribe. This is about them."

"Not necessarily," Will said. "I'm starting to think—you know, the place she was left? The Indian burial ground? That might have been just to get us chasing our tails. Not any deeper meaning."

I wasn't willing to go there. Not yet, anyway. "I'd still like to talk to him," I said.

"Yeah, sure."

"I went to see the team at *Weekend Waypoints*," I said, anxious to keep his interest. "It was the director, his name is Adam, it was him who suggested they cover the pow-wow. But he says he suggested a bunch of other pow-wows, too, so it might not mean anything."

"What other pow-wows?"

I frowned, trying to visualize the conversation. "One in Vermont," I said slowly. "Maybe the Algonquin? Can't remember what the others were. Is it important?"

"Might be," he said. "Good chance someone from the Wampanoag would have been at all the others."

That was something I hadn't considered. "Why?"

He sighed. "We just see the pow-wows as spectacle," he said. "But they're not. They're deeply meaningful to the tribes. They call it homecoming, and it's both an obligation and an honor to show up for others. At the grand entry, everyone's led by men carrying the different nations' flags. And—"

"Wait," I interrupted. "What's a grand entry?"

"The start of every day of the pow-wow. Before they do all the other stuff—the dances, the songs, the drumming. They line up in a specific order. Not by tribes, but by gender and age. And they enter the central performance area, with the flag-bearers first, so that by the time the tiniest children are in it's become a sort of spiral, with everyone dancing. It's a sign of respect, to be part of another tribe's pow-wow."

I didn't say anything. It had finally struck me it was us who weren't showing respect. I was pretty accustomed to tourists not showing respect, and it irritated *me*, even in Provincetown, and I wasn't even guarding centuries-old rituals.

Will asked, "Are you still there?"

"Yeah. I'm here. Just thinking." I cleared my throat if not my mind. "Looking at it from the program's point of view," I said, "how would it be viewed by the Wampanoag, to have all these people there recording, and probably encouraging a lot more tourists to come to the pow-wow?"

"Don't think it would be a problem," said Will. "I mean, there are parts of the pow-wow they don't want people recording, they ask everyone to put their cameras away. But the TV people know that, I'd guess. And it's educational. The less mystery there is about the event, and the kind of life it portrays, the less chance there is of white people othering the tribe. That's why we've covered it at the newspaper, anyway. We've done stuff like a day in the life—you know, the way some religious orders are doing, bringing viewers into the hidden world of the native tribe so it doesn't seem as—foreign, I guess would be the word."

"I think this is Wampanoag-specific," I said slowly. "Sure, they may send representatives to other pow-wows, but that would be catch as catch can, wouldn't it? If someone means to hurt the tribe, it would be on their own territory. And Juliet was producing the segment. I think if something happens—"

"Wait," said Will. "Something happens? It already has. She's dead."

"I know, I know," I said, a little flippantly. "But I just think that was the beginning of something, not the end."

"Because of the note?"

I shrugged, then remembered he couldn't see me. "Maybe. I'm pretty Cape-specific. But, listen, what if somebody didn't want the program to get recorded? It's a good motive, and they kind of underlined it by leaving her in the Indian graveyard."

"Who would care, though?" asked Will.

"And there's the other thing," I said, ignoring his question; I was trying out my own angle. "Juliet's brother-in-law is Wampanoag. Do you remember that whole embezzling scandal?" He was probably too young to have been working for the paper when it happened. Actually, he might be too young to have been *alive* when it happened.

I'd have to do the math. But he was a reporter, he would have looked into recent history.

Yep. "I read about it," said Will. "Old news."

"Maybe not so old. Rick Thatcher—that's the brother-in-law—was involved in the whole federal recognition movement. I don't think he was involved in the embezzlement—he would have been charged, and besides, it sounds to me less like a conspiracy and more about two greedy men lining their own pockets, which happens every day. But maybe he knows something someone wants kept secret? Especially now with the casino in Taunton becoming a reality?"

"I don't know." His voice was laced with doubt. "It was a long time ago. Why would it come up again now?"

"They're still trying to get investors for the casino," I said. "Not a good time for secrets to surface."

"Maybe." He was humoring me.

"One of the researchers on the show seemed to know a lot more about the Wampanoag than the others," I said, remembering Fred, fingering his Buddhist prayer beads. He could pronounce tribal names. "Maybe I'll talk to him."

"Okay. And I'm running down a couple of ideas," said Will. "I'll tell you about them if anything comes of it."

"And arrange another meeting with Derek?" I added. It sounded like he was wrapping up; I didn't want him to forget.

"Yeah, sure."

"There's something else," I said uncomfortably. "My ex-husband called."

"Really? Not exactly on your bingo card. What did he want?"

I'd have preferred to keep Noah out of my bingo game altogether, much less on my card. "He's going to trial. Not just on the hospital screwup, but it sounds like he might have killed his wife."

"*What?*"

Ali had said the same thing, when deep in the night I'd remembered the conversation and had told him about it. "He tried to bribe me, offered me something he knew I'd want, in exchange for lying to the court. Giving him an alibi for when she was killed."

There was a pause, then Will said, "You're going to tell me these two deaths are connected."

"I don't *know!*" I said, a little wildly. Ali had immediately gone there, too. "I don't see how they can be. But, yeah, they happened at the same time. Her and Juliet. And he's been coming down to the Cape, and I never knew..." I'd burst into tears when I told that part to Ali; I wasn't going to do it again now. I steadied myself. "If he did do it, he'd been planning it for a while. At least a couple of weeks, anyway. I don't see how he could have foreseen that Juliet would be doing the show, and I sure as hell don't see how that connects to whatever was going on in their marriage." He'd divorced *me*; maybe I was just lucky. "He wouldn't kill Juliet just so he'd have something over me. And, anyway, you don't kill two people in one night."

"It's been done," said Will calmly. "What's her name?"

"Who? Oh, his wife? Alice. I don't know her last name; maybe she took his when they got married."

"I'll look into it," he said. "How did you leave it with him?"

"I hung up on him," I said. "He has to know I wouldn't—perjure myself." Not even for my own alibi. Not even for the house in Cambridge. "I wouldn't."

"Of course you wouldn't." He sounded matter-of-fact and I tried to pull some of his calm through the phone; my pulse was racing again. "Leave it with me, Sydney. I'll ask some questions. And I'll get you that meeting with Derek."

I stared at the phone for a minute or two after he disconnected. What now? I hadn't even gotten Cally's contact information, I realized. I'd make a dreadful reporter.

I called Bruce instead; at least I had *his* number. "Sydney. Any news?"

Everyone seemed to be asking me that.

"No," I said. "Not about Juliet. I wondered if Cally had come up with anything on Rick Thatcher."

"Don't know. She's not here right now." There was a pause. "I'm coming down a day early," he said. "The team will be down just for the day, but I want to revisit the place they found her. Maybe if I retrace her steps… I have a reservation at the MidCape Resort. That's where she spent the night before she disappeared."

"They'll have cleaned the room," I said. Okay, maybe not the most compassionate response. And then, thinking about it, I added, "How do you know that? Where she spent the night?" I knew, but only because Will had told me and Ali.

"I told you. We're as good at investigations as the news team. We just investigate different things."

I hoped they'd be as good at investigating Rick Thatcher. "Who's coming for the pow-wow recording?" I asked. "The same crew from Provincetown?"

"Different lighting guy; Jake's on vacation. Adam said he might come down early with me, take a look at the set-up ahead of time. I think he's a little over-prepared there; don't really need the director until the actual shoot. But he's conscientious, that's not a bad thing."

"How are you managing without Juliet?" I asked. "You said the pow-wow was her project."

"Yeah. Adam's come through there. He shared some of the pre-shoot chores with me—normally that would have been Juliet. But like I told you, we work as a team."

"What kind of chores?"

"Talking to the organizers, getting permits from the tribal police, setting up interviews, all that sort of thing. Juliet and I share those out." He paused. "We *used* to share them out," he amended.

"Interviews?" I asked. "With Stacey?"

"She's good at what she does," he said loyally.

"There won't be a dressing room for her in Mashpee," I said, probably sounding nasty. I wasn't sure why she rubbed me the wrong way so strongly.

To my surprise, he hooted with laughter. "She'll have to survive," he said.

I smiled, too; I couldn't help it. "I'm going to the pow-wow," I said. "Probably my husband will be there, too."

"Well, make sure you come over and say hello," he said. "I'll be distracted, but don't let that bother you."

Like I would ever dream of being bothered enough to not go over and ask more questions. "I won't," I assured him.

"The end of an era," Bruce said unexpectedly. "It's the last program that was really Juliet's, that she was excited about. And I've had two resignations." He paused. "Maybe she was easier to work with than I am."

"More likely they were thinking of resigning anyway," I said, trying to sound reassuring. "And with changes coming—I assume you'll be hiring for her position, right?—they probably saw it as a good time to do it. Who resigned?"

He seemed to be digesting my opinion. "Who? Oh, Jennie. You didn't meet her, she's out on maternity leave. And Adam; he's had a really good offer from a show out of New York."

"Well, there you go. He was planning on resigning anyway. Did Jennie say why she wants to leave?"

"I expect," he said austerely, "that having a baby is resetting her priorities."

So: nothing out of the ordinary. And, just like that, another line of inquiry bites the dust. "You'll have a bunch of hiring to do," I said. Three positions—that sounded like a lot to be dealing with.

"Not a bad thing," said Bruce unexpectedly. "There's always churn. The kids learn the ropes with us and move on. I think it keeps things interesting. Juliet—well, that's another issue. She'll be hard to... replace."

"I can imagine." We shared a brief moment of gloom.

He cleared his throat. "It's not just for the programming," he said. "Juliet's the one brought me onto the team. But the station has been making noises for a long time about changes they want in the show. Just the usual, trimming the budget—you know how bad things have been, trying to get federal grants. We might end up losing some positions."

"But not Juliet's, surely?"

"Don't know. The executive producer's starting to think we don't need two producers on every episode. She would've survived, she has seniority, and I don't think there's anyone in the business who can think of *Weekend Waypoints* without her. She practically started it."

"You, then?" I asked with as much sympathy as I could muster.

"Don't know," he said. "It's just one more thing to worry about."

He sounded discouraged. "Call me when you get here tomorrow," I offered. "We could have dinner or something." *Or something? What does that even mean?*

Bruce didn't notice anything amiss. "Super," he said. "You choose the place. We'll have a drink to Juliet's memory."

No talk, I noticed, of including Adam in the celebration. Maybe the team wasn't quite as tight as they wanted us to believe. "Sounds good," I said. "Talk to you then."

Will had texted me while I was on the phone. *Derek can see you at one o'clock. Meet him in front of the tribal community and government center.*

I texted him back, unconsciously echoing Bruce. *Super*, I wrote. *Thanks! Will you be there too?*

Unclear if I can find time. I'll try if you think useful.

Don't worry about me, I texted. *Do what you need to do.*

And it was after that that things got very weird indeed.

Chapter Seventeen

The first thing that happened was Mirela showing up.

Not exactly at my front door; I was keeping Margo's secrets. And when I saw Mirela's picture appear on my phone, all I thought was, *Good. We're in for a nice long chat, and I can bounce some ideas off her.*

"Sunshine," said Mirela, "are you in hiding for a purpose?"

What? "I'm not in hiding," I said. "I'm at Margo's house. I told you that—where I'm staying."

"Well, then you must give me an address," she said. "I have come to see you. I am right now sitting beside a very small airport waiting for you to invite me."

The airport—for general aviation, the "runways" being nothing but flattened grass—was only a couple of miles away. "You're here?" I asked, stupidly.

"Of course I am here. You asked me to come. What is wrong with you, sunshine?"

Good question. "Stay there," I said. "I'll come to you." *What is she really doing here?*

Mirela gave me an exaggerated sigh. "If you must."

Wally was, as usual, nowhere to be found. I told him I was going out anyway, grabbed my keys and my purse, punched in the Secret Code, and was out of there.

Mirela was waiting at one of the pull-offs apparently designed for plane-spotting, except that in the myriad times I'd been there I'd never once seen an airplane doing anything but sitting. And I'd looked; over the past year, for reasons that were totally obscure even to me, I'd developed a minor obsession with airplanes and flying, and spent an inordinate amount of time on YouTube watching videos from Mentour Pilot, 74 Gear, and Pilot View.

She was noticeable in her new car, a scarlet Jaguar F-Type. And she wasn't best pleased: these days, no-one made Mirela wait. "Sunshine. It would have been easier for you to give me the address."

She was probably right; Mirela wasn't in any way involved with the person who wished Margo harm, and she was good at keeping secrets. "You could have told me you were coming," I said defensively.

"I am here now. You said I should come to support you. So here I am."

I said that? "What did you do with Lily?" I asked instead, seizing on something irrelevant to get her to talk. Besides, if I knew my goddaughter, she'd have wanted to come along on anything that even hinted at a promise of adventure. *And* she was on her summer vacation.

"Lily is fine, sunshine. She is staying with George for a few days." George was Mirela's gallery manager, a cushy job if ever there was one, as Mirela's paintings pretty much sell themselves. George lived deep in Provincetown's West End with his husband, four corgis, and an art collection that would put some museums to shame. He also had lost a daughter to leukemia, and cheerfully took Lily into his life whenever Mirela needed it; she'd gotten rid of the nanny when Lily was six and already exhibiting a wider vocabulary than her minder.

I sighed. We weren't going to have a conversation about anything remotely subversive in what amounted to a lay-by. And Mirela would never consciously harm anyone. "Okay," I said. "Just follow me. We'll go to Margo's."

She shook her head, looking at me with wonder in her eyes. "This is what I proposed, sunshine," she said.

"I know. I always follow your opinions—at a safe distance."

"Then lead on, MacDuff," she said.

Really? And now you quote Shakespeare? "Just follow me," I said and got back into the Grey Goose. She followed, but with way too short a distance for it to feel safe; her new sports car had a lot more power than my Honda Civic. *Yeah, you should have just given her the address when she asked for it.*

We went back along roads that twisted and turned and made it to Margo's without Mirela actually having—or causing—an accident. A minor miracle, all things considered. She loved to drive, but was notoriously bad at it.

I punched in The Code and moments later we were ensconced in comfortable chairs in the three-seasons room. "Sure you don't want anything to drink?'

"No, sunshine, I want to hear what is happening which is making you so frightened," Mirela said.

So much for small talk. I said, "I think at least some of this is connected to the pow-wow. A pow-wow is—"

"I know what it is," she said.

"Okay. You know we could have done this on the phone, right?"

"What is this connection between the pow-wow and your mysteries?"

I sighed. It was feeling less clear every time I tried to articulate it. I wasn't sure it was supposed to work that way. "I think Rick Thatcher will be there," I said. "I still don't know why, but it feels like he's at the center of everything. He has ancestors buried in the cemetery where they found Juliet's body. And in the past—"

"I know," she interrupted. "You told me this already, sunshine. You believe he was part of a scandal in the tribe. But that was a long time ago."

"It was, but…" I allowed my voice to trail off; I didn't know what to say next.

"Then you need to speak with him," she said. "I am surprised you do not think of this yourself."

And since when are you this interested in one of my mysteries? "I was getting around to it," I said defensively. "Just trying to think of what to ask." *I could start with, Did you kill anybody recently?*

Possibly not the best approach.

"You always know what to ask, sunshine," Mirela said. "Why is it you perceive this as more difficult?"

"Because he's Wampanoag."

She raised her eyebrows. "That sounds like racism," she said.

"It's not!" I protested. "In fact, it's just the opposite. Indigenous people have gotten short shrift around just about everything since the first Europeans came over. I don't want to be culturally insensitive, and it seems to me that singling out one of the tribal members as a suspect isn't all that respectful, if that's even what I'm doing. I just don't want to be rude."

"I see." She thought about it for a moment. "If he agrees to speak with you, at least then you will know."

"I don't think my prowess—or lack thereof—at asking questions is going to exactly overwhelm him," I said tartly.

"But you believe he is behind the murder," she countered. "Perhaps even behind the disappearance of the girl from the tribe."

It was sounding more and more absurd. "I don't know," I confessed. "I thought so for a while, but now I'm wondering if it was all in my mind."

"Many things are all in your mind," she said. "Perhaps this is not."

We'd gone from her believing it to not believing it and back again in very short order. And an idea was starting to hit me over the head. "Ali asked you to come, didn't he?"

"It does not matter, sunshine," she said. "I am here now."

"When?" I demanded. "When did he ask you to come and help?"

"It does not matter," she said again, sounding like it mattered a lot.

I thought about Ali, investigating a possible trafficker, warning me off any lines of inquiry I might choose to pursue. Ali, away in Boston where he couldn't keep me safe. Ali, hearing about another murder and a connection that went deep into my past life, my first marriage. "This is about you keeping an eye on me, isn't it?"

"Does it matter?" she asked rhetorically, and then answered herself. "It does not."

"Yeah, it does," I said. "He doesn't think I should be alone. He kept trying to get me back to P'town. And when that didn't work, he brought in the cavalry."

"Please? What is the cavalry?"

"Backup," I said. "Someone to look after me."

"Sunshine, you must admit, you are not very good at looking after yourself. I could give you some examples—"

"Never mind." The truth was, even though I was sounding snippy about it, I was grateful she was there. And grateful, too, that my husband wanted to protect me—though I would never let anyone, least of all Ali, know that was my reaction. "Okay. You're here now."

"I will come with you to interview this man, this Rick Thatcher. If you think it was him, it would be important for him to know you are not alone."

Right. Since Ali couldn't be there, seeing as it was outside of his purview. And he trusted Mirela, even though apparently he couldn't trust me. "Did you even bring luggage?"

"Please, sunshine?"

"A suitcase," I said. "You're planning on staying?"

"Of course I do. I have never seen a pow-wow, me. Luggage, this is a suitcase?"

"Among other things," I said. I wasn't really up for a conversation about English vocabulary.

She nodded, storing the word away. "Where do we start?"

"With lunch," I said firmly. "I have an appointment at one o'clock to speak with one of the tribal elders."

"Then *we* have this appointment," she said. "I will accompany you. And now you will tell me what we do about lunch."

I gave up. There's no derailing Mirela once she fixes an intention in her mind. "Let's see what's in the kitchen," I said.

"That is always a good place to start," she said, nodding. "And then we solve your mystery."

"Mysteries," I said. "Not just one."

"We shall see."

But first, of course, we saw about lunch.

***

We got to the tribal compound early, but Derek had still beaten us there. "You're lucky it's me you're meeting," he informed us. "Most of us are typically late. Indian time, you know."

I didn't jump on that; if he wanted to say 'Indian', it was his prerogative. But I didn't ask him about his remark—somehow, I thought, that would be racist, coming from me. In this instance, I was the tourist.

"This is Mirela," I said instead.

He shook her hand. "Derek Collins," he said gravely.

Mirela is courtesy personified when she chooses to be. "It is an honor to meet you," she said.

"Let's walk around the grounds," Derek suggested. "I'm grateful anytime I don't have to be in an office."

There were more posters here, Skye smiling and happy in the photo, the message frantic, detailing her name and the date of her disappearance, the same number to call. It was a grim reminder the tribal police had a lot on their hands.

We strolled out back, into a field of sorts dotted with tall trees, picnic tables, and benches, all very pastoral and pleasant. The trees offered the kind of shade that's hard to come by on the Outer Cape.

I was especially grateful for them this afternoon: it was hotter than hot, and they provided blessed relief. A couple of benches were sitting facing each other under one of the trees. Derek gestured toward them, and I sank with relief into the shade.

"How can I help you?" he asked. I glanced at Mirela, but her face was giving nothing away. "Maybe first a general introduction to the Wampanoag?" I suggested. "Just to put Mirela in the picture."

He seemed unsurprised; I would bet he had to do this with some frequency. "All right," he said. "Once upon a time, all of southeastern Massachusetts and a good part of Rhode Island was the home of the Wampanoag Nation, made up of sixty-seven distinct tribes. They included the Nauset and the Pamet."

His eyes were on me; he knew I was from the Outer Cape. There was a famous "sharpening rock" used for centuries by the Nauset; you can see it, over at Fort Hill in Eastham. And in Wellfleet you can see the grave of a woman disinterred during an excavation for a new house—her stone (and presumably body) now sits at the head of the Great Island walking trail. The stone reads, somewhat unfortunately, that her family and tribe "gave of themselves and their land that this great nation might be born and grow."

No-one, of course, had asked either her or her tribe whether they wished to make that sacrifice.

The sharpening stone and the grave are still there; the people, not so much. "When the European traders and then settlers came, they brought diseases that decimated the population. But they also brought a system of governance that was unlike any of our tribal practices or values. We held the land sacred; they saw it as opportunity. Most of those tribal communities were killed in battles that the colonists started, so they could steal the land." He paused. "These days, only six visible tribal communities remain, and only the Mashpee and the Aquinnah are still on their ancestral homelands— but on very small portions of them."

The Aquinnah Wampanoag were on Martha's Vineyard. From my reading, I knew "Aquinnah" means "at the end of the island," and that is indeed where they live, out at Gay Head. They were the ones who began the Wampanoag Language Reclamation Project: the only instance of a language becoming completely dead… and being deliberately brought back to life.

Jessie Little Doe Baird—herself a Mashpee Wampanoag—had a dream in which her ancestors told her to "bring the language home." And she did: she worked with Ken Hale and Norvin Richards from MIT (the premier linguistic center in North America, which surprised me a little: I'd always thought of MIT as math-oriented) and over a number of years painstakingly located documents written in words from the seventeenth and eighteenth centuries, then drawing from the spoken languages of neighboring tribal communities to figure out pronunciations.

There's a Wampanoag saying that those who break a circle must reconnect it, and Ken Hale traced his ancestry back to Roger Williams, who'd "settled" Rhode Island, bringing *that* circle round again.

"It's so unfair," I said without thinking. I could imagine his response: you *think*? But he didn't say it.

"It is our history," he said simply.

Mirela, not one to normally be patient with anything historical, unexpectedly said, "We saw the same thing at my home, in Bulgaria. We were colonized by the Ottoman Turks for five centuries, until the Russians came—and colonized us for more centuries. We still spoke Turkish until the national movement in the twentieth century." I stared at her in disbelief. *Mirela* interested in history? Curiouser and curiouser…

Derek nodded but didn't comment. Just as well.

I cleared my throat. "A lot of people who live on Cape Cod don't even know you exist," I said.

"Yes," he agreed. "We're hoping our pow-wows do something to change that. To bring our presence and stories and culture into their awareness. So they can feel blessed we are still here."

I wasn't so sure about that; with my vast experience of tourists, I feared that visitors to the pow-wows might regard the tribes as spectacles at a zoo. Maybe I was wrong; maybe they'd see it as educational. One could hope.

Anyway, it was time to get down to the essentials. "Tell us," I said, "about Rick Thatcher."

He didn't seem surprised. I had a feeling nothing would surprise this man. "Rick is a hero to his people," he said gravely. "Back when things were going badly, he kept working for federal recognition. He was one of those who kept the flame alive. And counseled many of us." He glanced at me. "You know he is a psychotherapist, right?"

I nodded. "He has an office in Boston," I said.

"That's so more tribes can access his services," said Derek. He caught my look of surprise. "We've always been here," he said, perhaps unconsciously echoing the title of a film I'd watched online about the language recovery project. "We still are. And we all experience many of the same challenges and joys experienced by other tribes. Rick is a beacon in a world that doesn't understand the importance of our presence." He stopped talking, sat back on the bench.

Mirela wasn't having any of it. Though her very recent interest in history drew a few parallels, the two cultures couldn't have been farther apart. The Wampanoag are slow and thoughtful and deliberate; Mirela rushes in where angels fear to tread. "What other tribes?" she asked Derek now, apparently wanting him to pick up the pace. I could have strangled her.

Perhaps not the best metaphor to use.

Derek smiled as though he knew exactly what she wanted; but he answered readily enough. "The Pequot and the Narragansett—they're also federally recognized—along with some state-recognized tribes, the Nipmuc, the Mi'kmaq, the Penacook, and the Herring Pond Wampanoag." He paused. "It might not surprise you to know that individuals within these tribes need someone to help them sort their feelings, their heritage, their connection to a land that was taken from them, to ancestors whose lives were lost to occupying Europeans."

Put that way, it wasn't surprising at all. My own Irish ancestors had experienced some racism and oppression when they, much later, emigrated to America; but they'd never been wiped out as a people. I could almost imagine what that felt like.

Almost.

"Tell us about Rick," I said, again trying to sound encouraging. I needn't have bothered: even in just two meetings spent with Derek, I had recognized the Wampanoag had different social skills from the white people I'd grown up around: they had clear boundaries and were pensive, extraordinarily kind, and certainly not given to sharing anything they hadn't first thought about.

Derek had thought about what I might ask, no doubt, in the time between Will's call to him and our meeting. "He is Wampanoag," he said slowly, which was beginning to tell me a lot about Rick. "What he does, he does out of love for his people."

That pretty much precluded him being involved in Skye's disappearance.

Derek was still talking. "He honors his ancestors and his family," he said. "For us, family is everything. The blood in our veins is there from centuries of Wampanoag ancestors. Rick honors that."

"But he married outside of the tribe," Mirela observed, again to my surprise.

His eyes, if anything, reflected merriment. "Maybe that's why he worked so hard to get us federal recognition," he said. "One of the obstacles was exactly that: our many years of marriage outside the tribe. The feds said we couldn't assert an ongoing existence because there had been so much intermarriage with Black and European-Americans. In the past, that tended to be mostly Black people— partly because we had so much in common with them around the prejudices of the white people. But intermarriage was necessary even from the beginning, with so many men killed in battles with the English."

A long pause, which thankfully neither Mirela nor I broke. I was beginning to recognize that people from my culture were inclined to fill silences, that courtesy seemed to require constant communication, constant verbiage; the Wampanoag felt no such need.

Finally Derek said, "Rick married outside the tribe for love. It happens, and there's no shame in it. But I believe that's one of the reasons he's worked so hard to support us."

That made sense; we've all had to make difficult decisions, and that was a whopper. But totally understandable: if Eloise was anything like her sister, then there was a lot there to love. "Do you know his wife? Eloise?" I asked.

The dark eyes looked amused. "We all know each other's families," he said. "And Eloise has also done work for us. Especially around the casino project. She is part of the family, now. One of us. Not Womp, but what you would understand as an ally."

Rick was receding faster and faster as a suspect in either Skye's disappearance or Juliet's murder. And it occurred to me for the first time that the method used in Juliet's death was relevant: strangling someone means staying with their consciousness until they died. You have to look at the victim, and, perhaps more importantly, endure them looking at you. A little like the abyss, though far more personal. I just couldn't see this man strangling his sister-in-law, watching her struggle and in pain as her life slipped away, the panic in her eyes. It didn't compute.

And abducting a member of his own tribe? That was becoming unthinkable.

So I had to think of something else.

Chapter Eighteen

Derek was watching me. I had the oddest feeling he was reading my mind. "The first time I met Eloise," he said, "was before they married. But Rick had already spoken of his intentions. He took a few of us to visit her."

"And you liked what you saw?" I was still arranging the pieces to the puzzle in my mind, sliding names around like on the little plastic boards where you have to line the pieces up so they present a clear picture. Devastatingly hard to do.

"She was respectful," he said. "We arrived and waited for her to come to the door. And she understood." He caught Mirela starting to open her mouth. "In our culture, it is rude to assume you have a right to enter anybody's house," he said. "You must first give the person time to assimilate your presence, time to decide whether or not they want to open the door. We even have a social song about it, in which the people who want to visit sing to ask for permission."

"But Eloise said yes," I said.

"Eloise said yes," he agreed. "She learned some native crafts. Like making jewelry out of abalone shells. You will see her at the pow-wow; she has a booth there."

He knew I was going to the pow-wow. Not a tremendous mental leap, but I wondered who'd been talking to him. Maybe Will. "What about beadwork?" I asked. "Does she know anything about that?"

He shook his head. "I do not think so."

I pulled out my phone and went to the camera roll where I'd photographed the wampum and the envelope where it was stored.

"Here," I said, passing the phone to him. "Does this mean anything to you?"

He hadn't seen it before. Even in a face that gave nothing away, I could sense an undercurrent of something—surprise, interest, comfort. "Do you know what this is?" he asked me.

"It's a wampum belt," I said. "But that's all I know. It looks as if Rick gave it to Juliet—it was in her apartment. I don't think the police noticed it—or if they did, they discounted it as relating to her murder. Probably thought it was just art."

He looked up at me. "Is that what you think?"

I shook my head. "I think there's a message there," I said.

Mirela had contained herself long enough. "What is this wampum belt?" she demanded.

Derek smiled and turned his gaze back to the photograph. "Wampum is made from shells. Usually it is only two colors, white and purple," he said. "White beads are more common. The purple ones are highly prized. Their color is only found at the hinge and edge of the quahog shell." He looked up again. "You are right that they once served as a communication device," he said. "A sort of visual language."

Mirela was entranced. I made a mental note to explore her sudden interest in native culture later. "So it could take the place of what the—" *invaders*, I almost said— "Europeans saw as a contract?" I asked.

"Wampum predates the settler culture—some beads have been dated as far back as four thousand years ago," said Derek. "But the colonists weren't versed in our ways. They only saw wampum as currency. We know better."

"So wampum tell stories," I said, doggedly returning to my idea. "Can they contain other messages?" This was all admittedly fascinating, but I wanted to get back to Rick and Juliet.

Derek thought about it. "It's pretty nuanced," he said. "Not the most direct way of communicating. I mean, yeah, there are meanings woven into the belts, but they're only understood by the communities that exchange them. Back in the day, they were diplomatic in nature. Nowadays it's more like an ongoing narrative of survivance."

"Survivance?" asked Mirela. "I do not know this word." I was glad she'd asked, as I didn't, either.

"The conjunction between resistance and survival," said Derek. "It reminds us that not only have we survived centuries of genocide, but that we keep our cultures alive. For sure they're worn as ornaments now, but they still speak in a language we can all recognize. It's about memory and promise. It connects the past to the present and even the future."

I could see Mirela assimilating and storing the expression. I realized, then, that while she might well have come up-Cape to support and maybe even protect me, this was a concept she would someday set ablaze on canvas.

I opened my mouth to say something to bring the discussion back to this particular belt, but Derek wasn't finished. "Wampum was highly prized, because the process of cutting the shells into small cubes, drilling holes into them, and then filing them into cylinders— all without breaking them—requires great skill and delicacy. It still is," he said. And then, as though reading my mind, he added, "They're considered sacred and powerful. When someone holds a string of wampum, they are holding the embodiment of authority and truth."

I thought about that for a moment. "So this belt is telling the truth."

Derek nodded. "Words we can trust," he said.

And now for the sixty-four-thousand-dollar question. "So what does it mean?" I asked. "Can you read it?"

He shook his head. "I can't. But if you can send me this image, I will take it to some of our elders. Earl, our former sachem, will be sure to know."

Damn. So near and yet… "Of course I'll send it to you," I said. "And, Derek… the sooner, the better." I knew by now that rushing something important would be as foreign a concept to the Wampanoag as the meaning of their beadwork was to white people, but I had no choice. The pow-wow was approaching quickly, and we needed information, like… yesterday.

He wasn't happy about it, but he also was realistic. "I will try," he said.

"Thank you. Um—what's a number I can text it to?"

He told me, and I sent the photo right away. Mirela asked, "Who is a sachem?"

He smiled involuntarily at her pronunciation. "A chief," he said.

We were running out of time. Perhaps the retired chief could help, but I'd already decided to go straight to the source. Rick Thatcher would remember his truthful message to his white sister-in-law—who presumably couldn't read the message in the beads.

So why had he done it?

***

"Bruce Peterson will be here tomorrow," I informed Mirela. "I'm having dinner with him tomorrow night."

"*We* are having dinner with him tomorrow night," corrected Mirela.

I glared at her. "I didn't hear me inviting you to go along," I said. I knew I was sounding defensive, but I was on edge.

She dismissed my remark with a graceful wave of her hand.

We were back at Margo's house. It was too hot to sit even in the airy three-seasons room, and I'd finally given in and cranked up the air conditioning. Mirela had made some iced tea and we were sipping it in the living room.

Wally was a little confused by Mirela's presence. I thought I probably still had an edge over her—after all, I was the human providing his meals—but she was fast encroaching on our relationship: he'd already allowed her to pet him. Twice.

The heat was definitely making me cranky.

"And for dinner tonight," Mirela said, "I will take you and Ali out somewhere nice." She had a glint in her eyes that told me she already knew what I'd say.

So I said it. "At Bleu?"

"If we must."

"Oh, we must."

She sat back on the sofa with a satisfied smile. "Today," she said, "I think you will want to see this Rick Thatcher."

"I'm not going up to Boston again," I said. I'd had quite enough of that particular trip already. Never twice in one week… and preferably not twice in one month, either.

"He does not live in Boston," she said.

I had no idea how to get to Taunton from Marstons Mills, though Waze would undoubtedly give me directions in the soothing Alan Alda-esque voice I'd selected. It was a poor excuse. I did want to talk with him. I just wasn't sure simply showing up at his house would strike quite the right note. *You could always stand outside and sing the social song Derek talked about. Please let me in!*

Maybe Eloise would let me in. After all, it was her sister's death I was investigating; she would probably welcome any help in that direction.

Not that I had much help to offer.

I sighed and settled on a compromise: a phone call to make sure they were willing to talk to me. Since arriving in Provincetown, I've gone from a never-ever-pick-up-the-phone attitude to one that grudgingly admits that to do my job correctly, the phone is a necessary tool. Still, this was a strange request.

Mirela sensed my indecision. "Give me the number," she said. "I will make this call for you."

"I think they're going to find it weird enough that I'm calling; someone with a Bulgarian accent will take it into farce." I picked up my phone and found the number I'd copied from Juliet's address book. Deep breath. What did one say? *Oh, I'm wondering if perhaps you killed your sister-in-law, and wanted to see what you'd tell me about it.*

That was nonsense. I had all but crossed him off the very short list. I got voicemail, of course; possibly easier. "Hi. This message is for Rick Thatcher. My name is Sydney Riley, and I'm helping the police with their inquiries into Juliet Mills' death." Well, that was almost true. I took a breath. "And I wondered if I might drop by this afternoon." It was approaching three o'clock; not much of the afternoon left. "Or tomorrow sometime? Let me know, and thanks." I rattled off my number and disconnected.

Mirela had read my mind and was scrolling on her phone. "It is only an hour to go from here to Taunton," she said.

"I'm not going until they get back to me," I said.

Time to touch base with Will. I got *his* voicemail, too. "Hey Will, it's Sydney. Call me back, okay? I'd hoped to see you this afternoon; I think I maybe got some clues." Well, not really, but his silence was getting on my nerves a little.

Mirela was watching me. "What you need, sunshine, is to do something that has no relationship to your inquiry," she said. "I shall telephone Ali and tell him of our dinner plans. And then we will go shopping."

I blinked at her. "I don't need anything," I said.

"And that is when shopping is the most fun," she responded. "We will go to Hyannis. I will drive."

"Not a chance in the world," I said. Mirela makes up her own rules around driving, particularly when it comes to the speed limit. I wasn't going to intentionally shorten my life.

And then the second weird thing happened.

Chapter Nineteen

Will Fortier disappeared.

We were deep in Trader Joe's when my phone rang. *Excellent*, I thought: *It's Rick getting back to me.* I left my shopping cart where it was and bolted for the store entrance; I may be sometimes unconscious around the finer points of etiquette, but even I knew you don't talk on the phone when you're in a public place.

Besides, I wasn't sure I wanted anyone to overhear even just my end of this particular conversation.

"Sydney Riley," I said.

"Oh, good," said a voice I didn't recognize. "Thanks for picking up. This is Theresa Larsen at *The Enterprise.*"

I had again another image of the bridge of the Star Trek starship. "Yes, hello," I said.

"We're trying to connect with Will Fortier," she said. "His notes say he was working with you on a story."

Well, okay, maybe. "We are," I agreed. "He hasn't checked in with you?" *Oh, good, Riley. She just said that.*

"No," she said, and I could sense rather than hear the edge of concern running through her voice.

"I haven't seen him for a couple of days," I said. "We spoke this morning on the phone, but that's all. Was he supposed to check in with you?"

"It's worrying," she said, trying no doubt to keep that worry at bay. "If you hear from him, would you ask him to give me a ring?"

"Of course," I said. I stood for a moment in the shade of the building, where it was minimally cooler than in the sun. There was a hollow feeling in the pit of my stomach. Far too many people were disappearing. *Breathe, Riley. Just breathe.*

I called Will immediately, of course, and got voicemail again. "Just give me a call so I know you're all right."

I took another deep breath and plunged back into Trader Joe's. I caught up with Mirela in the cheese section, where she was apparently weighing the merits of two possibilities. "I do not know, sunshine," she said doubtfully. "It is all so… bland."

"Will Fortier's gone," I said. "The reporter?"

She put the cheeses down and turned to me. "It does not have to mean anything," she said.

"Or it could mean a lot," I said. "I wish I knew where he lives."

"Sunshine, listen to me. He is a reporter. This is a very major story. He only needs some space in which to work. Perhaps he is with somebody and could not interrupt the conversation."

Possible, but not nearly as comforting as she meant for it to be. On impulse, I grabbed my phone again and texted Margo. *No one can find Will,* I texted. *Where does he go when he wants to be alone?* For all I knew, he could be back at her house, waiting for me.

To my surprise, she answered right away. *He never wants to be alone. Tell me what happened.*

I don't know, I texted back. *He was maybe going to meet with me in Mashpee, and didn't show, and now his editor says she can't reach him. We've both been leaving VMs.*

Margo responded immediately. *His favorite hangout is Finn's in Hyannis. Brew pub, craft beers. You could check there.*

I was getting too anxious to be diverted, though I did wonder briefly whether Margo, thirty years deep into AA, hung out there with Will. Their relationship continued to puzzle me. *Okay,* I texted.

Let me know, okay?

I will.

I turned back to the cheese selection and Mirela. "Detour," I said.

We went through the checkout and loaded bags into the Grey Goose. I'd managed to locate Finn's, and Waze took us there, the feeling of dread rising inside me. So far two people had disappeared without a trace, and now one of them was dead and the other still a big question mark. I didn't have high hopes of finding Will at the brew pub, happily consuming one beer too many.

But we went anyway. And he wasn't.

Finn's had a modern, crisp vibe. I found a bartender creating a flight of beers and almost got derailed (Mirela's *shining things*), but then gathered my wits and asked him if he knew Will Fortier. His reaction made it clear Margo had been right. "Will? Sure," he said, pushing the flight over to a guy sitting three stools down. "Why?"

"Have you seen him today?" It was four-thirty, time for regulars to be claiming their seats at the bar.

He shook his head. "Not today," he said. He appealed to a staff member who was polishing glasses at the other end of the bar. "Hey, Cary, you seen Will Fortier?"

The other guy paused and considered the question. "He was here Monday," he offered.

Two days ago... The coldness in my stomach fluttered. "Not since then?"

"I was off yesterday," he said.

This was getting us nowhere. "If he comes in, could you ask him to call Sydney?" I asked.

The first bartender shoved a pad of paper across the bar. "Write it down," he said. "We'll never remember otherwise." He caught sight of Mirela behind me and reacted the way straight men always did. I almost told him to close his mouth.

I scribbled my name and number on the pad and added, "Ask Will Fortier to call me."

Mirela was giving the bartender her hundred-kilowatt smile. Time to leave before this got out of hand. "Thank you," I said, and I grabbed her arm. "Let's get out of here."

I texted Margo, who was clearly worried, and we got back in the car. "Turn the air conditioning up," I urged Mirela as I handled navigation back on Main Street; even with the short time we'd been outside, I could feel sweat trickling down my back.

Since nothing else seemed to make any sense, we ended up back at Margo's house, where Will predictably was not waiting for us. This couldn't be good.

My phone rang just as I was punching in the Secret Code, and I flubbed it twice because I was trying so hard to get inside and answer the call at the same time. My phone announced the caller as "unknown," which I generally allow to go to voicemail; but I wasn't taking any chances today. "Sydney Riley," I managed to announce.

"This is Rick Thatcher," a man's voice responded. It was as gentle and honey-soft as Derek's. "You wanted to talk with me?"

"Oh, yes, thanks for returning my call." I swept Will's situation as far to the side as I could manage, located my notebook, and sat down on the sofa. To my surprise, Wally joined me there right away, already purring. "I was hoping I might come and talk with you."

"In Taunton?" He sounded vaguely amused.

"Wherever you'd like," I said.

He waited a few beats before responding; white people could learn something from the courtesy of waiting until one was sure the other person had finished speaking. I thought about all the times I interrupted someone, and felt ashamed. "Derek said you might call," he said. "I'd be happy to talk with you. I'm taking the day off tomorrow to prepare for the pow-wow, so I'll be down in Mashpee."

I hesitated; I'd love to have a quiet place for the conversation, but I'd already brought too many people to Margo's house. And then an idea fought itself through my worries to my consciousness. "Would you meet me at Oneil's Kitchen?" I asked. Two birds, one stone: I could ask Oneil himself about Will, as they seemed to be friends.

Again that moment of waiting, and then he said, "That would be fine. Would ten o'clock work?"

"Absolutely," I said. "How will I know you?"

"Oh, Sydney Riley, I will know *you*," he said, and the undercurrent of amusement was there again. I wondered what he thought was so funny.

"Thank you," I said. "See you then."

Mirela arrived with glasses of her iced tea. I was pretty sure I needed something a little stronger, but accepted the glass anyway. "He'll be in Mashpee tomorrow," I told her.

"Good. Then we can enjoy our dinner in peace."

I'd forgotten we were going to Bleu, and it was a strong token of my anxiety that I hadn't remembered.

Bleu's food is *always* memorable.

***

Ali met us at the restaurant. The host took one look at Mirela and ushered us to one of the best tables, because—well, *Mirela*.

The escargots were perfect, and I barely tasted them. And my palate didn't even do justice to the bottle of Saint-Estèphe Mirela and I shared (I know, I know, but I *like* red wine with fish). The pan-seared scallops—a dish I always order at Bleu—were no less lovely than they'd be normally, but these weren't normal times.

We were barely seated when I asked Ali, "Have you found her?"

"No," he said. "Don't you want to just enjoy your food? You haven't even looked at the menu yet."

"We need wine," Mirela decided, and looked around expectantly. Magically, our waiter appeared; she has that effect on people.

Ali must have been really tired; he capitulated at once. Or maybe he just knows me. "I have a lead on the guy, though."

"They're letting you stay on the case? Even though you don't believe she was trafficked?"

He sipped his sparkling water. "That's just my opinion," he said. "Not everybody on my team agrees."

Mirela said, "What is this? You do not think the missing woman is being—trafficked?"

"I didn't catch her up on that part," I told Ali. "And *we're* going to have a conversation about you sending Mirela to watch over me." Fair warning.

He was unaffected by the threat. "No-one tells Mirela what to do," he reminded me.

"Please, tell me what this is about," said Mirela.

"It's possible I'm wrong," admitted Ali, and then the waiter appeared, opened the bottle of wine (looking expectantly at Mirela; she was clearly the one who counted), and at her nod he filled our wine glasses and took our order. Ali waited until he'd gone and then continued. "She doesn't fit the classic pattern," he said. "Generally, traffickers have some idea what they're going to do with the victim. They already have someone lined up to sell her to." He paused. "Or if it's a smaller operation where he's the one doing everything, he gets her started working right away, so she doesn't have time to think about what's happening to her. But neither of those things happened with Skye. Instead, they kept her trapped inside a nondescript apartment for a week. That doesn't fit."

"Sokanon," I said suddenly. "We should give her the respect of using her real name."

"I think she's back on the Cape," said Ali, undeterred. "And that's not just my idea, either. Kerry Thomas—that's the woman we arrested in Boston—says they're here."

I paused, my wine glass halfway to my lips. "You got his name? Who is it?"

Ali shook his head. "Didn't get that yet. She has a first-tier lawyer checking out everything she says. My guess is, they're holding that back to get a better deal for her. It's close to a miracle she's told us anything."

"She admitted to trafficking?"

"Only peripherally. Says she's subletting the apartment, and when he brought Skye—okay, Sokanon—to stay with her, she didn't realize at first what was happening. She claims as soon as she did, she made him and the girl both leave. Said she was shocked to learn the girl wasn't there voluntarily."

I'm shocked! Shocked to find that gambling is going on in here.

I shook my head to clear it of *Casablanca*. "Really? Even though she never let her out of sight?"

He shrugged. "I didn't say it was the *best* excuse."

I felt frustration wash over me. "So you're no closer than before. Did she at least describe him?"

"Oh, yeah. As nondescript as she could manage."

Our first course arrived, and I started fiddling with the escargots. "How nondescript?"

He was negotiating his Brie-and-onion-confit tart. "White guy in his twenties, about five feet nine, some kind of scientific nautical background."

"Which apparently didn't pay enough."

"Maybe it wasn't about the money," said Ali.

"What else is it about?" asked Mirela, looking up from her rillettes.

He shrugged. "Could be a number of things," he said. "Revenge. A hate crime against the Wampanoag. A ransom demand—that's where my money is—ransom her during something sacred, like the pow-wow."

Which was, I reminded myself, the day after tomorrow.

Mirela frowned. "If it is revenge, revenge against who?"

I managed to stop myself from correcting her grammar. "And where do I come into it?" I asked.

"Can't see a connection right now," said Ali. "It still might not have anything to do with Juliet's death, *cara*."

I had already decided it did. "Isn't that a little too much of a coincidence?"

"Coincidences do exist, you know."

"But doesn't it feel like a little much?" I demanded. "Bad things can coexist, I know, I know, but really, there isn't very much crime on the Cape, and two major crimes have been committed, and they both involve the tribe." Three crimes, I thought, if you included my first husband's second wife. For the first time, I wondered why there hadn't been anything in the news or on Facebook about her. If Noah thought it was going to trial, then it had to have been clearly a homicide. But it had nothing to do with the Wampanoag.

The last thing I'd talked to Will about was Noah. And then Will disappeared. The cold claw of fear was clutching at my stomach again.

Ali looked scandalized—he knows about a whole *lot* of hidden crime on the Cape—but didn't say anything.

"It might not be about Cape Cod itself," Mirela said judiciously. "This mysterious man—he could be bringing all this crime here with him."

I had a sudden image of some sort of darkness encroaching on us, moving down the coast, sliming its way across the bridges. What was the destructive event from *The Neverending Story*? War? Climate change? "Even if that's true," I said, "something is still gathering here now. With deep roots in the Wampanoag? And the pow-wow?" The "Nothing", that was it. A dark force that's never really specifically revealed, that threatens to engulf the wonderful world of Fantasia.

The waiter came and removed our plates, and Mirela gave him another look at her smile. He actually turned red. A few minutes later he returned with the main dishes.

"I do think there's something connecting the pow-wow with her kidnapping," Ali said.

"So you'll be there?" I asked.

"We'll have a presence there," he said. "But not in enforcement. The tribal police have been briefed. It's their gig. They'll have that part in hand."

Yep: The Nothing was alive and well.

Mirela had gotten impatient with the conversation. "And now we will enjoy our food," she announced, and we didn't talk about it again.

Chapter Twenty

Mirela went to bed, and I tried to feel no bitterness in observing Wally curling up next to her. Apparently cats respond to her the same way men do.

Ali and I sat up for a while in the three-seasons room; it had finally gotten cool enough, and there was a nice evening breeze flowing through. "I want to talk about your ex," said Ali.

I stiffened; if I never had to talk about Noah again, I'd be nothing but delighted. "Why? I demanded. Noah as abductor? It seemed too cartoonish to contemplate.

"Because he's threatened you."

"Okay," I said cautiously.

"Tell me again," said Ali, "exactly what he said to you."

"Why? Do you think he's behind any of this?" *This* could point in a number of different directions, of course.

"I think he's dangerous," Ali said.

And here I was, thinking we could dismiss him. I took a deep breath. "He's in trouble, but not just the trouble we've been seeing in the news. There's something personal, too." Another breath. "He offered me the title to our—to his house, the one in Cambridge. Said he already has the paperwork finished."

He nodded; I may not have talked much about my former life, but I did talk a lot about that house. "In exchange for what, exactly, *cara?*"

I curled my legs under me and settled in. "Well, that's the thing," I said. "He's going to trial. Some of it's part of the hospital stuff— you know, the recent deaths and the mismanagement of funds." A nice way to say *embezzlement*. "But that wasn't what he was talking about. He says his wife committed suicide recently, but apparently the cops aren't seeing it that way. He wants me to give him an alibi."

"To perjure yourself."

"Pretty much," I agreed. "But there's more than that." The feeling of being watched was creeping up on me again, and I was glad the sofa had a solid wall behind it. "He knew a lot about me, Ali," I said, and even I could hear the fear in my voice. "He knows about the inn. He's been spending a lot of time on the Cape, apparently, and that's just weird because he's never cared about the Cape before; we'd never even visited here. But it turns out he's been here a lot. I think—well, what I think is he's been keeping an eye on me, all these years. I just don't know why. I mean, *he* left *me*. If either of us was still hanging onto the past, you'd think it would be me."

I couldn't read Ali's expression, but he cut straight to the issue. "Gifting someone a piece of property isn't like a normal closing," he said. "It takes time. Lawyers are involved."

I nodded miserably.

"So he knew she was going to die weeks ago when he initiated the transferal."

I nodded again. "Yeah, that was my thought, too. He was—he was pretty angry with me, actually. Blamed me for his infidelity."

"You know," he said almost conversationally, "if he blamed you, this could fit together. The making you suffer part."

"I thought of that," I said. "First Juliet, and then Alice."

There was a longish silence, and I couldn't take it. "What are you thinking?" I knew what he was thinking.

"I'm thinking, if you did agree to give him an alibi—and I know you wouldn't, *cara*—but if you did, there would be something about it, something that showed you were lying. Torture you about Juliet, and then get you arrested for perjury. Kind of mess up your life."

"But how would he know about Juliet? And the connection to the Wampanoag? That's not anything he'd know about!"

"You haven't been reading the news," he said tiredly. "The media—legacy media, social media—they've been all over it. Remember, until you spoke with him, you didn't even know he'd been on the Cape. He could have been following you all this time, trying to see an angle in." He took a deep breath. "*Cara*, you're not safe here."

"Like I was in Provincetown?" I asked flippantly. "He knows about the inn. And no-one knows where Margo lives."

"I think we have to assume he knows everything," said Ali.

"And Juliet? How would he know about *her*?" An idea occurred. "I'm seeing Bruce Peterson tomorrow," I said. "I can ask him—you know, if anything happened that seemed normal at the time but on reflection might not have been?" I paused. "I could even show him Noah's picture… no, that won't work, I don't have any." I knew that for sure: I'd dramatically and ritually burned them all, along with every bit of personal stuff—letters, notes, anything with his handwriting on it. I'd gone through my digital photos, too, even the ones I'd liked. Banished them all. Banished *him*.

Or so I'd thought.

Ali sighed. "Ask the Google," he said wearily; he'd picked up the expression from me. "There'll be images online; he's been in the news enough." He stood up, stretched. "I'm going to bed. You have to promise me, *cara*, that you'll check in with me all day. Right? Anytime you get a call, anytime you leave this house."

"You sound like a cop."

"I *am* a cop," he said. "Promise?"

I nodded. "I'll be there in a minute," I said. "I have to sort some of this in my head."

He leaned over and kissed my forehead. "Come in soon," he said. "You need to rest."

Well, that—or figure out if a man I'd once loved was someone who wished me a great deal of harm indeed.

***

The morning brought no more clarity.

One day until the pow-wow began. I knew people had been arriving in Mashpee over the last couple of days; I'd driven by the tribal compound and had seen a scattering of brightly colored tents springing up on the grounds in front of the offices. All the guests from other tribes, dancers, drummers, merchants, cooks, and not one of them aware of the sickly feeling I had in my stomach, or what it meant.

The tribal police knew, though, and I took some comfort in that.

Ali was already in the kitchen, fiddling with Margo's high-tech espresso machine. He doesn't drink coffee—not for theological reasons, as Islam is divided on that subject; he just doesn't care for it—but he understands my need to mainline it. "*Ecco, la bella signora*," he said as I lurched in.

"You don't even speak Italian," I growled.

"I could say it in Arabic, but it's not as pretty," he said, handing me a cup filled with thick dark liquid. "How are you feeling? You had some bad dreams in the night."

"Did I?" It was all a blur, but I knew I wasn't sleeping well. The Nothing was approaching fast, and since I didn't know what it was, I couldn't do anything to stop it.

Instead, I drank the coffee in two gulps.

He leaned against the counter, sipping his own inevitable orange juice. "What are your plans for today?" he asked, his voice carefully casual.

I moaned and set the machine for another coffee. Waited while it made its mysterious noises and spat out more of the elixir. "I'm meeting Rick Thatcher at ten," I said. "And later I'm seeing Bruce Peterson. He's coming down for the pow-wow a day early. The director, too."

Mirela stumbled into the kitchen, which made the tiny room feel like a subway car at rush hour. She took the cup from my hand, poured sugar into it, and drank it all in one continuous motion. "That was for me," I complained.

"It is not yours now."

"Obviously." Mirela and I should definitely not live in the same space, as neither of us was at her best and brightest first thing in the morning.

Ali finished his juice and rinsed the glass. "Call me when you leave," he said, leaning over to kiss me.

"I will." I was already regretting my promise to keep him aware of my movements. Somehow, reporting on them lent them weight, a special significance. Right now I'd happily return to a life without significance.

I made some more coffee for both myself and Mirela, and we carried the cups into the living room. It was already getting hot. I told her about my conversation with Ali, and about Noah contacting me. "He might be behind all of this," I said.

She was awake enough to react. "It is better to know who it is than look for ghosts," she said. I imagined it probably sounded better, cleverer, in Bulgarian; we were apparently all about languages this morning.

"I just can't wrap my head around that level of hating someone," I confessed. "And someone who I loved, and who loved me. He really did, you know. At the beginning, anyway."

"How did you meet this first husband?" She made it sound like a proper noun: First Husband.

I finished my coffee and set the cup down on the coffee table. Remembering. "I was teaching film studies at UMass," I said. She looked at me blankly. "Um—the University of Massachusetts," I clarified. "One of my students collapsed in class, and she was transported to Massachusetts Medical. It's a hospital, a really famous one, in Boston. You've probably heard of it." She nodded. I took a deep breath. "I went with her, because she didn't have any family nearby we could call—she was on a student visa from Pakistan."

I remembered that afternoon and night with a strange clarity. In the ambulance they were taking her vitals, running a line into her arm. She came to when the EMTs were removing her hijab scarf, and she started struggling. I kept talking to her, saying it was okay, they had to do it to help her, anything I could think of saying to keep her calm.

And then the bright lights of the emergency room, the efficiency of the team as they lifted her from the gurney to the narrow bed, hooking her into machines. She coded and someone started doing chest compressions, which were far more raw and violent than anything I'd ever seen in the movies or on television.

Someone came and pulled me away from her cubicle, and a few minutes later a youngish man wearing blue scrubs came out and caught sight of me. "You're with the girl from the college?"

I nodded, willing him to not say what he was going to say. He said it anyway. "I'm sorry. We did everything we could."

I felt my legs give out from under me, and he caught me before I hit the floor. "Come over here," he said, guiding me to a couple of chairs in the center of the room, part of the nurses' station. And sat beside me.

It was Noah.

There's a strange closeness, I learned later, that develops between people who've experienced a disaster together. People who survive a plane crash, for example; most of them have reunions for years after the event. People who've been held hostage together, or survived a fire or a building collapsing, or even just being together in an institution or a cruise ship locked down during the pandemic. So maybe it wasn't surprising that I felt an odd and instant and incredibly intense connection to Noah.

He gave me his card that evening—he was running the place, he couldn't spend much time talking to me—and I called him the next day, still feeling bereft, imagining the call her parents in Karachi had received, wondering if there had been any signs I'd missed in class, wondering if I could have saved her. I dreaded the next day, when I'd have to hold my class without her, when I'd be lecturing to a smattering of students and one forever-empty chair.

We met for a coffee after his shift was over, and then had dinner in a nice restaurant neither of us could really afford a few nights later, and it wasn't difficult to fall for him. He was apparently a brilliant doctor, the youngest-ever chief of emergency medicine at an acclaimed teaching hospital, handsome and clever. We talked about everything—our pasts, our present, our dreams for the future; I even told him about Alexandra, which surprised me; I never talked about her.

We got married three months later.

And, yes, I knew I'd always share him with his work, but that was okay: I wanted to. It felt like a mission. I was teaching classes about films, for heaven's sake; he was saving *lives*. I wanted to be there and let him blow off steam after the horrible things he saw on a daily basis. I wanted to comfort him when he "lost one."

And while what he'd said on the phone was right—the sex *had* tapered off eventually, I'd thought that was normal: over time you don't have the same raw energy and desire you had at the start of a relationship. Life gets in the way. He was always tired; I was always busy.

But I'd thought we were okay.

I took a deep breath. "I think we disconnected over time," I said to Mirela. "But I didn't know, I never imagined, how much he hated me."

"It is the other side of the coin," she said seriously. "You can only hate intensely if you also loved intensely."

Mirela, the philosopher.

I stood up. "I need to get dressed," I said. "I'm meeting Rick at ten."

"So early!" she exclaimed, but she stood up, too. "And I am coming with you."

We didn't talk about Noah again.

***

Mirela loved Oneil's.

She was swept into a conversation with Oneil himself while I looked around, wondering which one of the people I was seeing was

Rick Thatcher. When she joined me at the table, she was in a sunny mood. "He is friends with Carmen," she said, picking up her menu.

"Who's Carmen?"

She looked at me as if I'd just inquired about the location of my inn. "She works at the Stop & Shop," she said, as though that settled it.

"But how did—" I was interrupted by a man who'd just stopped by our table. "Sydney Riley?" he asked.

I wouldn't have recognized him from his wedding picture. There, he'd been wearing a conventional tuxedo, and I hadn't been aware of his long hair. Today he was dressed casually in jeans and a loose-fitting shirt he hadn't tucked in; but he wore native jewelry around his neck, in his ears, on his fingers; and the hair was bound into a ponytail that reached halfway down his back. "Mr. Thatcher," I said, a little ridiculously, getting up and offering my hand for him to shake.

And still that expression of mild amusement. "You can call me Rick," he said.

"Yes, okay, thanks," I said. Why was I stammering? "Won't you sit down? Um—this is my friend, Mirela."

He didn't have that deer-in-the-headlights reaction to Mirela most men exhibit, and I liked him for it. By now he'd receded so far in the running for Murderer that I almost couldn't remember why I'd wanted this conversation, and was vaguely embarrassed I'd forced him into it.

Mirela didn't have any such inhibitions and jumped right in. "I am very sorry for your loss," she said. "For so many people, Juliet Mills was a beloved individual." I didn't think I could refer to anyone as an *individual* unless I was reading from a police report; she, on the other hand, carried it off.

"Thank you." A grave smile. "I ordered three coffees, is that all right?"

"More than all right," I said fervently. My two espressos hadn't done much to clear the cobwebs sticking to my mind. "But we should pay you—"

"It is my honor," he said. "We are a culture of hospitality. You are honored guests here in Mashpee."

"Thank you," said Mirela unexpectedly. I spared her a glance. She seemed to be much better at this than I was; I just rarely saw that side to her.

The coffees arrived, and the server fussed with creamers until Rick motioned her away. Like us, apparently he took his black.

I cleared my throat. "I've been reading about your work in getting the tribe federal recognition," I said. "It sounds like it's been an awful process."

He smiled at me. "And here was me, thinking you wanted to ask me if I killed my sister-in-law," he said.

Mirela giggled. I gave her what I hoped was a quelling glance. "I don't think you did," I said.

"That's a relief."

I had no idea where to go with this conversation. I knew from reading Tony Hillerman that the Navajos didn't speak of their deceased tribal members; I had no idea what the Wampanoag believed. "Is it all right to talk about her?" I asked.

"Thanks for asking," he said. "And it's all right. She's left a hole in everyone's heart."

"Did you—was there a funeral?" I asked. It had just occurred to me that I hadn't inquired before. *Too busy being a crime-stopper, Riley?*

Again that gentle smile. "There will be a memorial service," he said. "After the investigation is over. She went to church in Boston, at Trinity in Copley Square. There will be something there. She wasn't an enrolled member of the tribe, but she was family to us. So we'll also have a memorial here, and many of us will go to her grave and leave gifts there. So—a blending of the two cultures." He paused. "Ever since I married Eloise, Juliet's been very much a friend to us."

I was staring at him. Okay: I'll fully admit I've gotten taken in by people, trusted people I shouldn't have trusted, relied on my feelings rather than my brain, but if Rick Thatcher was a killer, then I was Queen of the May. "I'm so sorry," I said inadequately. "We know about the young woman who's disappeared, too. It seems like a lot to deal with, all at once."

Rick drank some coffee, then looked up. "Do you have time for a story?" he asked diffidently.

"Yes," said Mirela. She seemed to find him fascinating.

"There's a big community with neighborhoods and a recreational facility—well, all sorts of things, really, even restaurants and a golf club—in Mashpee. It's called New Seabury," Rick said. "It was created for wealthy white people, people who came from the mainland, people who didn't know the history. By 1976, there was a lot of anti-native racism coming out of that lack of understanding." He took a long breath, let it out. "We are always celebrating, you have to understand: we're grateful for the riches the Earth gives us. Over at Twelve Acres, we'd built a replica of a traditional Wampanoag village, and in July we had a celebration there."

He paused, as if to give us space to say something. But I couldn't see where this was going, and so for once I had the sense to keep my mouth shut. "Later that night," Rick said, "a group of young men were drumming and singing, or just hanging out together, sitting around the fire. The people in New Seabury said they were afraid of the drumming, some even thought it was hostile." He shook his head. "They made a noise complaint, and the police arrived. But not just any police. Police in tactical gear, with shields and nightsticks. They beat some of the native men, and arrested some of them. My father was one of the men arrested."

There was a moment of silence. I didn't know what to say. I was imagining the campfire, the faces around it, the storytelling. And the wealthy neighbors, the gentrification of the town, the fear and the racism. I thought of my own tribe in Provincetown, and the wealthy people coming in, wanting to change everything. Thinking of ways to make the town theirs.

But at least we weren't in physical danger from the new people. Or at least not yet.

"One of the policemen actually said it was in retribution for Custer," Rick said, without underlining the absurdity and bigotry of the remark. "It went to trial that winter. The media took hold of it, calling them the Mashpee Nine. They were all acquitted."

"I've never heard of that," I said. "I mean, I wasn't born yet, but you'd think something that big would still be known. Taught in schools, that sort of thing."

He smiled. "You'd think," he agreed. "There's a book written about it, and a film, but they're not well known outside of indigenous circles." He shifted slightly in his chair. "The reason I'm telling you this now is we've seen an uptick in police presence since Juliet was killed. Not on tribal land, but around Mashpee. It's a hot summer, people are on edge. And the white people around here? They're quick to blame the tribe. It wouldn't be difficult for something like that to happen again."

And here we were in July… again.

I cleared my throat. "I am so sorry for that," I said, the words totally inadequate.

"Thank you," he said with some dignity.

Mirela said, "We will find out who did it."

I shot her another look. Maybe Mirela was succumbing to *bright shining things* now, too. But I was also beginning to understand how deep the issues around Juliet's death ran, and that went double for Skye, wherever she was. "You think something will happen at the pow-wow," I said. It wasn't a question.

"It's possible."

Damn. And that was happening tomorrow. No way to find her killer in time.

Then I remembered something. "You gave Juliet a wampum belt," I said.

He looked, if anything, amused. "I did."

"I found it in her apartment," I said. "It's beautiful. I'll give it back to you if you'd like." Ali certainly wouldn't approve, and I was probably violating some law in offering it, but I didn't really care. I'd already violated half a dozen, probably, in taking it out of the apartment in the first place.

"Thank you," he said again.

"Sydney thinks there is a message in the beads," said Mirela. "Is that true?"

"There is," he conceded. "But it has nothing to do with Juliet's death."

I spoke without thinking. "Why are you so sure?"

He smiled. "It takes many hours to create wampum strings, and many more to weave them into a belt," he said. "My auntie made it for Juliet last year. The message was to say we love her as family."

I felt slightly deflated. He was right: there couldn't be any connection between an expression of love and inclusivity and the recipient being killed a year later. *What did you expect, Riley? For some spooky message to be written out for you like the plot of one of those mystery novels?*

Well, now that you mention it, yes.

"We'll be at the pow-wow," I told Rick. "Tomorrow."

"It's three days, you know," he said. "You'll want to pace yourself. And—just be careful. We have plenty of security, but there are already people in town who think we killed her. The word *savage* was used. There haven't been any clear threats, but—well, like I said. We don't want a repetition of what the Mashpee Nine had to go through."

I shivered. "No," I agreed. So now we had everything in place for a lot of people to potentially get hurt. Delightful.

My phone vibrated, and I looked at the incoming text: a number I didn't recognize, but the sender clarified immediately: *Hey its Cally from WW I sent you an email with some files on Rick. I don't see anything criminal on them tho.* I ignored the punctuation—or lack thereof—and almost smiled; she was underscoring my own conclusions.

In her novel *They Came to Baghdad,* Agatha Christie writes about all sorts of different people converging on the city for various devious reasons, a confrontation brewing as they each drew closer. I was starting to feel the same about this pow-wow.

I really hoped the result wasn't going to be the same.

Chapter Twenty-One

"What happens now?" asked Mirela once we were back in the car.

I held up a finger; I was already calling Will. This time the voicemail message was more disturbing: "You have reached 555-236-1932. The mailbox is full and cannot take any more messages. Good-bye."

"Something's happened to him," I said to Mirela.

"I think you are correct, sunshine," she agreed. I was surprised; Mirela's bad feelings had in the past consistently proved to be uncannily on point.

"But what do we do about it? That's the question."

"There is nothing we can do," she said.

"I hate it when you're right." But I couldn't stop thinking about it. "How does Will's disappearance fit in?"

"Perhaps it does not," said Mirela, playing devil's advocate. "Perhaps he has discovered something in his reporting that made him dangerous to someone. It might not even relate to this case—you do not know."

"Of course it relates. It's stretching credulity a little too far to say that three people have disappeared and the disappearances aren't related. But you're right: he's a danger to someone." I took a breath. "But to whom? The guy who abducted Skye? The person who murdered Juliet? Whoever it is who wants to put me in the middle of it all?"

"Perhaps they are all the same person," Mirela suggested, contradicting her own words.

"Then that person sure has more energy than I do." I started the car and cranked up the air conditioning.

"He is under pressure," Mirela said thoughtfully. "That is good. It means he will make mistakes."

Like trying to get me to provide him with an alibi for when his wife died, I thought. That was a mistake on his part. I couldn't imagine how he'd figured I might say yes. Even with the house as bait.

Had any of Will's questions led him to Noah?

Back at Margo's house, Mirela disappeared into the guest room to phone Lily. I couldn't light anywhere, finding myself jumping up and pacing every time I tried to make myself sit. I tried reading and couldn't keep focused enough to absorb any of it. I doomscrolled through my phone for a little while, but even the political threads on Reddit (my usual guilty pleasure) couldn't keep my attention.

I put the television on, but within moments the Boston news channel broadcast a picture of Skye Taylor, and a reporter noted that she had still not been found. Somebody had some pull, to get that onto the regular broadcast, I thought; but I flicked it off again as stories about flooding somewhere near Worcester came on.

Wally came into the room and delivered a couple of sneezes. Thus reminded of the conversation in the waiting room at the vet's, I looked up Thea's old number on my phone, hoping she hadn't changed it.

She hadn't. The warmth of Jamaica was in her voice, rich and filled with sunlight. "Sydney Riley! I haven't heard that voice in a long while!"

"I heard you were back in Provincetown," I said. "So I thought I'd give you a call." Never mind that I was using her to keep my mind off other, darker things. But there was another reason for the call, too, and the feelings tumbled over me as soon as I heard her voice. I missed her. We'd met under questionable circumstances, but had developed a strong friendship afterward, not unlike the bond I'd felt with Noah. We had been through something together. She'd been an integral part of the Provincetown I loved, the Jamaican community that kept the town running, cleaning the inns, cooking in the restaurants, collecting the trash, virtually unnoticed by visitors and summer residents, but seen and appreciated by those of us who work there year-round.

And, in Thea's case, healing the sick and the wounded. It had been hard to say good-bye when eventually she'd moved to Brooklyn to help open a medical clinic. We'd promised to stay in touch... and hadn't.

"Just for a week," she said now. "I went over to the inn to see you, but the fellow at the front desk said you weren't around. I said that's impossible, Sydney Riley never takes a vacation!"

"I'm taking care of someone's cat while they're away," I said. "Not exactly a vacation. What brings you back to the Cape?"

"I missed it," she said. "That's the simple truth. I went by my house yesterday, well, where I used to live, just to look at it. I do love that house."

"I know you do," I said. She'd lived in the Octagon House in the West End, as beautiful in its own way as the house in Cambridge I'd so loved. *But no-one's offering it to you as a bribe.* It was an odd little parallel experience we were living here. "A lot of good memories."

"And a few bad ones," she said. "You don't need to be so careful, Sydney. It's not as if I'd forgotten those, too, eh?"

"I don't suppose you *could*," I said.

"We were only married for about five minutes," she said. She paused, and then added, "But it was a very long five minutes!"

"You can say that again," I agreed fervently. And not just for Thea; for me, too. "Did you—do you ever hear from Emma?"

"No," she said, and I could sense the curiosity in her voice. "Why would I?"

"No reason," I said. "I was just—thinking of her, the other day." And wondering if she might be considering some sort of retribution; maybe I'd leave that part out of the conversation.

"Well, don't," she said. "That chapter's over. But—well, I may as well say it now: I'm going to move back."

"To P'town?" I was surprised—if it's hard to leave, it's harder still to come back. I knew of several people who'd decamped, citing the high cost of living, the unaffordability of housing, the restaurant prices that take even the tourists aback, the influx of wealthy individuals and corporations that wanted to turn the town into their own Disneyesque playground: "Provincetown," noted one of those individuals on social media, "is a good place to park your money." But for all its shifting priorities, all its inequities and disappointments, the town still drew people in, the kinds of people who gather at a place like Land's End, the eccentric, the lost, the creative—sometimes, the broken.

An alleyway cut between Commercial Street and the harbor ended at the ruins of the Old Reliable Fish House, itself once a bustling restaurant, falling into disrepair, home to the homeless, slated for conversion (by another new LLC) into a hotel and high-end condominium complex. One of the buskers who slept there said to me once, "I'm not homeless; Provincetown is my home."

I wondered where he'd go once the developers were finished.

And then those who left and answered the pull of the town to return find out there's no coming back: not enough rentals to go around, and the price of owning far beyond their means.

Thea was different in one sense: she had some money. She'd made it through medical school and residencies on grants and loans and dollar-bill donations from the ever-supportive Jamaican community, and had worked her way into repayment and beyond. She'd come to practice at the Outer Cape clinic after fulfilling those obligations, the same impulse that had finally led her to Brooklyn, not the gentrified Brooklyn of hipsters but the streets where immigrants sold clothing on racks set up on the sidewalks.

Still, she owned the Octagon House, rented out these several years since she'd left, and presumably could reclaim at the end of the lease.

"Of course, to P'town," she said.

"But won't it—doesn't it—*remind* you?"

"Sydney," Thea said calmly, "I am the one coming back. Not Emma."

For that matter, Emma probably could have, too. The Cape has a tradition of accepting errant ne'er-do-wells back into the fold. Back in the day, pirates had lived here for years, their families absorbed into the communities. And even today, so many broken people have made it their home that their eccentricities and even outright crimes were glossed over. The community, the real community, took care of its own.

In the 1960s, a local man called Tony Costa had become the Cape's only documented serial killer, at least since Europeans had killed off indigenous people. He went to trial, was convicted, and suicided a few years later in prison. His widow and his children carried on living in Provincetown—she was from an old local fishing family, her grandmother was one of the faces included in the big permanent art installation on the pier celebrating Portuguese matriarchs—and the community cared for them, even referring to him as

"Tony Chop-Chop," the dark humor somehow lessening his importance.

And a lot of washashores came here to start over again, some more successfully than others. But this was no village from a horror story; people assimilated, life went on. It's one of the reasons Provincetown is so welcoming of misfits, even today.

No one comes to Provincetown by accident, I remembered saying to Stacey.

And now it seemed another Person with a Past was returning. I didn't know whether to believe that Thea hadn't had some contact with Emma, that her timing for returning was entirely coincidental.

Emma had never disappeared from our list of possible suspects. Maybe I'd been naïve to think she had.

***

Bruce Peterson had called while I was still on the phone with Thea. I could hear Mirela's voice in the guest room, laughing at something Lily said. I pressed buttons and he picked up right away. "Sydney!"

"Hey, Bruce," I said. "Are you at the Cape?"

"At the MidCape Resort, yeah," he said. "It's where Juliet—"

"I know," I interrupted. I had a feeling of time rushing toward me, accelerating, drawing me into a place I was no longer sure I wanted to go. I had to do something, anything, to slow it down.

"It's an odd place for her to choose," he said, oblivious to my thoughts. "Juliet was forever seeking out gems, you know? Little-known places, special places we could share with the audience. Bed-and-breakfasts run by former entertainers, or people with a passion for garden gnomes. Your inn, too. But this place is big and commercial. It isn't like her, to stay in a resort like this."

"Maybe she didn't choose it," I said absently. Apparently nothing Juliet had done in the last couple of days of her life was "like her." And yet there we were.

I should have understood then, of course. I could have unraveled the whole mess if I had just been paying attention. It's the first thing I learned about solving puzzles, back before I had any myself to solve, just reading Golden Age mystery authors. Something happens, something changes, that makes it impossible for Person A to achieve their goals without doing away with Person B. Look for the variation in a theme, the sudden change, the break in routine, and it will lead you, however obliquely, to the answer. People establish patterns in their lives, whether consciously or not, and anytime a pattern is disrupted, it means something.

But I was too deep in my personal drama to see it.

"Let's meet," I said impulsively to Bruce; if I spent another hour pacing Margo's house I was going to go mad. "I have to give you back the keys to her apartment anyway." The wampum to Rick, the keys to Bruce; it sounded like I was wrapping things up, but in truth I was more confused than ever. "What are your plans? What are you going to do today?"

"I thought I might try and find out why she stayed here," he said, intent, a dog still worrying the same bone. "It wasn't like her, to pick a place like this. Maybe I can see who made the reservation, and when. That would help. Know if she came here on purpose, or if someone made her."

"That's a good idea," I said without thinking. In fact, it was a spectacularly good idea; I'd been too enmired in my own false trails to think of it. "Maybe the police already have. They won't tell you, though, will they? Isn't it confidential?" In truth, I had no idea whether it was or not.

He laughed. "I work for *Weekend Waypoints*," he said. "You'd be surprised what people will tell me."

He had me there. "Can I come?" I asked. "I can be there in half an hour."

A pause, then, "Sure," he said. "Why not? It helps, you know, to be doing something—not just waiting for someone else to figure it out."

A whole lot of professional people were trying to figure it out, but I was hardly in a position to point that out, being myself of strictly amateur status. "I get that," I acknowledged.

His voice turned brisk, the voice of a media producer. "I'll meet you over at the office," he said. "Let's say—one o'clock?"

"Okay. Um—my friend Mirela will probably come, too. My husband has apparently designated her as my bodyguard."

"The artist? Really?" He sounded startled. "Is she some kind of martial arts expert?"

I almost laughed then, picturing Mirela drop-kicking bad guys. Maybe she could, at that. "I think it's more to keep my worst ideas at bay," I said. "See you soon."

Mirela herself had finished with her conversation; she'd wandered back into the kitchen and was poking around in the refrigerator. "We have no tonic," she announced. I'd gotten her hooked on Fever-Tree, too.

"We can get some while we're out," I said. "Come on, the investigation calls."

"Excuse me?"

"We're meeting Bruce Peterson," I said. "You don't have to come."

She gave me a withering look. "I will get my purse."

I grabbed my own and got ready for the locking-the-house routine; I'd finally memorized the code to Margo's security system. "Meet you at the car," I said and opened the front door.

Ali was standing there, just reaching for the keypad. "You gave me a heart attack!" I exclaimed and laughed.

He wasn't smiling. "What?" I demanded.

"*Cara.*" He took my hand. "Let's go inside."

The cold feeling was back, twisting around my gut. "What?" I said again. "No, let's not go inside. Tell me now."

He was still holding my hand, and I pulled it away. "What?" I asked again, though by then I knew.

"I'm sorry," he said. "It's Will Fortier." He took a deep breath. "He's dead."

Chapter Twenty-Two

I hadn't exactly *not* expected it to happen: the tension had been building and there was no other explanation, really, for Will's silence and his overflowing voicemail and his non-communication with his editor. But it still shocked me. Disappearances and deaths seemed to have been featured on the menu this week.

I retreated into the living room, and Ali and Mirela followed me there. "How?" I asked.

"Strangled," Ali said.

"Like Juliet." I was imagining it, Will with his trying-so-hard beard, his ridiculous man-bun. Will, looking into the eyes of the person killing him. Will, dead.

I'm not going to cry, I thought.

I cried.

Ali sensibly didn't try to comfort me; he knows when it will be helpful and when it won't. After a few moments Mirela asked, "Was he also in that graveyard?"

Her question stirred me to sniffle my way back into coherence. "Please say there wasn't a note in his pocket," I said.

Ali didn't say anything.

Mirela shot him a look and came to sit beside me on the sofa. "Sunshine, this is not your fault," she said.

Oh, but it is.

Ali said, tonelessly, "He was in his car, parked near a place called Moody Pond, in the Quashnet Woods—that's Mashpee conservation land. There wasn't a note, but—" He took a very deep breath. "They used a Sharpie to write on his forehead."

No one moved for a moment. I started to say something and found I couldn't speak. Mirela was the one to ask it. "What did it say?"

He knew he had to answer, I thought, and it was killing him; he was trying to be kind. I swallowed hard and helped him with it, repeating her words. "What did it say?"

He glanced from me to Mirela and back again. "For Sydney Riley," he said.

Maybe I should just kill myself. That way, no-one else has to die.

Or maybe that's the point.

There was no expletive strong enough to voice what I was feeling—shock, despair, the sense of having passed through a curtain and found a whole other world of darkness waiting there. *Breathe, Riley. Just breathe. That's all you have to do right now.*

It was more than either Juliet or Will could manage anymore.

I stood up. "I'm meeting Bruce Peterson," I said. My legs were shaking.

Ali reacted then, a hand on my arm. "You need to stay here," he said. "We can give him a call. You're in no state to drive anywhere."

"Then you can drive me! Or Mirela!" I shook his hand off me.

"*Cara*," said Ali, "it isn't safe for you to go out there. Not today, and absolutely not tomorrow."

"What, so I sit here while everyone else around me gets killed? Are you for real? Somehow I got them into this. I'm not waiting for anyone else to get picked off!"

Mirela said, gently, "Perhaps that is the intention."

I whirled on her. "Or maybe that's just what they want you to think! Maybe all this is meant to get me sitting around, scared, waiting for the grand finale!"

"Or perhaps it is to lure you," she said.

I didn't know where she'd found that word, but it worked. I started a fresh set of sobs. "People around me are dying, not me. It's you that needs to be in hiding, or Ali, or…" My voice trailed off, belatedly following my thoughts, which were disjointed as hell. And I was still crying. "I can't do this! I can't have anyone else…"

Ali stood up and put his arms around me, and this time I let him do it. "*Cara*, it's so hard, I know. We'll figure it out, I promise. We've got a lot of people helping us. Smart people, experienced people. Take a deep breath, *cara*… there. You're okay. It's going to be okay."

That was so patently untrue I started crying all over again. This was never, ever going to be okay.

Ali's brain, unlike mine, seemed to be working, and he knew exactly what would calm me: focusing on the task. He kept holding me and said, his voice close to my ear, "It was pretty bold, when you think of it. You spoke to him in the morning, and he was found in the evening, so someone strangled him—which takes some time and would be obvious if anyone saw it—and moved his body, all of it in broad daylight. You have to wonder about someone who can do that."

On a really hot day, too. In a town filled with visitors, tourists, people arriving for the pow-wow. My brain showed a vestige of interest. It wouldn't have been easy.

Either someone really, really wanted Will dead… or they really, really wanted me scared. They'd accomplished both.

"I want to see him," I said.

Ali released me from the hug he'd held me in, shaking his head. "You can't, *cara*."

"Why not? Because of that—that Sharpie—I have some rights here!"

"He's already been transported," Ali said. "I'm sorry."

"Then I'll go to Sandwich!" Even to my own ears, I was sounding a little hysterical. The Office of the Chief Medical Examiner explores cause and manner of death for anyone on the Cape whose death is unexplained, unexpected, violent, or potentially the result of misuse of drugs or alcohol. People don't just walk in there. The State Police—again—are the gatekeepers, and I was quite sure they didn't want me within miles of the facility.

And yet… I wanted to see him. To say I was sorry. To tell Will I hadn't meant to bring this horror show down upon him.

As though reading my thoughts, Ali said, "You know, this isn't on you. It was his job. He was going to investigate, no matter what. With or without you. Reporters routinely stir up hornet's nests. He could have discovered something that made it necessary to silence him—the message for you was just the frosting on top. That's a real possibility." He took a deep breath. "You've got to think beyond yourself."

I knew he was right. I was hysterical because someone had decided I should be; and it was true that I hadn't done anything directly to cause Juliet's death, or Will's … at some level I did understand this wasn't about me. Or at least not all about me.

It might be, however about… "Margo!" I gasped. "We have to tell Margo!"

"We will," said Ali. "Give yourself a little time first, *cara.*"

Mirela said, diffidently, "And Bruce Peterson is waiting for us."

I'd forgotten him, of course. I'd forgotten just about everything but how I was feeling. I took a couple of deep breaths. Before I could open my mouth, Ali said, "Call him. You're not going out there."

We were about to have another fight; I could feel it coming on. "The pow-wow is tomorrow," I said. "We have to—"

"Every single law enforcement agency in the region knows the pow-wow is tomorrow," said Ali. "*You* don't have to do anything, Sydney. We'll handle it. We have procedures. We're good at what we do."

Apparently not at keeping people alive, I thought, but didn't say it. That was just me snapping at other people to assuage my own feelings of guilt. I tried another tack. "Maybe it'll keep both Bruce and me safe, if we're together today," I said. "Look, he just wants to feel like he's doing something. He and Juliet worked together for about a million years. It's really probably just him wanting to be talking about her. I'm the one who said we should get together, not him. And he's at that resort place, there's no way anybody's going to figure out we're there."

"I will go with her," announced Mirela, changing sides.

"You can't keep her safe," Ali countered.

"He will not wish to hurt her when there is someone to witness it," Mirela said.

"Maybe you two could stop talking as if I wasn't in the room," I said. "And I am going. To see Bruce Peterson, and to attend the pow-wow. If nothing else, I owe it to Will. And Juliet. And anybody else this guy chooses to target."

"Even if it's you?"

"Especially if it's me," I said with feeling.

Ali's phone started chiming. He released my arm and tugged it out of his pocket. "Damn. I have to take this. Don't go anywhere." He left the room, already swiping the phone to answer.

I turned to Mirela. "Let's go."

It was one of the few times in my life I'd ever seen her uncertain. "Ali said—"

"I don't care," I said. "Come with me, or don't come. Your choice." I took a deep breath. "This isn't over."

She stood up. "I will come."

***

We found Bruce in the MidCape Resort's front office, talking with someone whose nametag helpfully identified her as Marie. He looked startled to see us. "Thought you weren't coming," he said.

"Just waylaid," I said, trying to keep my voice even and normal. Wasn't sure I quite managed it. "This is my friend Mirela. Did you find out anything about Juliet?"

Marie said, "I was telling Mr. Peterson about—"

He interrupted her. "She was here alone," he said. "Let's go see her suite. It's open, but won't be for much longer."

"Okay." I glanced at Marie. "Did you find out who made the arrangements for her to stay here? The reservation?"

"Only the email," she said.

"I'll tell you about it," said Bruce. He turned to her. "Thanks for all your help. Let's go, Sydney."

"I have it right here," she said, turning the screen of her monitor around to face us. Mirela and I both leaned in. It was from an account called simply *JulietWeekendWaypoints (at) gmail.com*. I glanced at Bruce. "Is this her usual account?"

He shook his head. "We have our own domain," he said.

The message ran, *Reservation for one week only, starting July 28. One person. Will arrive late, so please leave key and directions at the front desk. Please reply with whatever address needed to send the payment electronically.*

I looked up at Marie. "And you replied?"

She nodded. "Venmo," she said.

"That's a clue, isn't it?" I asked Bruce. "Someone can track down the Venmo account holder, right?"

He nodded. "I'll let the Boston police know."

"And the tribal police," I said. "They're the ones investigating her death." She was probably in Sandwich, too, now that I thought about it. Juliet and Will, lying in adjoining refrigerated drawers, dead—literally—by the same hands.

Marie cleared her throat. "I don't know if this matters," she said tentatively, "but it was odd. One person—that isn't our usual clientele. The smallest unit is a two-bedroom that accommodates up to six people. Some of them are rentals, some are condos, but the point is, we usually have families stay here."

"Are there other places in Mashpee that would have been more appropriate for a single person?" I asked.

"Not in Mashpee," she said doubtfully. "But we're not far from a number of towns—like Hyannis or Falmouth. In fact, we only accommodated her for the one week because we'd had a cancellation. And then when we saw she left after one night… well, it was just a little strange."

I said, hoping I could get the words out without breaking down again, "Did a reporter come and ask you about her? Someone from *The Enterprise*?"

She nodded. "Will Fortier. I know him. He saw the suite before it had been cleaned, actually. He asked about her, too. I told him the same thing I told you."

I already knew he'd been here; I'd hoped mentioning him might shake something additional loose from her mind. "Thank you," I said.

But Will knew about the Venmo account, and he'd had a couple of days to look into it. What had it told him? Something that got him too close to the killer?

We headed out into the resort grounds, the heat mitigated somewhat by the shade cast by the tall evergreens around the property. "That's why she chose to stay here," I said suddenly.

Bruce looked at me quizzically. "Why?"

"Because the payment could be made without anyone seeing her."

He shook his head. "I don't think she made that reservation," he said. "That's not an email address she'd use, to start with; we have work emails. And she'd have identified herself, told them where she worked—we usually get a discount when we do. Everyone wants to be on the show."

"But perhaps she did not want anyone to know that she was already on the Cape," said Mirela tentatively.

"Couldn't be," I said, thinking it through. I looked at Bruce. "Remember? She wouldn't do the two shows back-to-back the way everyone wanted to do them. She said she had to do something first." I frowned, trying to remember. "Something to do with her sister? Or with Rick?" He might have slipped off my list of suspects, but that didn't mean Rick Thatcher didn't hold the key to understanding Juliet's last twenty-four hours. I should have asked him.

We were approaching a low ranch-style building, attractive and welcoming. Bruce had an electronic key, and we went in.

And it told us, naturally, exactly nothing. Cleaned since Juliet's stay, it was neat, sterile, utterly nondescript. A place for families to stay—one of the bedrooms had twin beds—while out exploring the Cape or lounging by the pool. I'd wondered about the cleaning staff, but it was highly unlikely anyone would remember what had been in the suite a week ago.

If Bruce was right, the reservation hadn't been made by Juliet.

Which meant it had been made by her killer.

What could have enticed her to follow his directions? I was more and more inclined to think she hadn't come here alone, that she might have come here under duress, or even unconscious. There would have been people about, but families tended to have earlier bedtimes, and anyway he'd shown he was willing to take chances: he drove Will's Jeep with Will's body in it to that parking area in Quashnet Woods in, as Ali had pointed out, broad daylight.

I was starting to get a feeling about this man—and it had to be a man, he'd handled dead weight without turning a hair—and he was emerging as ruthless and determined.

But still I didn't see the connection with me.

Chapter Twenty-Three

Ali called me twice, and both times I let the call go to voicemail. He finally gave up and texted. *Hope you're being careful. I have a lead on Skye and need to follow up. See you when I see you.*

I winced at the tone. Whatever happened, I had some serious fence-mending to do there. No time to think about it now.

What I *was* thinking was that it was the afternoon before the pow-wow, and I still wasn't any closer to determining why someone wanted to kill two people and involve me in their deaths. Nor whether any of it was connected to the disappearance of a young indigenous woman.

We ended up at a chain coffee shop in the Mashpee Commons. "Where's Adam?" I asked Bruce. "Wasn't he coming down with you?"

"He's here," he said. "Over at the pow-wow grounds. Doing something electrical."

I didn't ask what, since *something electrical* pretty much covered my own understanding of such things. "I don't suppose we could go over there," I said tentatively. The pow-wow was being held in the same grounds behind the tribal offices where only yesterday we'd met with Derek. Not long after Will had been killed: he'd said he'd try to join us. I put the thought away. I was sure the place looked quite different now, with vendors setting up their tents and stands, and an area prepared for the dances and the drumming. Perhaps it would help to see it that way.

Bruce shook his head. "Wouldn't even let me in," he said. "But Adam's been great. He's really stepped up to the plate in organizing this, taking over Juliet's work." He sipped his coffee. "The crew's getting in tomorrow morning around nine. The Grand Entry—you know about that?—is scheduled for eleven-thirty or so, apparently there's some flexibility about the exact start time, so they'll have time to set up and even do a couple of interviews before it starts."

That made sense; I couldn't quite imagine Stacey the red-haired "talent" wishing to cede center stage to anyone; and if the forecast was correct, it was going to be a scorcher of a day. Not good for preserving hairstyles or makeup; best to get it done early.

Because I couldn't think of anything else to say, and I didn't want to listen to my own panic-riddled thoughts, I asked Bruce, "Isn't Adam one of the people who's leaving the show?"

He nodded. "Got an offer from a national show in New York," he said.

"You'll miss him, won't you? Sounds like he's been really helpful."

"He's good," he said. "I'm not surprised he's getting picked up by the nationals, it was only a matter of time. I knew *Waypoints* was exactly that for him, a transition." He drank more coffee. "We were a means to an end. He applied because he wanted to relocate to Boston, start fresh. He kind of threw himself into the work once we offered him the job." He paused, then added, looking at me, "He had a tragedy year before last—his brother died. Took him a while to get over that. I guess they were close."

"I'm sorry to hear that," I said, the words automatic.

"What happened to his brother?" asked Mirela, joining us in the small talk. Maybe she didn't want to be thinking too much, either. "Was he ill?" I knew that in her culture, the word *cancer* was avoided, as though speaking it meant calling it into being.

"He was murdered, actually," said Bruce. "Literally stabbed in the back."

"Poor Adam," I said with feeling. There were an awful lot of murders happening around us. "Did they get whoever killed him?"

He shrugged. "Didn't matter," he said. "The guy was already serving a life sentence." He was looking at his watch, preparing to say something about leaving.

I wasn't ready to leave. I wanted the afternoon to last forever, so I didn't have to face whatever was going to happen the next day. Besides, Bruce needed the whole picture. "Did you hear about Will Fortier?" I asked. I'd managed to spend almost two hours not thinking about him, but the tears were pressing against my eyes again. Too many murders. Too much death.

"Who's Will Fortier?" Obviously he hadn't heard.

Mirela answered, but she was watching me. "He was a reporter," she said. "He was writing about Juliet Mills."

"What happened?"

"He was strangled yesterday," I said. "Just like Juliet."

He put his cup down with a bang that earned us a look from the other tables. "What?"

I didn't look at him, didn't look at anything, forced my gaze away so I could concentrate on not crying. I'd liked Will. Even saw us, in some way, as partners, trying to ferret out the truth. But he was a professional, and if I'd learned anything over the past week, I was an amateur, and not a terribly skilled one at that. Will was the real hero here.

Which had made him a target. Well, that, and the whole being associated with me thing.

Bruce was shaking his head. "Aren't the police doing *anything?*" he demanded. "This is getting out of hand."

"I'm sure they're doing something," I said, a little irritated. Any moment now he was going to say, *it wasn't like him to get killed*. "I know several agencies are involved. It's—it gets confusing, with more than one jurisdiction wanting to take it on." Or not; I had a feeling if I were in law enforcement, I'd gladly surrender this one to anyone else interested in solving it. And "getting out of hand" seemed a flippant remark—Will was *dead*.

I wasn't in law enforcement. There was no other agency I could pass my issues on to. Whether I wanted it or not, this one was on me.

***

Mirela's phone was ringing just as we let ourselves into the house. "Hello?" The person on the other line said something, and she looked across at me. "Yes," she said finally, and handed me her phone. "It is for you, sunshine."

I took it from her, a little mystified. "Hello? This is Sydney."

"It's a fine thing when I have to telephone someone else to get a chance to speak to my daughter!"

My mother. Because of course.

"I was going to call you back, Ma," I said. She'd only left me three voicemails.

"I tried calling Ali," she said. Once upon a time she'd referred to him as "that man," now she called him on a regular basis. I wasn't sure I hadn't liked it better before. "He's getting to be like you, not answering his phone."

"He's working, Ma. He doesn't take my calls, either. What is it?"

"What is what?"

Breathe, Riley. "What is it you're calling about?"

"Well, I wanted to catch you up on the plans."

I was going to go insane and she would still be talking. "Ma. What plans? What are you talking about?"

"The *wedding*," she said. "Really, you should pay attention. You were the one who told me to talk to that nice man at your inn. What is his name, again?"

I had no idea what she was talking about. "I have no idea what you're talking about," I told her.

An exaggerated sigh. "The man who's doing your old job. The wedding planner."

Light dawned. "Right," I said. Her friend's granddaughter's wedding. It felt as though years had passed since that conversation. "Erik Dombroski," I said. "He's the events coordinator."

"Yes, well, he was very nice and he had plenty of time to talk with me, not like some other people I could mention." She paused for emphasis. "He's going to take care of all the details."

"Well, he would, wouldn't he? It's his job."

"Don't you start taking a tone with me, Sydney Riley. I don't remember you being as helpful when that was *your* job. But he was so sweet, and didn't rush me one little bit. We went over *everything*. Such a nice young man. And he even went ahead and reserved rooms for all of us."

"You're coming too?"

"Well, of course I'm coming, *and* your father. Grace says her granddaughter doesn't like planning these things, and was very grateful when I volunteered to step in."

I'll bet she was, I thought. I had a feeling Mike and I were going to have to give Erik a substantial bonus for this one. Combat pay. "It will be nice to see you," I lied.

"It's a crime that I have to plan someone else's wedding to have the opportunity to stay at my own daughter's inn," she said tartly.

No, I thought; that's not exactly a crime. Not even in the running. "Ma? Is that what you called to tell me?"

Another sigh. "All right. I can see you're busy and I'm interrupting." My mother, the martyr. "I was thinking about that time when we came to visit you, and we went on a whale watch. Do you even remember that?"

Every painful moment of it. For someone who lived by the ocean, I wasn't overly fond of actually being out on it; I was always aware of the depths below the boat. And of course some other memorable things had happened to me in Cape Cod Bay, not many of them good. "Of course I remember it, Ma."

"Well, my thought was, we could include a whale watch in the wedding activities. I'm sure the guests would all find it interesting. And I wanted to ask you about it, because I remember there was that nice young man who was the guide. You really have so many nice young men in that town." It had taken her some time to realize that, in P'town, many if not most of the nice young men happened to be gay. If nothing else, her visits to the Race Point Inn had finally started challenging some of her stereotypical thinking.

"He was a naturalist," she said, "isn't that the word? Who told us all about the whales and the birds and all the rest." My mother, keenly into nature. "I couldn't remember his name, and I wanted to see if we could reserve a trip with him. So informative. What was his name?"

"Kai Bennett," I said. "He's not there anymore, Ma."

"No? How disappointing! I liked him."

I didn't remind her Kai had gone to prison. Didn't really need that discussion. "Anyone from the Center for Coastal Studies will be great," I said. "They're all scientists. I'm sure Erik will connect you with someone you'll like." Yes; he was definitely going to have to get a bonus.

There was a muffled conversation on the other end, and then she came back. "Your father says he wants to go on the whale watch, this time. I told him so much about it. You should invite us down, Sydney. The summer's not going to last forever."

Yeah, as soon as I figure out why people around me are dropping like flies, I'll be sure to enjoy a whale watch with you. I didn't even like whale watches; there's something about knowing a whole ecosystem is going about its business right under your feet, filled with mysterious creatures and leviathans and even the legend of a monster (take that, Loch Ness) that makes me feel a little… unsafe. Besides, I'd have to put them up at the inn, and make restaurant reservations and… it was all too much to contemplate. "Let's talk about it later, Ma."

"If you answer your phone," she said, "we'll be sure to plan it."

I sighed, ended the call, gave the phone back to Mirela. Nobody understands that I get my sarcasm directly from my mother.

There was still something I had to do. I couldn't put it off any longer. I picked up my phone and stared at it for a while, thinking of how best to say what I had to say, and finally opened up the text-message app and touched Margo's photo. *Are you there?*

She was. *Any news on Will?*

I took a deep breath. *I'm so sorry, Margo.*

There was a long pause, then: *No. He can't be.*

I'm so sorry.

Another pause, and then my phone rang. "What happened to him?" Margo's voice demanded.

"He might have been getting too close to someone," I said. "I don't know. I don't know who his contacts were, so I can't find out.

His newspaper will know, they're probably working with the police now to find out, but… I don't have any way of knowing what they're doing, or how they're doing it." I was babbling too much.

"How did he die?"

I swallowed. "Someone strangled him." I tried to rally. Margo was an attorney, she'd want all the facts in front of her, preferably on a yellow legal pad. I said, "You remember we couldn't find him? And his editor was saying he was out of contact. And his voicemail was full."

"I know. I tried it."

I took another deep breath. "I spoke to him yesterday morning. On the phone. He was going to maybe meet up with us later— Mirela's here with me. But he didn't come. And someone found him—I don't know who. He was in his Jeep, it was parked in some conservation land in Mashpee."

She knew right away what that meant. "Someplace some hiker would find him fairly quickly," she said, and I sensed she wasn't talking to me. I hadn't even made that connection.

"Ali said they were taking a big risk, getting him there, leaving him there. And in daylight."

Margo said, still sounding as if she was reasoning it out for herself. "Why? What is it that's coming, that's this big? They're clearing the stage for something."

"Something at the pow-wow," I said. I was probably making a mistake, sounding so confident about something for which I had no real evidence; it wasn't the first time I let my feelings run away with me. But they were strong, and I didn't have anything else to fall back on.

A kidnapping. Two identical deaths. And the connective tissue was me… and Ali. Me, mostly, because the note and the Sharpie message were completely about me; but what if this was something coming back to haunt Ali, and I was the way they chose to get to him?

Margo was pursuing her own thoughts. "Was he looking at the pow-wow?" she asked. "I don't remember hearing anything about that."

"He was looking at who killed Juliet Mills," I said. "And she was heading to the pow-wow. Professionally, I mean. *Weekend Waypoints* was doing a show about the pow-wow, so yeah, I think he was looking at the pow-wow."

"I'm coming back," she said, and her voice was brisk.

"The pow-wow is tomorrow," I said. "You can't get here in time—"

"The pow-wow lasts three days," she said crisply.

I didn't argue. People don't argue with Margo, in general, unless they're in court and being paid to do it. Instead, after a pause, I said, "Margo? I'm sorry if I'm intruding, I don't mean to—and you can tell me it's none of my business, but—well, what is it—what was it— between you and Will?"

"What d'you mean?"

I shrugged, even though she couldn't see me. "You weren't ro- mantically involved," I said. "But I could tell you were close. And he—knew—your house, knew things about you. Maybe it's none of my business…" But maybe, I thought, giving her a chance to think about him and remember him wouldn't be a bad thing right now, either.

I was right. There was a sigh, then Margo said, "I've known Will since he was two years old. His mother was a beautiful, creative, exceptional person, an artist. But she couldn't control her addiction. She tried, she did rehab, she went to meetings, but ultimately she couldn't." She cleared her throat. "I was part of an interdisciplinary team ensuring Will and his sister were given placements in the foster system, and those placements scrutinized. And then, over the years, the kids came to me—for supervised visits with Janey, that was his mother's name, and even for holidays and vacations when their placements weren't exactly always homey. Sort of like an aunt."

A fairy godmother, rather, I thought, but didn't say anything. I had a feeling it was helping Margo to talk about her and Will.

"The system doesn't always work," she said. "I liked Janey, I wanted her to succeed. She loved those kids to bits. But this thing inside that wanted to kill her was stronger." A sigh. "Priscilla—that's Will's sister—moved away as soon as she could. She's living in Maryland now. But over the years, Will and I spent a lot of time together. He never really left the area, just went to Boston for school, and came back when he got the job with *The Enterprise.* We still consider each other family." I noted the present tense, didn't say anything.

Margo sighed. "Janey finally killed herself a while back—well, eight years ago. So I'm the closest to family he has, me and Priscilla. I'll have to tell her."

So there was no mystery about how Will had known his way through Margo's house, or how she'd known which brewpub was his favorite. Just a lot of grief. And, also, a lot of love. I imagined him arriving with a duffle bag, joking with Margo in the kitchen while they made pasta together, arguing over who got the remote.

"I have to tell you something else," I said. I found my hands were trembling.

"Yes?" Her voice was distracted; I wondered if she was crying.

I took a deep breath. "Margo, this one's on me, too. You know Juliet Mills had a message in her pocket, a note saying I was meant to be responsible for her death? Well, Will did, too."

She sounded calm. "It would have surprised me if he hadn't," she said. "You know as well as I do, Mashpee isn't a hotbed of crime. Of course these two homicides are related. And you are, somehow, the key to finding out who killed them, and why."

Sometimes I couldn't distinguish Margo the person from Margo the lawyer. Maybe she couldn't, either. Maybe it's one of those professions that you *are*, rather than being something you *do*.

I didn't feel much like a key. More along the lines of Lady Macbeth. But that wasn't helping anything.

"I'll talk to the district attorney," she was saying. "Should be home tomorrow. I'll see you then, Sydney."

"Margo," I said. "I—I'm sorry. Really sorry."

"Yes," she said, and her voice was dimmer. She needed to get off the phone. "I'll see you soon." A decisive click, and she was gone.

I sat for a long time, holding the phone uselessly in my hands. Shadows moved around the room. Wally came in, jumped up on the sofa beside me, and settled in. Mirela came out of her bedroom, caught sight of me, started to say something, and stopped herself. She turned on the television instead, but she was as restless as I was, and after scrolling through entertainment options for a few minutes she turned it off again.

No haunting Billy Joel music tonight. No fears of what might be out there, trying to get in.

I was becoming more afraid of what might be inside me, waiting to get out.

Chapter Twenty-Four

Sometime back when I was in school and devouring novels—
something I probably should take up again, there's nothing like
reading fiction to help one cope with the world's grimmer realities—
I read a story about a couple of murders that took place somewhere
in the Arctic after a plane crashed there. The novel was called *Night
Without End.*

I could have used that exact same title for that Thursday night,
the night before the pow-wow, the night where I had to either figure
things out or know that something very bad was going to happen.
Or, possibly, both.

Ali was somewhere working late, and Mirela was watching a
movie on Netflix. We'd put together something approximating a
meal, ate it in near-silence, cleaned up afterward.

In Provincetown, in the winter, we get wild destructive storms
coming off the Atlantic, screaming with wind and rain or snow as
they hit land; they're called nor'easters, named after the direction
from which the strongest winds typically blow over the Northeast
states, including New England and the Mid-Atlantic states. If there's
sunshine at all before the storm hits, it tends to be what we call a
"snow sun," the orb surrounded by a haze, warning of what's on the
way. Whenever we see a snow sun, we don't even need to check the
weather forecast—we know something is coming.

I sat alone in the darkness of Margo's three-seasons room and
felt the cold glow of a snow sun in my chest.

What did I know?

I knew a young indigenous woman had been taken against her will, held in an apartment in Boston for a week by a couple, one of whom was still unknown and somewhere lurking.

I knew one of the producers of a popular television show had been strangled, and her death connected her to both the Mashpee Wampanoag tribe and me.

I knew a reporter was investigating both the disappearance and the death, and that he in turn had been strangled, his body left near Wampanoag land, a scrawled message connecting him to me as well.

I knew there was an uneasy relationship between the tribe and the non-indigenous inhabitants of both Mashpee and Taunton. That a casino was being built after a difficult and fraught history, that it would be an economic lifeline for the tribe and a source of friction with the local non-indigenous community. That the first killing connected to the casino through family ties.

I knew a number of law enforcement agencies—including the one that employed my husband—were jockeying for control over investigating the two deaths and the disappearance.

I knew the messages left for me implied the deaths were connected, somehow, to my past, but I didn't see how. I had quite accidentally learned that someone from my past, long gone, had reappeared in Provincetown, but I wasn't seeing a correlation between that fact and the events of the past week.

I knew that my former husband had been more involved in my life post-divorce than I'd thought, that he was in trouble, had possibly even murdered his wife, and wanted to bribe me to give him an alibi. I couldn't see how he was connected to any of the rest of it, though. And he certainly hadn't killed Juliet, if in fact he was busily killing Alice at the same time.

All in all, I knew rather a lot. What I didn't know was what it all meant.

I got up, restless, walked into the kitchen, pulled a Diet Coke from the refrigerator, and held the can against my forehead. Maybe I could think more coherently if it wasn't so damned hot.

I leaned against the refrigerator and thought some more. The one thing I felt strongly about was the one thing for which there was no evidence—that somehow everything was going to come together at the Wampanoag pow-wow. Why was I so sure that was going to provide resolution?

Wishful thinking?

Well, no. Or at least, not entirely. The pow-wow was part of both mysteries from the beginning: Skye Taylor was scheduled to be one of the dancers at the event, and Juliet Mills had planned a program around it. And then both Skye and Juliet disappeared.

I fell asleep on the sofa in the three-seasons room, and awoke with Ali's hand on my shoulder. "Come on, *cara*, let's get you to bed."

I blinked blearily at him. "What time is it?"

"Past midnight. You're exhausted. Come on, I'll help you."

We staggered into the bedroom together, and I was back asleep the moment my head touched the pillow. I dreamt of drums and distant thunder and running through thick underbrush, and woke to a headache and more than a little panic.

It was early. Ali was meeting someone from the tribal police well before the festivities got underway, and I had decided to try and hitch a ride with the *Weekend Waypoints* crew, if they weren't there already. Which, come to think of it, they probably were.

We stood in Margo's small kitchen, drinking espresso and comparing notes. "I will come in a while," said Mirela. "I must speak to

Lily's teacher on Zoom first." Why on earth the teacher had any complaints about my goddaughter, especially in the summer, I had no idea; time to pursue that later. "Will you be all right?" she asked me.

"Of course I will," I said robustly.

"You won't find a place to park within a mile of the event if you don't go early," said Ali; he'd done his homework on how past pow-wows were run.

Mirela just smiled, that cat-with-the-cream look she sometimes got when she thought someone was underestimating her. And she was probably right; princess parking was the least of her superpowers.

I was feeling twitchy and probably shouldn't have been drinking coffee. I called Bruce instead. "Hey. Where are you? Did your people arrive? I was going to try and catch a ride with you."

He sounded as strung-out as I felt. "We're setting up now," he said. "Problem is, so's everybody else."

I glanced at my watch: eight-thirty. "I'm on my way," I said.

Ali was already halfway out the door. "Promise me you'll stay with the crew until Mirela gets there," he said to me. "I don't want you out there on your own."

"I promise," I said, and even sort of meant it.

He shook his head and sighed. "Be careful, is all," he said, and kissed me. "I'll see you out there."

Mirela had taken her third coffee back to bed with her. I eschewed a shower on the premise that I was going to be sweating profusely anyway, and pulled on a sleeveless summer dress, shoved my feet into the most comfortable flats I had, and tied up my hair into a knot so it wouldn't be on my neck. Deep breath.

There were cars already parked on Great Neck Road near the tribal center; I tucked the Grey Goose in among them and set off.

I paid my entry fee at a makeshift table—where a young woman in a t-shirt and jeans asked me if I was "tribal"—and noted a sign telling potential dancers that they had to register and get a number.

There was music in the air already, coming from loudspeakers, something vaguely Andean, flutes and strings, and I reminded myself that indigenous people from all over participated in each other's pow-wows. Why wouldn't South America be represented?

The grounds were unrecognizable as the place where we'd sat and talked with Derek. A large central space, an arena of sorts, was ringed by rows of portable beach chairs, two- and three-deep, many of them already occupied, often in clusters that looked like family groups, most with coolers in their midst. They were arranged under canopy tents providing shade as well as delineating who sat where. On one side was a larger tent, where people who looked official were bustling about; that's where the Andean musicians were playing, microphones and speakers floating their music in the air.

More canopy tents also ringed the outer perimeter of the field. The ones closest to the entrance seemed to belong to various nonprofit organizations; my eye was drawn, immediately, to the sign that read Violence Against Indigenous Women. I swallowed. How easy to forget, in the midst of everything, how this had all started.

I wondered if Skye was safe. I wondered if she was *alive*.

Beyond the central staging area, and stretching out on two more sides, were the stalls where goods were being sold: smudge sticks and skirts, beadwork and leather goods and oddly shaped musical instruments. Many of the vendors were still setting out their wares, and I chatted for a moment with a young man who made jewelry. "I used to live here," he said. "It got too expensive, so I moved to Montana. But my auntie sends me the abalone."

The food sellers were still just setting up, too, and as it seemed none of them was offering coffee—the only thing that would have tempted me at the moment—I went instead in search of *Weekend Waypoints*.

They'd brought the same two vehicles they'd had in Provincetown, a van to transport the people and a second one filled with equipment; the vans had been shunted off to one side of the right-hand driveway, with a flow of people entering the pow-wow moving by beside them.

Adam Bennett, the director was sitting behind the wheel of the people-carrying van, eating an apple and staring at a sheet of paper. He glanced up as I approached. "Hey. Sydney. What's up?"

"Just checking in," I said cheerfully. "You don't have any coffee, by chance, do you?"

He grinned and held up a large YETI insulated container. "Always prepared," he said. "Hop in."

I went to the other side and clambered into the passenger seat. He located a cardboard cup and handed me the YETI. "Enjoy."

"You're a lifesaver," I said. I didn't really need the coffee. I needed to not be alone. I poured it carefully and put the container back on the floor. "Are you already all set up?" I asked. If I remembered correctly, it had taken quite some time to set up for their work at the Race Point Inn, and that shoot had had certain advantages, including a building that wasn't moving. Here, everything seemed to be in motion.

"More or less," Adam said. "Nothing's really happening yet. Stacey got an interview in the can, and we got some early shots of some of them setting up, but nothing's really happening until they do the Grand Entry thing."

He passed the paper across to me: a schedule. It looked largely the same as the pamphlet I'd been handed when I paid to get in, but well annotated, with names and angles and shots included, all in bright colors and with circles and squiggly lines. I handed it back. "Don't speak the language," I said.

He looked startled. "Wampanoag?"

I shook my head. "Director-ese," I said.

Adam grinned. "A lot of it's just B-roll," he said. "Just the guys walking around and filming—the crowds, all those costumes, then the drumming and dancing and all that. Try and get some close-ups of some cute kids. We'll add narration over it back in the studio. Stacey's interviewing one of the council members now, and then someone's taking her over to taste some of the food on camera and talk about it. Maybe an interview with one of the dancers, I'm waiting for them to get back to me on that one."

"Sounds simple enough," I said, even though I knew it wasn't. I'd been on the receiving end of their interviews and B-rolls.

He shrugged and finished his apple. "Just another day at the office," he said cheerfully.

"Where's Bruce?" I asked. "I thought he'd be the one here." It seemed to me that maybe the director should be doing something besides sitting around and eating breakfast.

"Bruce is hands-on," he said, unperturbed.

"He didn't seem that way in Provincetown," I pointed out.

He was looking at his paper. "Juliet was in charge," he said. "That was her thing. Everybody's got their own vibe, their own way of doing things."

"He was hoping to find out what happened to Juliet," I said. "Did he get any closer?"

"Yeah, that whole *maybe if I can stay in the same place she stayed her ghost will speak to me* thing? Don't think it did much." Adam tossed the clipboard up onto the wide dashboard. "Maybe it'll never happen. Maybe it'll always be a mystery." He shrugged. "One *you* didn't manage to solve, after all."

Odd tone of voice, I thought. Almost accusatory. "He still wants to," I said defensively. "I still want to."

He looked at me. "Would it be your first?" he asked.

"My first what?"

"First time you didn't solve one of your little mysteries," he said. "What I heard is, you usually do. You get the bad guy."

I stirred uncomfortably. "It's not exactly like that—"

"Not what I heard," he said again. "Juliet called you a crime-stopper."

"That's ridiculous," I said. I didn't like the way the conversation was going. "Mostly it's been because I know a lot of people and … I guess I have a position that makes it easy for me to see the big picture. I mean, it's not like I do it professionally, or anything." I knew how lame that sounded. I also wondered why we were having this conversation in the first place.

"Sounds like you could, though." He smiled, as though to make the words less offensive. "You've done a lot of good for your community."

"I like to think so." I finished the coffee. "Thanks for this. I think I'll go and see if—"

Adam cut me off. "Didn't mean to insult you."

"You didn't." I smiled brightly. "We're all a little tired."

He took the cup back and tossed it behind him in the van; clearly he wouldn't be the one cleaning it out, later. "Yeah. I'll be honest with you, Sydney, I'll be glad when this shoot is over. Bad luck all around." He stretched. "You heard I'm leaving the show?"

I nodded. "Bruce said you had an offer out of New York," I said. "He seemed to think it was inevitable."

"Really? In what way?"

I shrugged; I was trying to find some way to exit semi-gracefully from the conversation and the van itself, and I wasn't finding it. "He says you're young and you're good, and that *Weekend Waypoints* was really just a stepping-stone for you on the way to bigger and better things. For what it's worth, he thinks you deserve it—the promotion, the bigger market, all that."

"He thinks that? Nice of him to share it with you," he said. "Never said that to me. He's right, though. I never planned on staying in Boston. You know how it is with a career: you go, you do the thing, you move on."

"And you've accomplished what you wanted to do here?" I asked. I wasn't really interested, but he was. *Okay, I'll play along.*

"Almost," he said. "When Bruce hired me, he knew it wasn't going to be for very long. Just needed to get a few things accomplished."

"I'm glad you did," I said politely.

He flashed me a grin. "And here I am, taking up your time, boasting about my resume," he said. "Maybe success is going to my head."

"I'm sure you'll do well in New York." I opened the door and slid out of the van. "D'you know where Bruce is now?"

He gestured. "Place isn't that big, you'll see him somewhere. Right now he's probably inside the building with Stacey, running her interview." He grimaced. "In the air conditioning, lucky bastard. They'll be out soon, though. We have to get into position for the start of the parade, and Stacey likes to make her own grand entrance in front of the cameras before we do that."

Thus reminded, I thought I should probably be thinking about where I wanted to be for the pow-wow's Grand Entry. And see if Ali had arrived. And about a million things that probably all amounted to nothing. "See you later," I said to Adam.

"Sure thing," he agreed.

I went to check out the other program van, but it was locked, and probably none of my business anyway, and as I turned away I tripped over some of the electrical cables feeding into it. *Watch what you're doing, Riley.* Breaking a bone was certainly not on the day's agenda.

The whole area had gotten more people-y, and the heat was already unrelenting. I probably should have brought a water bottle. I never remember to bring a water bottle, not anywhere. I wandered over to the food stands and bought a large lemonade, and that helped somewhat.

What I couldn't imagine would be standing in this heat wearing some of the regalia I was seeing. And some of it was truly spectacular.

Two small boys raced by, barefoot, wearing only some sort of soft, deerskin-fringed trousers, their hair long and black, their laughter delighted and loud. I smiled and made way for them. Some of the younger men wore very little indeed, bare-chested, handsome... but most of the tribal members were in riotous colors, swirling skirts and tunics, feathered headdresses, heavily beaded necklaces and armbands, fringe and shells, tattoos and soft moccasin shoes.

And among and around them, of course, the hapless tourists, most of them white, wearing shorts and t-shirts and looking far less at ease in the heat than were the indigenous participants in full—and, in some cases, heavy—tribal regalia.

The Andean musicians had been replaced with drumming, and I wandered over under the big canopy beside the arena to take a look. The drummers were all ages—and all men—perfectly synchronized, and singing something that sounded a lot like "yah way yah way ha ha."

A voice next to me said, "What you're hearing is what's known as vocables," and I looked up to see Derek standing there. He looked magnificent; gone were the jeans and t-shirt from our earlier meetings—he was wearing buckskin and feathers and beads and heaven knew what else. "I *was* wondering," I admitted.

He smiled. "We do a lot of songs that way," he said. "It's so tribes with different languages can all join in. Is this your first pow-wow?"

"It is," I admitted.

"And what do you think?"

I smiled. "It's breathtaking," I said. "Are the drum circles always men?"

He took a deep breath. "First of all," he said, "a drum *circle* is a bunch of white hippies in a forest somewhere, trying to get in touch with something. We have drum *groups.*"

I laughed. "Sorry," I said automatically. "Wow. White hippies—that's a vivid image."

He grinned. "It is, isn't it?" Another tribal member came by and exchanged a fist-bump with Derek, something I'd already been observing men doing—perhaps, like the vocables, it was a way of transcending tribal-specific greetings. "Don't worry," Derek said. "There's a lot to learn. You should come to pow-wows more often."

"I should," I agreed, fervently hoping the next one I attended wouldn't be quite as fraught as this one. Thus reminded, I asked, "Is there any news about the girl who was kidnapped?"

He shook his head. "She was one of the dancers," he said. "In a couple of the competitions. We will remember her then, and especially at fireball."

"Fireball?"

He nodded. "Tomorrow night, at dusk. Fireball is a game, but it's also a ceremony. Well, a lot of our games are like that. Fireball is a little like soccer, but you can use your hands and catch and throw the ball." He paused. "But first, the ball is soaked in kerosene and lit on fire."

I stared at him. "People grab a burning ball with their *hands*?"

"Pain is part of the point," he said. "The ceremonial aspect. What they do is carry the pain of somebody who is either sick or who has passed, to release that pain from them, as a warrior, and heal them, as well as heal themselves and their families."

"Don't they get burned?"

He nodded and held up his hands; I could see a network of old scars on them. "It is a young man's game," he conceded. "But it's also a healing ceremony. We don't allow cameras, no pictures. It's reverential." He glanced at me, and there was only the slightest smile on his face. "It's also a lot of fun."

I was imagining grabbing a ball that was literally engulfed in flames; the image was a little too vivid. I shivered. "Maybe I'll come back for that," I said. I might have to, if none of the things I was worried about happened today; the pow-wow was, after all, three days.

"Well," he said, his eyes moving around the tent and the still-empty arena. "Seems your friend has arrived. And I need to see some people."

I followed his gaze and there was Mirela, looking a little distracted. She caught sight of me at the same time, and waved. I waved back and turned to Derek. "I'll see you later?" I suggested.

"No doubt."

Mirela was dressed in a cool sleeveless dress and sandals, but she was still uncomfortable. "It is terrible, this heat," she announced when I'd made my way around to her.

"It is," I agreed. "Is Ali here? Have you seen him?"

"No," she said. "I must drink something, sunshine. Or I will die."

I smiled. "Lemonade," I suggested, and steered her out to the lineup of food tents. We each got a lemonade—and they were seriously good, nothing artificial in them, tangy and sharp and cold—and sat down at the base of one of the big trees. I had a feeling I was going to be chasing shade all day.

"I saw your friend," said Mirela.

"What friend?" I'd leaned my head against the tree trunk and closed my eyes. I didn't open them.

"The doctor."

I sat up suddenly, abruptly. "Thea? She's here?" That hadn't been on my bingo card.

Mirela nodded, sipped her lemonade. "She is here," she confirmed.

"Where?"

"I do not know, me. What do you think? I do not know if she saw me, or not."

"Was she alone?"

"She was alone when I saw her," Mirela said, and unconsciously echoed Adam's words. "It is not such a large place; you will find her, if you wish to."

I settled back against the tree again. I wasn't doing anything or going anywhere until I'd hydrated; and Mirela was right—despite the number of people who kept pouring in, the space wasn't ridiculously large, and there were tribal police stationed everywhere errant visitors might wander off to. I could find her.

For all of that, there was now something cold and heavy settling into my stomach.

Was *Thea* the wild card in this deck?

Chapter Twenty-Five

I'd like to be able to record that I spent the next hour getting some answers to some of my questions, but I didn't.

I did, on Derek's suggestion and despite the heat, try a cup of clam chowder—very different from the "New England" style I was accustomed to. "We didn't have milk before the Europeans came," he'd said, and this was indeed not the thick creamy slop that often passed for chowder in Cape Cod's myriad fried-seafood joints; this was a flavorful broth with whole clams, potatoes, onions, celery, dill weed, and some other flavors I couldn't place. Yep: I wasn't going back to the creamy chowder anytime soon.

Mirela was impatient and wandered off on her own; I caught up with her later by one of the crafts stands, where she was buying a pair of beaded earrings.

"Nice," I commented, and she turned to me. "Your friend Bruce is here," she said. "I have seen him, eating fried dough."

"Where?" I looked around.

She made an airy gesture with her hand. "Somewhere."

The loudspeakers sizzled and came to life, informing us it was time to line up for the Grand Entry. "Come on," I said. "Let's go somewhere where we can watch."

We ended up actually at the arena entrance, where the lineup was in full force, beginning with men holding aloft what looked to be very heavy flags: an American flag, a veterans flag, and then a succession of flags from various tribes; I was nearest the young man who carried the Narragansett flag, and wondered what it felt like to be doing something important while tourists clicked photographs all around you.

The closest I could think of was how older residents felt during the Portuguese Festival in Provincetown, when the bishop from Fall River came to St. Peter's and said the Fisherman's Mass, after which the statue of the saint was processed down to the pier for the Blessing of the Fleet. For many of us, that was a religious experience; but we were always aware of the people gawking at us.

It was also one of about five times in the year I actually went to Mass, so perhaps I shouldn't be getting so much holier-than-thou about the tourists. And maybe also remember that, here, I was one of them.

Someone whose name I didn't catch was the MC, but it was Derek who said the opening prayer, and then the drumming and singing began, and the flag-carriers entered the arena, dancing as they went. The tribe's medicine man stood at the arena entrance with a pot holding burning incense, and as people entered, he wafted the smoke over them. The flag carriers went into the arena and danced there, and as each group was announced and entered, the space filled up in a spiral of dancing, colors blurring, and I looked across the arena and caught sight of Bruce Peterson.

I put a hand on Mirela's shoulder. "I'll be back," I said, and slipped away before she could protest, back out through the spectators, working my way around the arena, the drumming and chanting less something you heard and more something you felt.

What I also felt was Mirela's eyes on me.

Bruce was talking into his phone, one hand up to his other ear to block off some of the noise. He caught sight of me and raised an elbow in greeting, and as I moved closer I could hear part of the conversation. "…get it all, or we won't have anything to work with," he was saying. "I'd like to have her ask someone about the meaning of the costumes, too. Okay." He clicked off and looked at me. "Enjoying yourself?"

"I am," I said.

"Juliet would have loved it," he said. "Not the heat, but everything else."

We walked away from the crowd still craning to catch a look at the various groups entering the arena. "Let's get into some air conditioning," Bruce said, and we went across to the *Weekend Waypoints* vans. Bruce waved me over to the one with seats; it was running now, I saw, with all the windows rolled up. "Be right there," he said, and seemed to wait as I clambered into the front seat again. He had a key to the other van, the one without windows, and unlocked it and just stuck his head in for a moment before closing it up and joining me.

"How do you keep these running?" I asked. "I'd think you'd run out of gas."

"There's a generator for the equipment," he said. "And a lot of extra gas cans. God, it's hot out there."

"Welcome to climate change," I said.

"Lots of things changing." He pulled yet another clipboard off the dashboard and consulted a list. "We're good so far," he said. "Two interviews in the can, and Stacey's holding up pretty well. She got one in when we first arrived, and after that she had one inside, so she's had a chance to reapply her makeup."

"Priorities," I said, smiling.

He looked up from his list. "She's talking to your friend Rick Thatcher," he said.

I hadn't seen him. It seemed I wasn't seeing a lot, which didn't augur well for my figuring out what else was going to happen here. "Bruce," I said, "do you think Juliet's killer is here?"

He looked startled. "Why would they be?"

I shrugged. "It's all so tightly connected to the Wampanoag," I said. "Okay, yeah, so maybe it's just a feeling I have, but it's a strong one. I think something's going to happen. And I think it's going to happen today."

"Why today?" He was back to scanning his list, uninterested, just making conversation.

I said, "Because you're here."

That earned me a look, fast and sharp. "What do you mean, because I'm here?"

I shrugged. "Not you per se, but *Weekend Waypoints*. All this started with Juliet, with her interest in the tribe, with her deciding you needed a couple of days between shooting at the Race Point and shooting here. It really does seem to be about her. And now here you are, in her place."

"Not her place; my place," he said, his voice sharp. "We're doing the show in her memory, but it's my show now."

"Okay," I said cautiously.

"And you're forgetting it could be just as much about you," he pointed out. "I don't want to be too obvious here, but it wasn't my name on that paper they found with Juliet."

"I know," I said. I couldn't think about that note without starting to hyperventilate again; I carefully took two long breaths. *I'm so sorry, Juliet. I'm so sorry, Will.* No matter how this resolved itself, no matter what happened, I was still wondering how I was going to live with that knowledge.

Which was, I reasoned, precisely what the killer apparently wanted. Me to be guilt-ridden for the rest of my life.

He was definitely on track to get his wish.

Another deep breath. "All the more reason it's going to happen today," I said to Bruce. "We're all here, aren't we? All in one place? This whole thing, it's been orchestrated, carefully orchestrated. The events all building on each other. It's over-the-top dramatic, isn't it, when you think about it? And you have to admit, a pow-wow is a really impressive backdrop. We're all here—you, me, my husband—" I didn't mention Thea. I still didn't know how, or even if, she fit into all this. "And the tribe. There's such a strong connection to the tribe, its recent history, just… everything." That sounded almost rational, I decided.

But I was still just trying to justify a feeling.

Bruce tossed his clipboard back onto the dash, just as Adam had done earlier. "So what is it, exactly, that you're expecting to happen?" He was stroking his beard, consciously or unconsciously looking like the professor he wasn't, wisdom and academic knowledge contrasting with what he had to be thinking was my silliness.

And he had me there: I had no idea. "I don't know… but I'm sure the killer is here."

"And will do what?" He paused. "Sydney, are you listening to yourself? I don't think you're right, but if you are, if he's here, the logical next victim is you."

And there it was.

I stared at him. Why hadn't I seen that? Ali had, I was sure; he'd tried to keep me away from the pow-wow. He'd made sure Mirela was with me at Margo's house, whenever I spoke to anyone, even here at the pow-wow; I knew what he was doing even as I dismissed it. *Because, yeah, Riley, you know so much more about all this than the man in law enforcement who loves you.*

Bruce was watching me with something like amusement. "I'm a little surprised you're here at all," he said. "You really didn't think about that?"

"I really didn't think about that," I said. But I was thinking about it then, and was back to wondering what the killer wanted from me. He'd already gotten into my head and my heart. Was this the endgame? Killing me, too?

And why? I still was back to that. Who had I hurt so much?

I had a sudden urge to flee: to leave everything behind, the Wampanoag, Margo's brooding house, Wally even… go home, where I belonged. In Provincetown. With my own tribe, the people I'd chosen as my family. Where even if occasionally my life had been in danger, at least it wasn't the result of careful long-term planning, but only a reaction to a situation; never personal. I wanted to go back to stressing over budgets and worrying about people offending Adrienne the diva chef. Back to our lovely penthouse apartment and Ali strolling out of his office for orange juice…

Ali. He was going to be here sometime, he'd said. I looked at Bruce. "I have to go," I said.

"You'll be back," he predicted. "You won't be able to stay away."

"Why? What's going to happen?"

He smiled. "Air conditioning," he said.

"You have a generator," I agreed. "Okay, maybe I'll be back. Right now I need to find my husband."

"Good luck with that." He bent his head over yet another list he'd unearthed from somewhere, and I opened the door and slid out of the van.

It was like walking into a wall of heat and humidity.

I took a deep breath and plunged in. Mirela was supposedly my bodyguard, so I'd best find her and give her a body to guard.

The dancing in the arena had begun, separate dances for men and women, the drums and singing an irresistible backbeat. I'm very white: while Latin dances are indeed enticing, I can't move terribly well to them. But this? I had to stop myself from joining in—it would have been both inappropriate and a disrespectful caricature, but I found it interesting that even as a non-native, this rhythm was finding its way into my bones.

I walked around the periphery, looking for Mirela and not finding her. The sun was reaching down through the trees and pounding anyone not in the shade; it was giving me a headache, and looking for Mirela I felt suddenly dizzy, the swirl of colors around me moving way too fast, too bright, too hot, too much noise, the drumming and the singing and the voices around me talking way too fast and …

Someone grabbed my elbow. "Sydney! Are you all right?"

I still felt like I was falling, but I managed to focus on his face. Rick Thatcher. He was frowning. "Come with me," he said, his hand still holding my arm as we threaded our way through the crowd. Holding me up. Holding me together.

He found a picnic table that was only partially occupied, and eased me onto the seat. A large disgruntled tourist grudgingly made room for me. "Stay here," Rick commanded and disappeared again into the blurry backdrop of color and movement. I closed my eyes. The sun was hot, too hot, and… "Here," said Rick. "Drink this." He had a bottle and was tipping cold water into my mouth. "Keep drinking."

I kept drinking, and slowly the world righted itself around me, the blurry colors coalesced into people moving around the perimeter of the arena, the drumming returned to where it belonged and not inside my head. I gulped water, then air, then water again and felt my breathing return to normal.

For the first time, I really looked at Rick. His regalia was every bit as colorful and intricate as anything anyone else was wearing, and his face even had markings on it. He fit here, he belonged here, and I felt bad I had ever suspected him of murder.

"Thank you," I managed to say.

"Finish it," he said, gesturing at the water bottle, and I did and felt everything settle into something approaching normalcy. "You should hydrate more, Sydney."

"I know. I—wasn't thinking clearly."

"No one does, when they get dehydrated, and the heat's doing you in," he said.

"Shouldn't be." I finished off the water. "I was just sitting in air conditioning. I don't know why this happened."

He took the bottle, thrust it into some sort of leather case slung across his back, and sat down next to me. "Builds up over time," he said. "You look like someone with a lot on your mind."

"You could say that," I said and nodded. "None of it is particularly helpful, though."

"Care to share?" He smiled gently. "I *am* a trained psychotherapist, after all."

I looked at him. "Don't you have things you need to be doing? I don't want to monopolize you… I'm really grateful, though. I think I was about to pass out." Which would have been the crowning touch on my lack of progress.

"Never mind all that," he said. "What's going on?"

I took a deep breath and sighed. "I wish I knew," I confessed. "I seem to be at the center of something I still know absolutely nothing about."

Talking about it helped, if not to show me any answers, at least to help the shadows in my story coalesce into some kind of order. Rick knew about most of it, anyway, but was a good listener—good at his job, I supposed. He didn't interrupt, and his expression didn't change a whole lot as I started winding down. "So that's it," I finally finished. "I'm afraid something's going to happen here today. Maybe someone else getting killed, even, someone else dying because the killer wants me to suffer. But it's everybody else that suffers, the victim, everyone who cares about the victim, the whole community."

Belatedly I realized that referring to his sister-in-law as "the victim" wasn't exactly thoughtful, but I was way past that now. "If this is really about me, I wish he'd just kill me and get it over with. I'd have preferred him to kill me in the first place, and then Juliet and Will would still be around." I hiccupped slightly, I was starting to cry again and trying to stop it at the same time I was talking. "I mean, it's totally egocentric of me to talk about how all this affects me, but— I'm never going to be able to forget. I'm never going to be able to forgive myself."

"Which is," he said gently, "the intention."

I sniffed. "I thought it might be you, at the beginning, you know?" I said, trying to lighten up a little.

"Yes, I did rather have that impression," Rick said.

"I was connecting everything to Taunton," I explained. "You know how they say, follow the money? And the money leads to the casino. And you were super-involved in the project…" My voice trailed off. *Breathe, Riley. Just breathe.* "I'm sorry," I said again, inadequately. "I did at one point think you might have killed Juliet, which is beyond stupid and disrespectful, she was your family. And I even wondered if you were behind Skye Taylor's disappearance."

He nodded. "I've been following along," he said gently.

"It wasn't that random," I said. "I mean, I know everybody's been talking about it, but it's true that down in Provincetown, I *have* been involved in some situations. Um—people have died, and I've been lucky enough to be in a position to help catch the killers. And after that happening for a few years—well, I guess I've gotten used to looking around me and putting labels on people. Like *potential killer.*" I sketched air-quotes around the word and grimaced. "Maybe I could be a little less analytical and a little more humane."

Rick took my hand. "Listen to me," he said. "From what I've heard—and you're right, people talk—you've helped a lot of people find some kind of peace after violence has been done. That's a tremendous gift you've given the people who aren't with us any longer, and the people who care about them." He paused. "Don't you think this targeting shows how successful you've been? The good you've done in the world?"

"I've still killed two people," I said.

"You haven't," he said, and his voice became brisk. "You're being maudlin. Don't you think you owe Juliet and Will Fortier the same effort you gave the other victims? Don't they deserve as much?"

"Of course they do," I said.

"Then snap out of it," he said. "You think something will happen here? Then do something."

I stared at him. "Like what?"

"Get something to eat," he said reasonably. "Drink some more. Don't be alone. You have a mind for this kind of thing; you'll figure it out. The pieces will fall into place." He squeezed my hand a final time, let it go, and stood up. "You all right?"

I nodded. *Snap out of it, Riley.*

"My wife's here," he said. "I'm going to go get some lunch with her. I'll be around."

I nodded again, managed to say thank you once more, watched him disappear into the crowd. The fat tourist sighed in relief and settled closer to me on the bench. I dashed at my eyes in case there were still tears there, took a long breath to steady myself, and left him to it.

Following Rick's edict, I drifted over to the food stalls, and finally caught sight of Mirela, who was eating something sweet and sloppy from a bowl. "This is good," she announced to me when I joined her.

"Let's stick together," I said.

"It was my intention, sunshine," she said. "Try this. It is a pudding."

She was right, it was good, thick with molasses and spiced with cinnamon and ginger. "Why is it that eating something hot on a hot day feels right?"

Mirela either didn't know, or didn't care to share. Okay, so much for my attempts at light banter. "Have you seen Ali?"

She nodded, swallowed the last bite of pudding. "He is here," she said. "He is talking to the police."

Since a great deal of Ali's life involved talking with the police, this was not much of a revelation. "Okay," I said. "Let's go find him."

She dumped her empty bowl into a nearby trash can. "I think he is over there," and she indicated the very edge of the periphery near the food stalls, where a couple of tribal police cruisers were parked, presumably to fence in the spectators; beyond them were still more tents, probably for the overflow of tribal visitors to the pow-wow.

Ali was, in fact, directing some sort of operation. There were a bunch of serious-looking people in body armor, mostly men but two women also, clustered around him; after he finished talking in a low, serious voice, they dispersed quietly, efficiently. I couldn't imagine doing anything, including crime-stopping, in those get-ups.

Ali caught my eye. "I wish you'd go someplace else," he said to me.

"Nice to see you, too."

"Are you okay, *cara?*" He clearly wanted me out of there. It was a little creepy.

"I'm fine. What's going on?"

He looked around, no doubt to assure himself no one else was close enough to hear him. They weren't; the parked tribal police SUVs saw to that. "Skye Taylor's here," he said.

"For sure?" It wasn't altogether surprising, but there'd been so many false leads around her disappearance. Then I realized what he could be saying. "She's—she's not dead, is she? She's here, alive?"

He nodded. "So they said. Came to me as a text."

He wasn't looking happy. "That's good, then, right? What's wrong?" I asked.

He took a deep breath, let it out. "There was no ransom demand," he said. "Not sure why they're giving her up now, with all this operation for nothing. It doesn't work for me."

"Where is she?" asked Mirela.

"Unclear," he said. "I've got some of my people over with tribal police searching the building first. It's supposedly unoccupied."

"Except for *Weekend Waypoints*," I said. "They're filming an interview in there, or at least they were about an hour or so ago."

He hadn't known that; I could see it in his expression. Maybe the various law enforcement agencies were still having territorial disputes, just as they'd done when Juliet was killed. "Okay, thanks," he said.

I didn't know if that meant we were dismissed or not. There was a moment of silence, punctuated only by the sound of drumming from the arena, switching rhythms; I imagined a new group of dancers coming on and performing. We couldn't hear anything else; we were far enough away from the crowds here. Perhaps that was why I heard my phone ding as a text came in.

I pulled it out of my pocket without a thought other than silencing it; I'd been getting a lot of spam lately. I glanced at the text, and drew in my breath quickly. "Ali," I said.

"Yes, what?" He looked up from the map he'd taken out and was examining; it seemed to be this section of the reservation. "Ali," I said again, and he caught the urgency then.

"What is it?"

I held out my iPhone for him to see it. A photograph: Skye Taylor, in a typical hostage shot, sitting on the floor with her knees drawn up to her chest, her wrists manacled, a cloth around her mouth.

She still looked beautiful.

The text read, *She's here. Recognize the place, Sydney?*

Ali looked from it to me. "Do you?"

"I'm not sure," I said unhappily. It was a small space, the wall behind her looked like metal.

Ali grabbed his walkie-talkie and spoke urgently into it. "Hakim," he said. "Just got a text from the perp. Hold tight." He turned back to me. "Try again. Is it familiar?"

I shook my head. It was, but I couldn't place it.

Then the phone dinged again and another message came through. *Just you and your husband,* it said.

"Answer it," said Ali.

"And say what?"

He thought for a few seconds. "Ask them where," he said.

And that was when it really started to get scary.

Chapter Twenty-Six

The answer came back immediately: *Call off the police.*

I looked at Ali. "Give me the phone," he said, his hand out. I gave it to him and watched over his shoulder as he punched in a reply. *Need more information before that can happen.*

Seconds crawled agonizingly by. There was something about that photo, something familiar, lapping irritatingly at the edges of my mind, like something you see out of the corner of your eye but that disappears when you try to focus on it. I knew that place. It wasn't in the tribal building; I'd only ever been in the entrance hall, and this was smaller, enclosed...

Another photograph: Skye, in the same position, but now with a gun held against her temple. All you could see of the person holding the gun was the lower part of a man's arm; impossible to see what he was wearing. And the text. *Don't think too hard. Call off the police or it's a body you're going to find.*

Ali seemed to know when he could push them and when he couldn't. He immediately keyed his walkie-talkie again. "Everyone. Hold your positions. I repeat, hold your positions. Sanchez, where are you?"

His set crackled and a male voice responded. "Second floor tribal building. Nobody here. I'm watching the area."

"Hold," said Ali tersely and handed me the walkie-talkie so he could text into my phone. *Done. What do you want?*

The answer came back immediately. *Just the happy couple. No one else. Sydney and Ali, sitting in a tree...*

Ali nodded, the gesture automatic as they couldn't see him. Or could they? I looked around. No drones overhead that I could see, but we were on a slight rise and anyone near the arena with a decent pair of binoculars could easily have us in their sights. And they'd waited to text me until I was standing near Ali.

He was typing. *Where?*

Sydney knows where. Come on, Sydney, you know you know it.

Ali was looking at me. "Do you?"

I shook my head. "It's familiar, but…"

He zoomed in on the photo. "Look again."

My hands were shaking as I took the phone back, passing the walkie-talkie to Mirela. Metal. A small metal space. Cramped. I looked more closely. A couple of electrical cords on the floor, and…

"It's a van," I said suddenly. "It's the *Weekend Waypoints* van."

"You sure?"

I nodded. "They have two vans, one with seats, the other for equipment, and it doesn't have windows in the back," I said. "It's the only thing that fits, but I don't see *how*. They don't have anything to do with her."

"Apparently they do," he said, and took the phone back. *Weekend Waypoints*, he texted.

Good girl, Sydney. I knew you could do it.

"Ask them who's talking," I said to Ali. "I can't believe anyone there is doing this."

Mirela said, a little diffidently, "They are the common denominator."

"What are you talking about?"

She seemed ridiculously calm. "The Wampanoag woman disappearing, Juliet Mills being killed, Will Fortier finding out something bad. Always a connection with the television show."

I shook my head. "I thought *I* was the connection," I said.

"It can be two things at once."

"But who? Which one?" A part of my brain, idiotically, was saying, *Stacey isn't smart enough…*

Ali had been thinking while we were talking, and his thoughts had paralleled mine. He typed, *Who am I speaking to? Who is this?*

Does it matter? Now you know where she is. You can come and get her. But just Sydney and Ali. I want both of you. Anyone else, and the girl's dead.

It matters, Ali typed. *Need to know what we're getting into.*

You're about to be a hero, that's what you're getting into. Our own Dudley Do-Right. Stop when you get close to the van. Do not go in, or she's dead. Do not call anyone for backup, or she's dead. There was a pause, then: *Go now.*

Ali and I looked at each other, then Ali typed, quickly, *This is Ali. Sydney isn't coming. I'll come alone.*

Then the Indian girl is dead.

"I have to go," I said. "You know I have to. Come on, we can't waste time."

He took back his walkie-talkie from Mirela and spoke into it. "Locate the two television vans. Do not go near them. Set up a perimeter around them, and don't let anybody through until I get there." He waited until he received a response, then looked at me. "Ready?"

I nodded. I'd been wrong about them, wrong about the anxious Bruce, the airhead Stacey, the competent Cally. I felt as if I were driving a car skidding out of control. "Ready," I said.

Mirela cried, "You cannot go! He will kill you both!"

Ali turned to her. "I want you to find Derek. You know him, right? Tell him what's happening."

"And what is happening, exactly? You and Sydney will die."

"Not if I can help it," said Ali, perhaps unconsciously touching the holstered Glock pistol on his belt. "Come on," he said to me.

We were as far away from the vans as we could possibly be. I followed him as he threaded his way through the crowd, everyone around us oblivious, taking pictures and eating fried bread and buying trinkets. I could feel my heart thudding in my chest, and I thought, absurdly, that this wasn't going to work if I passed out.

"What's the plan?" I managed to ask.

"We'll do as they say. For now." He still had the walkie-talkie in his hand and depressed the button. "Get ready to move."

"Copy that."

It was probably only a few minutes, but it felt like an eternity. The faces in the crowd became a blur as we moved through them, the riotous colors, the tourists and tribal members all merging into one, waves of people we had to fight our way through.

They'd already set up the perimeter; I had no idea how they'd managed it so quickly, but as we got closer, the people thinned out, and then we were standing near the vans. No one was sitting in the people-carrier one. No one was anywhere around. The other van, the one where they were holding Skye, was closed up tightly. We stopped a few feet away from it, making ourselves obvious targets.

I'd done something wrong. I hadn't figured anything out. And now it looked probable that one or both of us was about to die. It was the only conclusion. They were holding her for ransom, after all: we'd just gotten the price wrong.

The price was our lives.

Ali motioned for me to stop and handed me the phone. "Tell them we're here."

My hands were shaking. *Breathe, Riley,* I reminded myself, and steadied myself enough to text. *What now?*

Now, the answer came back, *Special Agent Hakim can come and get her.*

It was wrong. It felt wrong. "If they're in there, they have to know they won't get away with it," I said to Ali. "What are they *doing?*"

"Maybe they aren't there," he said. "Stay here."

I looked at the van. It seemed so innocuous, the cheerful *Weekend Waypoints* logo on the side, everything so ordinary. Just filming an event for their show. A fun-nothing show. A show that told people where to go on vacation.

Ali started walking toward the van.

And then I saw him. Everything suddenly stopped, resumed in unbearably slow motion. Not Bruce; Adam Bennett, the director, inching forward from behind the van, an electric wire in his hands. And Ali, reaching the door, putting out his hand, and I remembered Bruce's words: Adam wasn't around, he was "doing something electrical." And I screamed, "Don't touch that handle!"

Ali froze immediately. He was that good.

Adam dropped the wire and ran, and without thinking, I ran after him.

We were on the periphery of the grounds, the drumming still going on behind us, the singing, so beautiful and ordinary; but Adam was running toward the entrance, toward the road, and he was going to get away. I don't remember what I was thinking, just running. He'd wanted my husband dead, he'd already killed at least two people, and he couldn't do that.

No one stopped him.

If he made it to the road and could get around the parked cars lined up on either side of it, he could disappear into the nearby wealthy suburb of New Seabury, the one that had displaced so many of the Wampanoag, and be gone, perhaps forever. Get away with it, with all of it.

I was starting to get a stitch in my side but I ran on, my breath becoming ragged, and I knew I was slowing down, I knew I couldn't make it. "Stop him!" I screamed at the top of what my lungs could manage, still running, and then there was a blur of color and Adam stumbled as a big bird tackled him, feathers and colors going down, and I realized it was Rick Thatcher.

We were in the midst of the tents set up in the front of the tribal land, the tents of the dancers and drummers and vendors who'd come here from so many tribes to be part of this beautiful ceremony. And in that moment I think I hated him as much for disrespecting their celebration as I did for him trying to kill Ali.

There were two tribal police officers there now, pulling Adam to his feet, placing him in handcuffs, and I just stood there, bent over, winded, sucking air in. *Just breathe, Riley. Just breathe.*

I straightened up eventually and made my way, far more slowly, back to the vehicles now clustered around the *Weekend Waypoint* vans; they'd moved quickly. Ali, I was thinking; I had to make sure Ali was okay.

The van door was open, and a uniformed officer was helping Skye out of it; someone had wrapped a blanket around her, and she was moving slowly and with some difficulty, but she was alive. She was alive, and she was home.

Ali was standing talking to a knot of people, most of them men, most of them in uniform. He caught sight of me and turned away from the group with his arms out, and I ran into them.

"You're okay, you're okay," I was sobbing, and he held me tight.

"*Cara. Cara.* Are you all right?"

I managed to nod and he tightened his arms around me even more. "It's over," he whispered. "It's all right, it's over."

But I wasn't so sure.

***

Things got a little blurry for me after that.

We ended up in the tribal offices, sitting in a nondescript conference room smelling of coffee, and I was shivering in the air conditioning—that alone felt odd, after being overheated all day. But maybe my body was reacting to the stress.

All the various alphabet branches were present: the state cops, the tribal police, the Mashpee police, a guy from the FBI, and a couple of Ali's people from the anti-trafficking squad.

It did seem as if it was over. Adam was in custody. No one could find Bruce Peterson, whether to tell him about Adam or to question him was unclear to me; but people were looking for him. At the very least he was losing his director sooner than he'd envisioned.

Stacey had reportedly fainted and had been transported to Cape Cod Hospital in Hyannis.

Mirela was sitting beside me, calm and collected and steadying me with her presence. Ali was still outside, looking after Skye Taylor, organizing things. The pow-wow had paused so Derek could make the happy announcement over the loudspeaker: Sokanon had been located, was healthy and well. A cheer had gone up from the crowd at the news. She had refused transportation to the hospital, and a Wampanoag doctor had checked her out on the spot; she was sitting with the tribal elders, watching the dancing resume.

She'd vowed to join them the next day.

The tribal police interviewed me, were calm and courteous and took my phone; presumably I'd get it back eventually. Mirela drifted away but joined us again after the interview when all the alphabet soup of law enforcement agencies assembled in the conference room. I only really recognized one of them—Detective Lieutenant Alice Whitney; it was clear from the look she gave me she didn't like me any better now than she had back in Marstons Mills.

I could live with that.

Mostly I could live with my husband being alive; I was having a delayed reaction to his near-death experience, shivering in the air conditioning. I had a tendency to take Ali for granted, and I was belatedly realizing how close I'd come—again—to losing him. I found my hands were shaking; I clasped them in my lap so it wouldn't show, but I knew the state cop was watching me and she was aware of how much I was shattered.

No doubt the others did, too, but they at least extended me the courtesy of not staring.

By now they were all mostly talking about how Adam had wired the electricity, talking about things I didn't even want to understand, saying he'd "tied in live to four hundred eighty volts" and other specifics concerning how he'd electrified the handle on the van's door. It was all a little sickening. I kept getting an image in my mind of Ali reaching for the handle and what would have happened to him if he'd touched it. I remembered reading Sylvia Plath's memoir and how she'd imagined the judicial killing of the Rosenbergs, likening their electrocutions to being burned alive all through their veins. And it had sickened Sylvia Plath, too, if I was remembering correctly.

They wanted to dissect the *how* of the murder attempt, but what I wanted to know was the *why*. I had to know. If Ali had died, it would have been because of me.

That was what was really clear. The note left in Juliet Mills's pocket: "Now Sydney Riley will know what it feels like to be responsible for a death." The message scrawled on Will Fortier's forehead: "For Sydney Riley." Adam hadn't needed to leave a message with Ali—he wanted to make me *watch* this death.

And I still had no idea why he hated me so much. My instinct had been correct: Skye Taylor's abduction was linked to the murders. Adam must have known from the start that anything involving human trafficking on the Cape would of necessity involve Ali. And killing him in front of me was a bit of a *pièce de résistance*, even I had to admit that. But I still didn't know why.

The voices droned on around me, and I was feeling colder and colder. If I had to stay there much longer, I was going to have to do something about that.

Mirela, beside me, had figured it out. "You are in shock. There is a sweater in my car," she whispered. "I will go and fetch it for you, sunshine."

"Give me the keys," I whispered back; unlike me, Mirela didn't leave her keys in her unlocked car. To be fair, her new Jaguar was higher on the list of Vehicles Most Likely To Be Stolen than was my Honda Civic. "I'll get it. I need the air."

She didn't argue, which had to be a first, pulling a fob from her purse and passing it to me under the table. Maybe now that the danger was over, she felt her babysitting duties were over. Or maybe she just realized that I needed some space on my own, now that there wasn't any adrenaline coursing through my veins. I could still taste it, though, metallic in my mouth. I stood up, announced to no one in particular that I'd be right back, and headed outside.

The heat hit me as soon as I was through the door, and it seemed absurd I was going for a sweater, but any action was better than sitting in a cold conference room listening to the postmortem. Ali was nowhere to be seen, and it only took me a few minutes to reach Mirela's car.

That was when the plan went awry.

I was sitting in the driver's seat, reaching into the sports car's absurdly small space behind me for the cashmere sweater—of course it was cashmere, it was Mirela's, after all—when the passenger door opened and Bruce Peterson got in. "Don't move," he said pleasantly.

My heart did a quick somersault, and not in a good way.

"I'll take the fob, too," he said, holding out his hand closest to me. I probably would have argued the point, except he had a gun in his other hand. Absurdly, I wondered if he knew Massachusetts has a mandatory eighteen-month sentence for carrying an illegal firearm; *like that would make a difference to him, Riley.*

I gave him the fob.

"Good girl." He didn't take his eyes off me.

I swallowed hard. If I couldn't figure out why Adam had it in for me, I could even less figure out why Bruce might. "It was Adam who killed them, wasn't it?" I asked.

"Partly." He was holding the gun in his right hand, low down; anyone passing by would just see two people sitting in a car having a conversation. Even if he didn't keep it pointing at me, I couldn't have escaped: you don't get into an F-Type so much as you put it on, like a garment. He'd have plenty of time to aim if I attempted to extricate myself.

Besides, I really wanted to know the answer.

Bruce was checking out the area; seeing we were alone, he relaxed slightly—I hadn't realized he'd been holding his breath, but I could feel it when he let it out. "Your reporter friend," he said. "Um—Fortier, wasn't that his name?"

"Will Fortier," I said.

"Right. That was Adam."

"And Juliet?"

"All mine," he said.

I shook my head. "I don't get it," I said. "Why?"

He was both scanning the area and keeping an eye on me. "We had the conversation, you and I, back in Boston," he said. "Adam wanted me to give you some clues. He thought that might be fun. Don't you remember?"

"You'll have to forgive me," I said acidly. "A few things have happened in the meantime."

Bruce gave an exaggerated sigh; apparently I'd been meant to memorize his every word. "Everyone's tightening their belts," he said. "*Weekend Waypoints* is still popular, sure, but we've got a lot of online competition, and they're looking to save money where they can."

I stared at him. I did remember. We'd been talking about Juliet's tenure on the show. I could hear Bruce's voice as clearly as if he'd just repeated the words. "The executive producer's starting to think we don't need two producers on every episode. She would've survived, she has seniority and I don't think there's anyone in the business who can think of *Weekend Waypoints* without her."

My eyes widened and I just stared at him. "Wait. You killed Juliet because you wanted her *job?*"

"You make it sound so crass," he complained. "I liked Juliet. I liked working with her; we just clicked. Don't get me wrong; I even learned a lot from her. But I was always going to be second-in-command anytime she was around, and, as I told you, they're looking to cut costs. Producers don't come cheap. I was the obvious layoff." He paused. "I'd have thought you might have figured that out."

I hadn't figured out anything, apparently.

Bruce went on. "I'd never find another job in the field if I lost this one, there's too much competition and I'm too old to start anything new. And I'm one of those people, Sydney, who doesn't have much of a life outside of my work. My work is everything."

It had been for Juliet, too, but I didn't bother pointing that out. He knew.

"And then there was the money," he added.

"What money?"

He smiled. "My job's everything," he said. "But a little insurance is never a bad idea."

"You stole money?" Something was starting to make a little sense here.

"Got it. Finally. The idea was to make it look like Adam took it," he said. "He was in a position to do the embezzlement from the department. Well, so was I; but Adam planned on disappearing as soon as we took care of your husband. I was going to stay on."

"With your precious job," I said.

He ignored me. "Looks like that's gonna be the way to go, now. And Juliet would have figured it out in the end, so that was another good reason to take care of her first."

"You and Adam planned this together?" If I kept asking inane questions, it made for extra time when I wasn't getting shot.

"Funny how life sometimes puts just the right person in your path," he said. "I don't know what I would've done if I hadn't run into Adam, if I hadn't hired him for the show. He knew all along, of course, it's why he applied. I didn't think anything of it, we always have churn. I suspect he did something to nudge the former director out the door. And Juliet was always okay with me making the hiring decisions."

"You—and Adam?" I asked, a little bemused, trying for flippant. "What's that about? I'd have though he was a little young for you."

He chuckled. "I do like your politically correct spirit, Sydney," he said. "No, we're not gay. It's what you might call a marriage of convenience. I wanted to do something about Juliet, and he wanted to do something about you."

And there it was again. "Why?" I wailed. "Why? "What did I do to him?"

"I told you that, too," Bruce said. "I gave you all the clues you needed, Sydney. We wanted to see how the famous Provincetown crime-stopper worked. Not too well, it would seem. I kept telling you and telling you." He gave an exaggerated sigh. "Okay, for those in the back of the room: remember yesterday, in Starbucks? When we were talking about Adam leaving the show? I told you his brother had died a couple of years back?"

I stared at him. I could in fact remember the conversation, though I'd paid it scant attention at the time. Bruce saying Adam had been through a lot, grieving the death of his brother, who had been "literally stabbed in the back." And when Mirela asked, idly, with only a vague polite interest in the response, whether they'd caught the brother's killer, Bruce had said...

Didn't matter because the guy was already serving a life sentence.

My blood really did feel cold, that same electric current running up and down my nerves. We'd been right: it was revenge, after all. Revenge for my helping put someone in prison, someone who'd gotten killed in some prison dispute, someone who would still be alive and healthy and walking the earth if it hadn't been for Sydney Riley.

It was one of the names on The List.

He watched me work it out, and when I did, it was blazingly, unforgivably obvious. "Kai Bennett," I said softly. Adam hadn't been shy about introducing himself to me; in fact, he'd done it three different times, extending his hand to shake mine, watching to see if I responded to his name. "Adam Bennett."

And I still hadn't caught on.

Not just that: my mother had even reminded me of it, obliquely, when she'd called about the whale watch. "That nice naturalist," she'd said, and I'd latched right onto it. "Kai Bennett. He isn't there anymore."

Yeah, I could have been a little more dense, but not by much.

"He killed two people," I said slowly, stupidly. "Kai did. *He* put himself in that prison. *He* put himself in that situation."

Bruce smiled. "You know, actually, I agree with you about that. Believe it or not. But—and here I'm speaking candidly, you understand—Adam is just a little obsessed. Fine: I don't have a problem with anyone's kinks." He shrugged. "But he'd been following you since Kai's trial, saw you give evidence, and that started this whole fixation he had. Well, you can imagine. Anyway, I went by his place one night for a drink after work, back when we were first thinking about doing this, doing a little planning, and do you know, he has a whole *closet* dedicated to you. Can you imagine? That's a little bit over the top. Real serial-killer vibe. Pictures of you, your family, your inn, your house in Cambridge…"

"I don't have a house in Cambridge," I said. My goosebumps had developed goosebumps.

Bruce ignored me. "And that whole messages thing? To get you all riled up about the past? That was great. Took the pressure off me. He got his revenge, and I got my job security, and some decent money on top of it. It was a win-win sort of thing." He paused, considering his words. "Well, not for Juliet or the reporter or your husband, maybe."

There was too much coming at me, too fast. Kai. Noah. A death closet. I took a deep breath and steadied myself.

It was also occurring to me that what we were doing wasn't terribly smart from Bruce's perspective. The longer we stayed sitting there, parked in front of the pow-wow, the greater the chances of a passer-by noticing us, of one of the law-enforcement types out looking for Bruce seeing him… or of Mirela coming to see what was taking me so long. This was all to my advantage, of course, but Bruce wasn't stupid. He had something in mind.

He wasn't finished. "I'm sorry about the reporter, by the way. He was collateral damage. I met him, did you know that? He interviewed me. I was sorry he had to go."

I seized on that. Maybe keeping him talking was a good thing. "Why?" I asked. "Why did he have to go? What did he find out?"

Bruce was following his own train of thought. "It's good we didn't have to take out anybody else," he said pleasantly. "Your Wampanoag friend was starting to have some ideas. I talked to him, too. Rick Thatcher. Juliet's brother-in-law. I didn't want that many bodies piling up."

It was the way he said her name that got me, more even than his casual mention of possibly needing to kill Rick. "You *liked* Juliet," I said. "How could you look her in the eyes while you were strangling her? How could you do that?"

It was the only question that really mattered, at the end of the day. *How could you do that?* And after more than a decade of being somewhat peripherally involved in murders, the question was still as fresh and real for me as it had been that first time, when I'd found

Barry's body floating in the pool at the inn: how can someone think their aims and desires and priorities were so important they made it acceptable to take someone else's life, their future, their whole being? How do you sleep at night? I remembered sitting in a booth at Chach's in Provincetown, asking Julie Agassi the same question. She hadn't been able to give me any comfort, any real answer. Either you thought that way, with you at the center of the universe, or you didn't.

Bruce did.

He wasn't interested in talking about Juliet. "So now here we are," he said.

I didn't like the sound of that, but okay, he was right. I'd have to shelve my philosophical musings for the moment. "What's your plan now?" I asked. "Adam's in custody, Ali's alive, Skye Taylor's alive. Adam's going to talk; you know he's going to talk, and after everything you've done, you've lost *Weekend Waypoints,* after all. No job, no embezzlement. This was all for *nothing.*"

That seemed, somehow, additionally unfair. Two people had died, and while Adam had gotten what he wanted, at least in terms of my feeling the deaths were on my shoulders, Bruce clearly hadn't. "There's nothing you can do about that, and there's nowhere you can go. They're looking for you, I heard them say so. If it were me, I'd be hightailing it out of here as fast as I could, but hey, you do you. What's the plan?"

He was in no hurry to tell me. "I think we'll just go for a drive," he said.

I hadn't exactly not expected it, but hearing the words still made me feel like I might throw up. "Killing me won't help," I said. Killing me would be astonishingly stupid, in fact, but I didn't think it would be helpful to point that out. Still, it was true: his goal had been to go on with his life here, in Boston, keeping his nice job and his nice home, and that was clearly no longer an option. He wasn't an idiot.

He had a Plan B. And I was apparently part of it.

295

Chapter Twenty-Seven

I kept talking; as long as I was talking, we weren't going anywhere. "And this is a really, really stupid car to take," I said. "I mean,
it's gorgeous, right? People stop and look at it when Mirela drives
anywhere." Given Mirela's driving, the fact of it still looking pristine
was a minor miracle in itself. "You really want to try and escape in a
car everyone watches? Listen: I have a Honda. A Civic, one that
looks like hundreds of other Civics. Let's take that one."

Something I'd said had bothered him. "Adam's not talking," he
said, suddenly.

"What on earth makes you say that?" I demanded.

"We have an arrangement."

"That's shot to hell now," I responded. "He didn't get what he
wanted, and you did. You got Juliet; congratulations. For him, this
was all just prelude. He wanted to avenge Kai. He wanted to see my
face while I watched my husband die horribly. That was his endgame. And he didn't get it. Whatever little pinky-promise you boys
had together went out the window when that happened; you're the
only thing he has to bargain with now." *Calm down, Riley; you don't have
to actually speed things up here.*

He looked, if anything, amused. "For someone who took so long
to figure out what was going on," he said, "you seem to have a lot of
opinions about things you don't understand."

"You try having a gun pointed at you," I said. "It clarifies thinking." Or something like that.

"Right." He sighed. "Love to go on chatting with you, Sydney,
but we have places to go, people to see." He looked around again;

no-one was paying any attention to us. The pow-wow was the draw; and for anyone craving a little more excitement, there was still activity around the *Weekend Waypoints* vehicles. Or so I presumed; as I'd said, I was pretty focused on the gun still pointing my way. "Start the car. And don't pretend you can't, that would be just too cliché, even for you."

"I wasn't planning on pretending anything." Of course I was planning to pretend I didn't know how the car worked. Or would have if I'd thought of it.

I pressed the starter button, and the Jaguar's engine roared nicely. I glanced at Bruce; he wasn't amused. "Seatbelt," he said, and fastened his own as I was clicking mine in place, no small feat while holding a gun. I'd be impressed, if I lived to tell the tale. "Pull onto the road, slowly," he said.

I did. I wasn't seeing what else I could do, and, besides, he wasn't going to shoot me while we were in motion; the one thing he didn't strike me as was suicidal. Traffic was moderate, latecomers to the pow-wow searching earnestly for somewhere to park their cars; as soon as I pulled out one lucky SUV—that was never going to fit into the space I'd left—started trying to maneuver in, which held up the flow behind us for some time.

I kept checking my mirrors, waiting for flashing blue lights. Someone must have noticed us. Mirela must have been getting concerned by now about the time it was taking me to fetch a sweater.

On the other hand, Mirela knew only too well my ability to be absorbed by *bright shining things*, as she'd put it. She might not be giving it any thought.

"Stay on Great Neck Road," said Bruce, pleasantly. "Through the rotary."

I'd hoped we could get onto Route 28, which was always very busy, with a whole lot of red lights where someone might notice us; and I actually legitimately missed the exit off the rotary because I was still coping with a car I'd never driven and a weapon pointing my way, along with traffic headed to the Mashpee Commons. "I'll do it, I'll do it," I said, a little desperately, and got it on the second try.

I wish I could say that in the twenty minutes we spent driving I'd come up with something to do; the truth was, I couldn't even come up with anything to say. That was all behind us now. There was just the car, and the roads, and Bruce.

I'd liked him, damn it. I thought briefly about saying so, decided not to, and then changed my mind; what the hell. "You seemed so nice," I complained.

"I *am* nice," said Bruce. "All I wanted was to keep my job. And, of course, have a little money set aside if I needed it. I did a decent job of setting Juliet up to take the fall for that, though. Her, or Adam. I had alternatives. It was a good plan."

"If it had worked," I pointed out.

He seemed to remember why we were there. "Just drive," he said.

Okay; we weren't finding common ground there. I shut up and drove.

After a while Great Neck Road fizzled out, and I saw with some shock we were in Marstons Mills, perilously close to Margo's house. What were we doing here? Did he know where I'd been staying? Were we going to barricade ourselves in her home and end things in a flurry of gunfire, a Billy-the-Kid moment? How had he found out? What was…?

But we passed by the turn that would have taken us to her place and kept going, and after another moment, Bruce said, "take a left here."

I saw the sign before I made the turn. "Here" was the small Cape Cod Airfield. The place where I'd tried unsuccessfully in the past to plane-spot. I hadn't seen this one coming; but then, I was starting to realize I hadn't seen a whole lot of things coming.

A few cars in the small dirt parking lot; a few general-aviation airplanes tied down, the bright red biplane used to take people up for rides, a few small propeller planes and a couple of larger ones that looked too heavy for the airfield's short runways but which obviously managed to land and take off. I hesitated, but Bruce pointed beyond the office. "Over there."

We were as bright as the biplane and far more incongruous. Someone was going to stop us, surely. There were people here, an airport manager, pilots, someone was going to say something. But we bumped our way past the building on the grass and a couple of people came out and stared at us, one with a cup of coffee still in his hand, but then we were beyond them and in front of us was a gleaming Cessna Skyhawk.

(Yes, I knew what it was. I can't help myself, I did mention a recent aviation obsession. More *bright shining things*. I recognized the plane. I had a feeling I might be about to experience it far more intimately than I'd imagined.)

"Pull in over there," Bruce said, pointing to a spot near the plane's right wingtip. The people in the parking lot had lost interest in us; anyone who can own and operate a private aircraft can certainly also afford an F-Type: the price of fuel alone would see to that, not to mention maintenance, hangarage, and so on… I let my thoughts drift that way for a moment. Much better than imagining my own potentially immediate demise.

I stopped the car. Bruce said, "Don't move until I tell you to, Sydney. Here's what's going to happen. We're getting into the airplane. Be careful approaching it, and watch your head, don't hit it on the wing. Do you understand?"

I nodded. I couldn't take my eyes off the plane, the big propeller.

"You're sitting in the front," Bruce said. "Get in, and we'll tell you what to do next.

Now, drop your keys behind you. Good. Take your seatbelt off. Okay. I want you to open your door, *slowly*, and get out, *slowly*. Do it."

I did it.

He got out and whipped around the Jaguar so fast I was barely conscious of him moving; now he was behind me, and I felt the gun's muzzle in my back.

I was pretty sure if I got into that airplane I was going to die. I was also pretty sure I would if I didn't, too, and there was no reason to hurry things up. For once, I didn't have to urge myself to breathe: I was gulping air like I'd never tasted it before.

"Go on," Bruce said from behind me.

I went on.

The cabin was a lot smaller than I'd anticipated; it was a bit of a squeeze, but I managed to watch my head and get in, awkwardly, and pull myself into the right-hand seat. Bruce was behind me, pulling the door shut, fastening it.

The pilot sitting in the left-hand seat glanced at me; he seemed young, but I couldn't tell much else about him, as he was wearing wraparound sunglasses and a headset. Paid lackey? Co-conspirator?

He was an unknown entity, and I certainly couldn't count on his help. If I got so far as to need it.

The pilot reached past me and pulled another belt across me, and then held up another headset. I fumbled it on.

Bruce's voice was immediately in my ear. "Stay still and shut up," he said, his voice tinny. "Most of all, don't touch anything. Don't move your feet. Don't move your hands. Don't do anything with the yoke. Do you understand?"

I nodded, then croaked something. I cleared my throat. "I understand."

The pilot was muttering, a long string of words in my headset I recognized vaguely from my YouTube viewing as preflight checks. "Elevator trim set for takeoff, mixture rich, throttle open to one-eighth inch, primer cold start, battery master on, gauges alive.." He reached over and literally just pushed a button—it was that easy—and the engine roared to life, the propeller started turning, and I thought again I was going to throw up. I swallowed, hard. The only thing I was sure about was that I was *not* going to die in a puddle of vomit.

Of course, just because I was interested in aviation didn't mean I wanted to actually aviate. Especially under these circumstances.

The voice was still in my ear, calm. "RPMs coming up, pressure coming up, pressure positive."

The Skyhawk started moving, bumping its way away from any chance of hope I might have of rescue, leaving buildings and people and other vehicles behind.

There were brakes on my side of the cockpit. I wondered if I should hit them. I wondered if that would mean delay (good) or death (bad).

"Trim set, mixture rich, magneto and masters on, prop on, fixed pitch…"

Bruce wasn't going to shoot me now. With the bumpy progress we were making across the grass, he could just as easily put a hole in the fuselage instead of putting one in me; but I also couldn't see how I could do anything to stop our progress. I could grab the yoke; I could …

"Nav lights on, controls full free and correct, oil temp coming up into the green…"

I tried closing my eyes but the not-insignificant bumps jarred them open again. What was going to happen once we were airborne? Why did he need me to come along on his little getaway?

"Flaps set ten degrees, visually confirm ten degrees, Ts and Ps in the green…"

We'd trundled our way down to the end of the field and were coming around to line up on what I imagined they called a runway. My heart was racing in time to the engine as the pilot revved it way up. I did the only thing I could think of. *Hail Mary, full of grace, the Lord is with you* …

Were they going to throw me out of the airplane? It would be tricky, but for all I knew, feasible. *Blessed are you among women…*

The voice droned on in my ear. "Check for traffic, clear base, clear final, line up on center line…" He could see a center line on the grass? *Holy Mary, Mother of God, pray for us sinners, now and at the hour of our death…* Which might be coming sooner rather than later.

The engine quieted momentarily and then started picking up again as we began moving in earnest, gathering speed as we went. I closed my eyes again. *Hail Mary, full of—* The pilot yelled an expletive and I opened my eyes and there it was in front of us, a police helicopter hovering over the field, low enough that we were going to hit it if we kept accelerating.

I made a mental note to thank Our Lady later.

***

There was still, of course, the little matter of the man in the backseat with a gun.

The Skyhawk came juddering to a stop, and the helicopter landed and some guys, most of them in tactical gear, came spilling out of it. They didn't matter: the only one I could see was Ali.

They surrounded the airplane and the pilot cut the engine. The propeller slowed and stopped, and the pilot took his hands off the controls and put them in the air, obviously deciding that in his case, discretion was the better part of valor.

The gunshot behind me was deafening.

Chapter Twenty-Eight

I was packing to go home.

Wally came out from wherever he'd been lurking to watch. I could almost read his mind. *Nice to have seen you, don't let the door hit you on your way out.*

Provincetown was calling. There were things to do. A yacht stranded in the harbor with mechanical problems had dumped eighteen annoyed, entitled people on the Race Point Inn. Lily wanted Mirela and Ali and me back for a long-planned visit to climb the Pilgrim Monument. We had dinner reservations at The Mews.

Adam Bennett was in custody and likely to stay there; eventually I'd have to go and testify against him, too. He was, or so I heard, completely unrepentant and furious he hadn't achieved his long-anticipated act of revenge.

The jury is still out on that one, actually. I was forever changed by what he'd done, and why; the revenge may have been partial from his point of view, but it was still pretty successful in its effects on me. He had something to remember when Kai's senseless death played over and over in his dreams.

The woman he'd hired to help with Skye's abduction and act as her jailer in Boston—Kerry Thomas—cut some sort of deal; I never heard exactly what. Margo was back with Wally and grieving the man she'd loved like a son.

And Skye Taylor danced at the Mashpee Wampanoag pow-wow, resplendent in a jingle dress she had made herself.

Bruce's final Plan B remained a mystery. It was shocking but not altogether surprising he'd chosen to kill himself; what I didn't understand was how he thought he'd get away. The pilot-owner of the Skyhawk had been engaged to take him—with or without me—to Beverly, another small airfield on the North Shore, but beyond that no one could trace what he meant to do. Some mysteries will always stay mysterious. Meantime, I had enough to cope with, quite a lot of Bruce's blood and other unspeakable things having been blasted over my head and shoulders. It took several very long hot showers for me to feel clean again, and that was just on the outside.

I had a feeling some intense therapy was in my future. Perhaps even with Rick Thatcher.

Ali and I had reached a new level in our relationship. We had taken greater risks with each other, and those risks had paid off. I resolved to pay more attention to his emotional needs, so different from mine.

Thea, who despite my suspicions had attended the pow-wow without ulterior motive and purely out of interest, moved back to Provincetown. "They're my people," she said, simply, when I asked her why. We all have tribes, federally recognized or not: the people we cherish, who live together in as much harmony as humans will ever achieve.

I was better positioned, now, to help my tribe; to stop moaning about what was happening to P'town and to instead support and sustain the town, to help empower others. There were people out there who wanted to make Provincetown into something it didn't want to be, and making snide remarks about it on Facebook was just a self-serving echo chamber: it wasn't going to help. We had to do more than that, *be* more than that.

In the meantime, with Mike's blessing and Wendy's help, I set up a permanent art gallery space at the inn, and invited the artists driven out of the old Cortile Gallery to show their work there. Mirela offered use of her studio space. Incremental changes, but it would all help. It wasn't about fighting back: it was about changing the rules. Wealth alone won't impart intelligence or empathy—but we had plenty of both.

And I now owned, it seemed, a house in Cambridge: Noah gave up on his quid pro quo; eventually he'd go to trial, and it seemed inevitable he would wind up in prison himself. He had, we learned later, indeed poisoned his wife, for reasons I had no interest in knowing. That was one trial I wasn't attending. The paperwork for the house was going through. I had absolutely no idea what I was going to do with it, but it was mine.

Ali and Mirela and I were all alive. That counted for everything.

***

On Saturday before we left, we were invited to sit with the elders at the pow-wow. Derek was there, and Rick and Eloise, and together we watched as Wampanoag and other tribal sisters performed a jingle dance.

And Skye Taylor was in the center of them all.

Author's Note

As usual, most of what I've written about here in terms of background is true.

Human trafficking is an underreported, ongoing cluster of crimes I guarantee is happening right now in whatever community you call home. In the United States, human trafficking formally became a federal crime in 2000 via the Trafficking Victims Protection Act. It is a global concern, however, and governments worldwide are moving in the direction of better enforcement.

My character Ali Hakim works for the DHS Center for Countering Human Trafficking, which advances counter-human trafficking law enforcement operations, protects victims, and enhances prevention. The CCHT provides identification and screening, enforcement and investigations, victim protection/assistance, and training and outreach.

***

The Mashpee Wampanoag (correctly rendered Wôpanâak) are one of three surviving tribes of the original sixty-nine in the Wampanoag Nation, though not all still live on their ancestral lands. Many people use the word "Indian" or "American Indian" to describe them; better to refer to indigenous people by their tribal affiliation, or as being "native."

The name Wampanoag means *People of the First Light*.

After an arduous process lasting more than three decades, the Mashpee Wampanoag were re-acknowledged as a federally recognized tribe in 2007. In 2015, the federal government declared 150 acres of land in Mashpee and 170 acres of land in Taunton as the tribe's initial reservation, on which the tribe can exercise full tribal sovereignty rights.

The Wampanoag currently comprises approximately 3,200 enrolled citizens. Most live in Massachusetts, where there are two federally acknowledged tribes, the Aquinnah Wampanoag and the Mashpee Wampanoag, as well as several smaller bands in areas like Herring Pond, Assonet, and Manomet. In the Caribbean Islands there are also descendants of Wampanoag people, those sold into slavery after losing the war with the English—known to history as King Philip's War—in the 1670s.

If you can, attend a pow-wow—any pow-wow. You're sure to find the experience enriching. Festivals aren't confined to the communities that give birth to them; they're invitations to witness each other's light, to celebrate the human impulse toward meaning and connection that transcends any single path.

For more information on the story included in one section of this novel, you can check out Paula Peters' excellent book and documentary, *Mashpee Nine: A Story of Cultural Justice*. And for general history, *This Land is Their Land: The Wampanoag Indians, Plymouth Colony, and the Troubled History of Thanksgiving* by David Silverman is quite good.

Lee Roscoe's *Wampanoag Art* will give you some stunning visuals.

Also worth reading is the novel *Caleb's Crossing*, by Geraldine Brooks, about a friendship between a Puritan minister's daughter and the first native person to attend Harvard in the 1660s.

A Time Must-Read book of 2025 and an NPR Books We Love pick, Joseph Lee's *Nothing More of this Land* and the accompanying workbook are explorations of indigenous identity across the world.

Himself an Aquinnah Wampanoag, Lee presents a panoramic view of the lives and challenges faced by native peoples; Adam Richard's accompanying workbook teaches how Lee's concepts can transform the way we all live.

***

As I mention in the story, Provincetown is changing rapidly. I realized just how much recently when I looked up something in an earlier Sydney Riley novel and realized that since I'd written it, businesses have closed or changed hands, people have moved away or passed away, and even the architecture of the town is different.

Those are normal changes. What is happening there now is anything but normal. If you'd like to explore more about a phenomenon that certainly isn't limited to Provincetown, you might take a look at *We Have Never Been Woke*, a development of Pierre Bourdieu's concept of symbolic capitalism by Musa ah-Gharbi.

Just for fun—did you notice the Easter egg name in this story? While "Mills" is a popular Wampanoag name, Juliet Mills is named for an English actress. Look her up—she was pretty fantastic.

Acknowledgments

My cup overfloweth with gratitude to and for Arthur Mahoney of Homeport Press, who I am fortunate enough to call my friend as well as my colleague. Sydney belongs to him as much as to me.

And again as always I thank all the beautiful people of Provincetown, who generously allow me to use so many of their own special selves in my books.

Thanks to Jane MacDonald who performed introductions to her beloved native friends, and to the Mashpee Wampanoag Nation: I've tried very hard here to get everything right, and if I failed, that failure is on me.

Garr Roosma helped me wend my way through the arcane language—and processes—of all things electrical. And many thanks to Lois Hirshberg and Janice Hank, co-chairs of Cape Cod PATH (People Against Human Trafficking), both for their time spent with me and also for everything they do.

To those who contribute in so many different and important ways to the creation of a Sydney story: Pat Medina, Colin Kegler, Chip Capelli, Carem Bennett, and Bob Allen. Thank you to my beautiful family—for loving me despite everything—Doni Angell, Anastasia Czarnecki-Weiss, and Jacob and Sydnia Czarnecki.

Thanks to Amy Raff, Deborah Karacozian, and Nan Cinnater of the Provincetown Public Library for fabulous book launch parties; and to Miladinka Milic for Sydney's amazing cover designs.

Thanks to my friend and colleague Bill Bowers for razor-sharp editing, and to my wonderful First Readers: Kimberlee Sams (who truly goes above and beyond), Corinne Diana (who sadly died as this was going to print), Margo Nash (yes, she's a real person!), Dianne Kopser, and A.C. Burch. And thanks to James Dooley (he knows why).

A tremendous thank-you to the lovely people in my daily writing accountability group, the Worm Zoom, and to its founder and owner, Mason Currey (read his books!), who have kept me working even when writing seemed impossible. Cally Booker, a weaver from Scotland, has especially creatively supportive (and I named a character after her!).

The internet gives me access to many great minds who have been unstinting with their assistance as questions have cropped up, and I am the luckiest of all novelists in having connections with so many really *really* smart people, among them the Wombats, the CEL, and many, many Reddit contributors, especially the folks on r/IndianCountry and r/Indigenous.

Any mistakes that remain here are mine, not theirs.

My gratitude goes out to you all, to everyone in my beautiful seaside home, and with apologies and thanks to anyone I might have inadvertently left out—for sometimes I am a bear of very little brain.

***

And of course I have to note that I'm one of the people benefiting from the illegal European settlements in the Americas, and would be remiss if I didn't acknowledge that I live and work on the unceded traditional and ancestral land of the Wampanoag, Pamet, and Nauset tribes. I am hoping that this novel is in some small way a step beyond that mere acknowledgment through sharing some native experiences and culture with a wider, mystery-reading audience.

About the Author

Jeannette de Beauvoir writes mystery and historical fiction (and often novels at the intersection of the two). She's also a poet whose work has appeared in a number of literary journals.

She's a member of the Authors Guild, the Mystery Writers of America, the Historical Novel Society, and the Association of Thriller Writers.

Her delight is to find characters true to the spaces in which they live. She herself lives and writes in a cottage in Provincetown, on Cape Cod, Massachusetts, and loves the collection of odd people who assemble at a place like Land's End.

Find out more at jeannettedebeauvoir.com.